'Brilliantly and movingly written.'

—Dorothy Koomson

'A moving, beautifully written, uplifting debut about mending broken hearts through friendship. The twists and turns make it impossible to put down.'

—Sarah J. Harris

'What a total joy!'

—Fanny Blake

For *Where We Belong*

'Incredibly moving and atmospheric.'

—Beth O'Leary

'Simply stunning.'

—Fionnuala Kearney

PRAISE FOR ANSTEY HARRIS

'It is brilliantly written, so many brilliant phrases which made me
sr ... I shall keep my fingers crossed that it is a huge hit. It
ιt to be, it's marvellous. I shall be recommending it to all.'

—Lesley Pearse

nstey Harris never disappoints. *When I First Held You*, is gripping,
art rending and extremely satisfying, from start to finish."

—Katie Fforde

powerful, compelling and affecting read."

—Heidi Swain

is is a hauntingly beautiful novel. The painful story of Judith
Jimmy is told with deep sensitivity in lyrical prose that was a
:o absorb, and the plot unfolds at a pace that keeps you turning
pages – such a winning combination.'

—Imogen Clark

s book has a very big heart. Full of hope and so beautifully
:ved.'

—Samuel Burr

pelling . . . A story of broken dreams and unexpected healing.
ιant to read this.'

—Sarah Ward

'*When I First Held You* is a wonderful kaleidoscope of passion, love, grief and misunderstandings . . . A stunning book – one to read and re-read many times'

—Celia Anderson

'Her most powerful and personal book yet. Evocative, emotional and original, every word has been expertly crafted'

—Catherine Isaac

For *The Truths and Triumphs of Grace Atherton*

'The real truth and triumph of this gem of a story is simple: it is one of the best and most gripping descriptions of heartbreak that either of us have ever read.'

—Richard and Judy

'Glorious on so many levels.'

—A. J. Pearce, author of *Dear Mrs Bird*

'Lose yourself among beautiful symphonies, the romantic cities of Europe and quirky characters . . . a triumph.'

—*Woman's Weekly*

'A powerful and passionate novel, awash with heartbreak but still an uplifting tale of friendship and rebirth. Five stars.'

—*Daily Express*

'Full of hope and charm.'

—Libby Page, author of *The Lido*

WHEN I
FIRST
HELD
YOU

ALSO BY ANSTEY HARRIS

The Truths and Triumphs of Grace Atherton

(also published as *Goodbye, Paris*)

Where We Belong

(also published as *The Museum of Forgotten Memories*)

WHEN I

FIRST

HELD

YOU

ANSTEY HARRIS

LAKE UNION
PUBLISHING

Text copyright © 2023 by Anstey Harris
All rights reserved.

Published by Lake Union Publishing, Seattle

www.apub.com

Amazon, the Amazon logo, and Lake Union Publishing are trademarks of Amazon.com, Inc., or its affiliates.

ISBN-13: 9781662503863
ISBN-10: 1662503865

Cover design by Emma Rogers

Printed in the United States of America

For my mothers, with love
Christine Jayne Harris 1945–70
Hazel Jane Baker née Choyce 1931–92

And for Rose McLoughlin,
every week of my life

Chapter One

For most customers who enter the shop, the thing they most want mending is the past. We can't do that: we can patch it, polish it, we can turn the past into a healthy memory to be built on – but we can't mend it. Once we explain that, they seem happier: content to have an emblem of that time restored, or a memento made usable again. Often, all they need is to talk.

The shop began life as a blue plastic laundry basket outside our garden gate. In it, Catherine would put every single thing that had made its way into our house but that we no longer wanted, or had never found a use for. Magically, every evening, the crate would clear again – as if there were fairies waiting to recycle those flimsy plant pots left after the seedlings had grown, goblins interested in a jumper with a bleach mark on the cuff, or a plastic bag full of plastic bags.

'One man's trash is another man's treasure,' Catherine would say, when she brought the grubby plastic basket in to fill it up again.

The proof, day after day, that almost anything can be recycled or repurposed led to the bigger conversation that got us here – to the Mending Shop – and, four years after Catherine's death, it's a way to re-invent me. She may have set the whole thing up just to re-use me, I wouldn't be surprised. For an artist,

Catherine had a methodical and pragmatic mind: she spent fifty years one step ahead of me and it still amazes me that I manage to live without her.

Usually the shop is a quiet place – a couple of volunteers beavering away at benches, the occasional customer in from the cold outside, a general air of concentrated purpose. I enjoy the peace in my little office; I have to raise my head above the parapet to deal with a crisis from time to time but I stay in here with the paperwork. Outside, in the shopfront proper, there are smells of solder, of paint, the occasional whiff of glue as something comes back together, comes back to life. We have customers – although not too many and no money changes hands – and we're all, the volunteers and I, quietly useful.

Today, I am standing by the front door herding cats: the space is filled with people despite the fact that it wasn't designed for that at all. We have long benches across the width of the room, each a few metres apart like school science labs. The walls around the edges are racked with shelves from floor to ceiling: shelves that hold things to be mended, things to be collected, and enough tools to fix anything except a broken heart. The shop wasn't set out for every volunteer, and a number of nosy locals, to all come in at once.

There is an excited buzz of conversation that warms the air and, despite my best efforts to be detached and above-it-all, makes me tingle with excitement.

'Judith,' a man calls from amongst the melee, 'could we get you into Make-up?' 'Make-up' means my tiny office. It sits, like an old-fashioned foreman's post, in the furthest corner of the long room. The cubicle doesn't really warrant a word as grand as office: it is plywood thin and the top half of it is glass so that I can look out at the workshop and, which happens far more often, so they can look in at me. There is a door of sorts but it doesn't quite fit properly and I worry that, if it does shut one day, I'll never be able to open it.

'Judith?' he asks again.

'Sorry, absolutely, I'm on my way.' Make-up isn't really my thing but, if I'm to be on television, I'd best try and look half-decent. Age and the very bright lights dotted all round the shop have bleached my skin enough.

In my office is a nice young woman called Angela, the daughter of one of our volunteers. She has offered to help me look less dishevelled for this morning. Angela sits me down in my swivel chair and just about finds room to squish herself in, between my feet and the door. She puffs powder on to my cheeks from a spectacular box of tricks, foofs and fluffs my hair with her fingers. 'I love your fringe,' she says, almost purring.

'Thank you.' I accept her compliment graciously and try not to think about the nail scissors and the bathroom mirror, the little snippets of grey and white that waft into the basin below as I save myself a trip to the hairdresser.

'Have you been on TV before?' she asks. I am perched on the edge of the chair. She is looming over me, dabbing my face with a silky cloth.

I remember the grainy footage of demonstrations, leaning in as close as possible to the screen during the news, hoping to see myself, hoping my parents wouldn't. I didn't, not until I was in my fifties. 'A placard of mine made it into a crowd scene on a march.' I leave my mouth open, ready to tell her what was on the banner when she asks, but she doesn't.

'Nearly there,' she says, smoothing my hair at the sides. She tucks a few stray ends behind my ear.

'I've been backstage in TV studios a few times,' I say, making conversation while the technical things happen outside the glass

3

sides of the cubicle. 'My late partner was an artist. She did lots of talk shows and interviews.'

She doesn't ask about Catherine either, who she was, what she painted.

'Done.'

The face in the mirror is a pantomime dame.

'It looks heavy like this, but it won't on the screen.'

I nod, I know it's true. I've seen Catherine, painted up like a butterfly, look completely like herself when we watched the programme through later. 'It's great, thanks.' I take a selfie of the pantomime-dame-me, which I'll send to a few close friends later, for a giggle.

The reporter is chatty and encouraging – I don't have time to be nervous.

'Welcome back to *Our High Street*.' The presenter smiles into the camera as he says it, an honest smile, full of support. 'Where we look at all the jobs you could do, if only you knew they existed.' His grin is wide and white and his hand flourishes across the shop. 'Judith Franklin is – right here on the High Street, right in the middle of a traditional county town – the owner of a "Mending Shop".'

The cameraman takes one step back to fit us both in the shot.

'A place where you can have your own object repaired or pick up one already done to replace something of yours that's broken. Is that an accurate description, Judith?'

My throat is a little dry, but I've never had the same problem with public speaking that I've had with more intimate truths, and my voice is strong. 'Absolutely, we exist to keep things out of landfill – first and foremost. We restore things that make people happy, and we turn things that might be thrown away into perfectly serviceable objects that get another life. Keep the plastic out of the sea, and keep people thinking about the planet.' It's a lecture I know off by heart. I've recited it to newspapers, on radio. I've recited it to friends and funders. Once I even had to say it to an angry customer whose beloved childhood pram had its wheels up-cycled – by some new and over-enthusiastic volunteers – into a go-cart for the youth centre. Our systems are more robust now.

'Why hasn't anyone done it before, Judith?' the reporter – his name is Ben – asks.

'It's a non-profit,' I say, feeling the heat under the powder on my cheeks, glad that it's hiding the flush the huge lights have brought up in my skin. 'No money changes hands here and we can't pay wages or bills in kindness and repairs. I'm sure a lot of people have thought about it, but haven't had the means to see it through.' I don't tell him that I can't find anyone else to take over, that I'm tired of running Catherine's shop but that it's me or no one.

Catherine spent a decade hiding from cancer, dodging and ducking its various attempts to overwhelm her. When, on its last call, she knew she wouldn't recover, Catherine told me to sell the paintings that leant up against the wall of her studio – the ones she'd finished but not exhibited yet – and put the money to good use: this good use.

'What's the point in holding on to them, babe?' she said. 'You have a house full of pictures, not enough walls, and a crappy social worker's pension. You don't need them to remember me.' She was sitting at the table in our garden when she said it, her feet propped up on a pale-blue slatted chair, a blanket over her knees despite the summer. 'You need money to go to New Zealand, or buy a camp-ervan, or do anything worthwhile.'

Ben cocks his head to one side like a bird. His soft pink shirt is open at the neck and the stubble on his chin – artfully trimmed – grazes the edge of its collar. 'Can you think of an object that encapsulates exactly what you're doing here, Judith?'

The shop is brightly lit, full of people. The old-fashioned gold letters painstakingly painted on to the glass cast an elongated message on the sanded floorboards. The back-to-front letters spelling out 'The Mending Shop' distort as the light floods through them.

A blue jumper sits on the fabric bench, the curls and coils of its wool dripping over the edge like intestines waiting to be sewn back in. On the plastics bench a yellow tractor, large enough for a child to sit on and zoom around these urban streets, waits with its steering wheel removed for someone to fix it. The shop is alive with stories, with other people's histories.

My favourite thing we have at the moment is a snow globe. A glass dome with an underwater scene made of tiny real shells and little flashes of fish which have been pinched out of clay. The work that has gone into the miniature scene is remarkable: the mermaid who sits in the centre of it wears scales so fine they might have come from a real fish, and two modestly placed minuscule clam shells. Over the years, the sea itself has evaporated. The glitter lies, immobile, on the toes of the mermaid, matted in her plaster hair. I haven't decided which bench it belongs on yet. At the moment, she's on the counter – like a talisman – with my laptop and the coffee machine, but I'm confident we'll work out what to do with her eventually.

Whether I will be able to part with her once her bubble has been topped back up and the silver fish are wet again, I don't know. Catherine made me swear an oath about clutter when we first opened the shop. She predicted – from fifty years of knowing everything about me – that I would fall in love with every broken object, need to find a home for every chipped heart. For each year without her, the oath gets progressively harder to keep.

I pick up the Kintsugi vase that sits on my desk, not for sale or rehoming. I curl my fingers around its slender neck, thinking of Catherine, of how she took it from the shelf in the gallery in Akita, her gentle nod that said it was ours. 'Sometimes they're accidental breaks,' she said, 'ones that no one meant to happen.' She put the vase down to take my strong hand in her slight and tiny ones. 'And sometimes the vase is broken on purpose – by the craftsman. But whichever way the break happens, the item is always stronger – richer – for being mended.' Catherine smiles in my memory and the solid-silver mend of her in my heart grows thicker, shines more deeply.

I sigh, at once mournful and comforted, and turn to Ben. 'This break . . .' I trace the crooked silver line on the vase with my finger and the cameraman moves closer to me.

'One second,' the cameraman says. 'Can you just turn round a little, rotate the vase towards me?'

'Start again at "This break . . ."' Ben says.

And I do. I trace the jagged line of metal, I show them the vase and how much more beautiful it is for its mend, and therefore for the damage it suffered in the first place.

'And each time an item is mended in our shop,' I tell them, 'it will accrue value, it'll gain a story. Every time we unpack something from newspapers, open a bubble-wrap parcel, the person who has brought it in will tell us about it: where it came from; how it was broken. Most importantly, they'll tell us why it needs to be mended. And then each object will grow, will become so much more than the negative space it would have served in landfill.' I put the vase back down. Everyone in the shop is quiet, listening.

'That's quite lovely,' says Ben. 'And the Mending Shop will become part of the history of the item.'

I nod, beaming. My answer has been even better than the rehearsals I've had in the bathroom at home – saying the words out loud to myself in the mirror, listening to them die away against the porcelain tiles and the silence.

'Each object that leaves here – mended – has another life: becomes something to someone else who needs it. That's at the very heart of . . .'

At the front of the room, behind the cluster of television crew, the door opens and someone steps into the shop.

He stands, undiminished by time, as tall and wide as the frame.

This must be how it feels when you die – when your whole life flashes before your eyes. It takes one click of the brain's mechanism to recognise someone you haven't seen for over fifty years. Another impossible moment to remember who they are and what they did.

Standing in the doorway like a time traveller is Jimmy McConnell.

Chapter Two

Jimmy McConnell's voice was as gentle as the powder that falls from chalk when it writes on a blackboard. His accent had the softness of the mist that hovers over lochs, below mountains purple with heather. That was what I remembered whenever I dreamt of him. I deliberately avoided the cliff edge of thinking about him in my waking hours, but my subconscious betrayed me too often.

'It *is* you.' The huge silhouette steps forward. His eyes are the same – the ghost-blue of an ice sculpture – his eyebrows are white now and long, wild. 'Jude Franklin.'

'Judith.'

'I'm James.' His laugh still has the baritone boom it had back then. 'Jimmy's long gone.' The names we wore back then have not survived.

I have thought about this moment for decades. I have played out what it would be like to see Jimmy McConnell, how it would feel to tell him how everything went for me – what he did. In my mind, I have smashed angry fists against him – and not in the powerless, pathetic way wronged women do in films. I am fit, solid, and strong.

In real life, that vigour is sucked from me. It seeps from my pores and what is left puffs, soft and impotent, from my mouth without forming any words.

Jimmy takes three easy strides through my shop towards me. The bystanders in his way part without his having to ask.

Jimmy speaks. Jimmy takes charge. Now as then.

'I saw your name on the job sheet. I mean, I'm retired, obviously, but it's my company. Jude-ith.' He juggles with the me he knew and the one who is unutterably changed.

Instinctively I shrink away towards the counter where Catherine's vase stands. Two halves of me – before, after – cleave quietly apart like a crack opened up with a chisel.

'You haven't changed a bit,' he says, even though it isn't true.

The TV crew and the volunteers blur into clouds of colour and noise behind him.

Jimmy McConnell makes even me look small – he always did, a full six inches taller than me, his shoulders built for farm work like the crofters of his family's past.

'Hey, James.' Ben has long since waved to the cameraman to stop filming. He greets Jimmy warmly, with that European thing where men shake one another's hands and then go in for a half-hug, an almost-kiss. 'Good to see you. What a treat.'

Ben turns and introduces Jimmy – James – to the rest of the team. 'James was still working full-time when I started,' he says. 'Taught me everything I know.'

James grins at everyone. A beam of confidence tracking round like a lighthouse, the same spell he could cast on a room as a young man. His teeth are still crooked but pearl-white: it makes him look harmless, detracts from his size, his obvious fearlessness. It is the enchantment he put me under fifty-something years ago.

'And you know Judith?' Ben asks.

'We go back a very long way.' James moves in for a hug, I steel myself. I hold my body taut, strong, resist the embrace with every fibre as his arms close around me.

He smells expensive.

'Before your parents were even born,' he says over my head to his audience, for that is what they are now after less than a minute of basking in his light.

I shake myself free. 'Where have you been?' I ask him. I am dizzy, too dizzy to even think of it as a strange question.

'James, can I . . . ?' Ben wants to finish up. 'We need to get on to the 5.45 a.m. tomorrow.'

I stand back where I was. But I am a different person now, they must be able to see that. They must be able to read the panic on my face creeping through the powder and the lipstick, crawling over my skin like fire ants.

'We're nearly done, Judith,' Ben says. 'Then I'll leave you and James to catch up.'

James's smile swings round in my direction and the warmth of it singes my cheeks. He grasps my hand before I can move it, squeezes it quickly before letting go. 'As you were, Ben. We've got all the time . . .' He bends slightly to speak to me. 'I hope?'

It's framed as a question but I ignore it. The words I would need to answer are buried deep inside me, wrestled and gagged into a quiet that took five decades to achieve.

'Thanks.' Ben takes back over.

The spotlight returns to me, and I can't imagine that I will remember my name.

The mermaid in the glitter shaker, her sparkles flat and stuck to the plastic rocks, turns her painted eyes towards me in support: she knows how it feels to be empty.

Ben finishes the interview with our contact details, arranges for the cameraman to have a last wander round the shop, looking in corners. Then they crowd back into their van with their big lights and microphones and they drive away.

'Nice to see OBs are just as brusque as they ever were,' James says – to me, I assume; there are only two volunteers left now the chance to be on TV has evaporated, and they've both gone straight back to whatever they were doing at their benches. 'Outside broadcasts,' James says, as if he's trying to open a conversation. 'They're always like that, like hurricanes.'

I am still silent – reeling from the fact that he, who tore through my life leaving utter devastation, could be so casual about the word hurricane – when he says: 'Can I take you for a drink? Dinner?' He glances at my left hand, checks for a ring so clumsily that I see him do it. 'Is there anyone waiting for you to get home?'

'My partner died, four years ago.' I have reduced her, Catherine, to 'my partner', to the anonymity, to the ambiguity. 'We were together almost fifty years.' No better. And no answer.

'Same,' James makes a rueful smile. 'Forty-eight years together. She died the year before last.' Gendered, honest: easier for them. The idea of Jimmy McConnell married, happy . . . I can't process the rest.

I am trying to pin him to the boy I knew: the eyes; the height; he's almost exactly the same, but James's voice is different to Jimmy's. His accent has mellowed and lightened, his voice is still the same languid bass, but it has lost its regional identity.

'I've lived in London for a long time,' he says.

I must have spoken out loud.

'My wife and I moved to London, in the seventies.'

My first thought is that he doesn't live near me, thank God. I am miles from London. An hour's drive even to the edges.

'Shall we go?' he asks me and I fumble for words, for keys. Once upon a time I prayed for this moment – far too long ago, of course, but it doesn't stop me leaving the shop with him, an auto-pilot of response, a one-time habit.

I met Jimmy McConnell on my first adventure. I had peeled away – silently – from the life my parents had: from Sundays at church; from the neighbours in our slick modern cul-de-sac who twitched and watched and commented; from school rules. I had run away.

The injustice of nuclear-missile testing, of the threat of war, was the cause that first fired me. Then, I was fifteen years old and the Cuban Missile Crisis was looming – it followed me to school every day. At church on Sundays, I flicked to the back of the Bible, to Revelations, and read the passages everyone said predicted this. The hooves that rumbled under the Four Horsemen drowned out Father Patrick's sermon. The grey grainy image of the Doomsday Clock was an icon to my friends and me. We thought of it often, drew it in pencil on the back of our schoolbooks, imagined it so close we could hear the second hand tick. Next to it, we would draw the symbol of the only weapon we had, the only chance of avoiding global catastrophe: the black, spidery fork of CND, the Campaign for Nuclear Disarmament.

'How will we know when it happens?' I asked my dad. I asked him often, swallowing down my panic to make the questions sound casual.

My dad's work was honest, long, and hard. He came home to my mum's cooked dinners, to her smile and hugs – no matter how tough or dull her own day had been – every single night. They worked all year for two weeks in Wales: Tenby, in a chalet. When I was fifteen, the point of that quiet happiness was completely lost on me.

'Know when what happens?' He would put his paper down in his lap, resigned to a question-and-answer session. My father was a good man and a kind one: even tired, he enjoyed the debate, proud of the spark of politics in his only child.

'When the hands meet at midnight. When they drop The Bomb.'

My father would stretch his legs out and I could see the shiny leather on the underside of his slippers.

'You'll know, duck,' he'd say. 'And then we have four minutes to get to safety.'

And he moved his hands apart in a stretching gesture. 'Boom.'

It is a warm afternoon and people are smiling. James and I walk down the High Street, side by side, for all the world as if we are friends. I wonder how long this can carry on before reality bites.

'Any ideas?' James says. 'About where to have a drink? Actually, something to eat would be great: I'm starving. It's your town. You do live here?'

I nod and, simultaneously, point to a pub on the corner. It has baskets of valerian, sage-green fronds hiding between loud reds and pinks, hanging from every conceivable corner. The menu is printed on a blackboard outside in huge curling letters of liquid chalk – 'Potatoes' is spelt wrong. I have never been in there before but I don't want James to start asking questions about where I live. The idea of him standing in my house with Catherine's paintings, walking across the spatters that stain her studio floor, makes me feel seasick.

We talk about the weather: James talks, I mostly focus on walking forwards, on quieting the voices of injustice shrieking like crows inside my head.

By the time he has put his hand on the brass plate of the pub door, the voices have given way to an overwhelming sadness.

'Judith.' He places his hand under my elbow, steadies me for a fraction of a second before I shake him off. 'I'm not a fool. I know there are conversations we need to have, it's why I came. It's OK. Just not out here, not in the street.' He lowers his voice as the door swings open and the gloom of the mahogany-varnished interior looms. 'And not in your lovely little shop.'

The pub has quotes about drinking stencilled on the walls and over the bar. I have time to read them while James goes to fetch a menu. I look at him leaning up against the bar, one foot on the brass rail that runs around in front of it just above floor level. From the back, James doesn't look seventy-six. His lightweight sweater is a tasteful teal blue, it fits well and is long enough even for his arms. He still wears jeans, turned up at the bottom, his shoes are brown brogues – immaculate. James's hair is white, not a grey hair left, and I can see that the light above him shines slightly glassy on the top of his head where his hair is thinning. He looks exactly what he is: an older man who has had a career in the media. He doesn't look dangerous, not to a stranger.

'Red wine,' he says and puts my glass down. He has a pint of something amber, a foaming cream top. We look like a couple and I move slightly away from him in my chair. 'I last saw you . . .' he says.

'I know where you last saw me, Jimmy. I do remember.' I am creeping out of my shocked shell, my voice unfurling. A lot of things have happened since I last saw him, things that changed me.

The last day that I saw James was a tangle of police and confusion and fear. The final image of him – until today – is burned into my memory: James, at the top of the steps in the squat we shared in Glasgow, a policeman at each side of him and his legs bicycling in the air, searching for purchase as they half-threw him down the steps. The other girls we shared with were scattered around me, crying, all except Polly Wright. Along the street more police cars wailed their way nearer and the boys from the squat scattered into ginnels and alleyways.

The last shape of James I saw was him curving into a comma as the policeman pushed him into the back of the car, screaming out as they slammed the doors on his ankle.

My fingers tense around the stem of my glass. 'Cheers,' I say with mock politeness.

'I'm going to eat,' says James. 'Anyway.' He means regardless of the outcome of this conversation. 'Are you still veggie?'

Strange, the things you remember about a person after fifty-six years. 'I am. You?'

'Off and on,' he says and smiles. 'Mostly off, if I'm honest.' The old Jimmy McConnell was not honest. 'The veggie burger looks good though. You?'

I nod. I'm not hungry, but I feel some – pointless – weakness in not eating when James does. 'Same. Thanks.' My thanks is churlish, but he doesn't react.

He goes to the bar and orders for us.

When he sits back down, James is silent for a moment. He puts his elbows on the table and leans his face into his hands. 'I'll start with "I'm sorry".'

I say nothing.

'It was a long time ago. But there are things I did then that would be easily as awful if I did them today. I know that. And I need a chance to explain it all – properly and in order.' He puts his hands in his lap. 'I never stopped thinking about you.'

I smother the tears that are welling up, filling the top of my nose and stopping me from breathing. Only when he touches my face do I realise the tears have spilled over, escaped.

'No.' I move my face away from his. 'Don't touch me.'

I go to lift my glass but I'm shaking too much. I misjudge the distance somehow and the glass upends and spirals across the table.

James jumps back, red wine pools where his fingers were. He stands up, rubbing the legs of his jeans. The wine has splattered them, darkened patches bloom over his thighs and crotch.

I don't apologise. I can't. He might mistake my apology for something else, some connection to 'then'. 'I need to leave.' I stand up opposite him, gunfighters.

'Let me drive you.' He calls over to the bar. 'Cancel our food. Sorry.' He waves a gesture to show that he doesn't need a refund. 'Thanks,' he says to the barman.

'I'll walk,' I say, not sure my wobbling legs will take me.

He shakes his head and I follow him out of the pub. The car is electric, silent, and the drive is surreal. I point wordlessly at turnings in the road until I say, 'Here.'

Jimmy McConnell is huge in my cottage hallway. He follows me through the house without asking.

'Are these original Catherine Rolfs?' He stops at the entrance to the sitting room. Two of Catherine's pictures of the South Downs hang side by side. They are an abstract swell of greens with the scent of red autumn leaves imagined across them.

'I have a print of hers at home. "Artemis. Waking." It was one of my wife's favourites.'

'Catherine was my partner.'

'How extraordinary.' He looks from me to the paintings, back again. 'Catherine Rolf. She was a phenomenal artist.' And then he remembers, adds, 'I'm sorry for your loss.' He – we – could be anyone, exchanging surface-level condolences.

'What do you want, Jimmy?' Catherine is on every side of me now, her paintings in front of me, left and right, on every wall. The tiny steel woman that she was has my back. Instinctively, I have walked the length of the house to her studio. The double doors

17

allow access to the garden, to fresh air, and I unclip the catch that lets them swing open. The pattern of her spattered paints is indelible on the boards beneath my feet.

James points to the director's chair by the open door and I nod. He is safer sitting down, smaller.

'Too much happened. And it can't be undone,' I say, warning him from the off.

'It wasn't what you think.'

I don't even bother to say, 'It never is', out loud. I'm sure he can hear me thinking it. Instead, I wriggle my foot free of my sandal and grind my toes into the set paint beneath them. 'You're wasting your time here,' I say. 'There's absolutely nothing you can ever say to set this right.'

A flash of cobalt blue peeks between my toes and I feel energised. 'And I have no desire to rake over old coals. Especially not in my own home.' They've never been old coals for me, those embers still burn if I get too close to them.

'I looked for you as soon as I could, Judith. And then I assumed you'd have changed your name. If I'd known you were Catherine Rolf's partner . . .'

'Meaning?' I am reinforced by anger now: a blur of cadmium yellow flares from the top edge of my foot.

'Meaning I could have easily found her, and then you – as a result.'

Catherine would never have led him to me.

'There are things I need to clear up.' James keeps talking as if I will eventually bend through the force of his repetition. 'Always have been.'

'You're going to have to leave,' I tell James McConnell. 'I'm not ready to have these conversations, and I have no interest in what you have to say.'

'We were kids,' he says, shaking his head. 'And . . .'

'And I didn't have to be this lonely.' My arm rises and I point at him, the end of my finger far too close to his face. 'I didn't have to be this lonely and . . . and . . .' I stride towards the front door, pull it open so hard that it grazes the end of my toes. 'And I'm angry. I've never stopped being angry – not in all these years. At the bottom of all of it, James McConnell—' It's everything I can do not to shout. 'At the very heart of it is you.'

James walks to the front door without a word. His smart brown shoes make no noise on the earthenware tiles of the hallway. His huge shoulders are still held high, unapologetic and unafraid. He turns towards me and his face is cold and blank. 'That will do,' he says, with a quiet anger. 'That's enough. I came here to explain and to fill in some gaps. I did not come here to be spoken to like that.'

I stand, sentry, with the door open, and neither of us speak as he passes through it.

He walks to his car without looking back.

I slam the door behind him and my house rocks to its foundations.

I don't sleep. I keep the window flung open wide despite the rain that sweeps through the garden in splatters and crashes. By the time I make a cup of tea at first light, the sun has speckled through and there is a puff-edged swathe of blue in the sky. 'Big enough to patch a sailor's trousers,' Catherine would have said.

Every time I closed my eyes last night, every attempt at resting my hammering brain was met with the same images. They loomed through the dark like the interminable slide shows my dad used to treat neighbours to after our annual trip to Wales. As I waited for sleep to save me, I heard the click-click of my dad's projector as it slid each slide of the past into place.

A still from my last sight of Jimmy McConnell, not much more than a boy. Another plastic slide drops in front of the lens: his face yesterday; his self-righteous, misplaced anger.

The slide that came back and back between every other one – the image that punctuated the night – is a photograph from the mid-sixties, white-edged and square.

By 4.30 a.m., as the peach dawn edged into the garden, I worked out the format of James's email address from my correspondence with Ben, and I messaged him, direct, blunt.

'You have a photograph of mine. At least, you had. I'm sure you understand exactly why I want it back.' I add my full address so that he can post it back to me. There are no kisses, no 'best regards'. There is nothing I wish him.

For me, I wish that Catherine were here, that I could tell her the outcome of a situation we talked about less and less each decade but that never truly went away.

Catherine and I met at work. Her heart wasn't in it: social work isn't the place for those with an artist's soul. It's a job where you have to be prepared to be witness and advocate for people you can't bear to leave alone, and then leave them all alone until the next day you're at work. Catherine was a million miles from being that person.

She was crying in the staff room when we met. We worked at a borough council in London: she'd been in a particularly awful meeting where a wife was being forced back to a marriage she didn't feel safe in, it was that or lose her children. Catherine had been reprimanded for offering the woman a bed on her sofa.

She was sitting at a low coffee table, reaching down to cradle her mug in two hands. I couldn't really see her face.

'I don't know how you do it.' I think I could have been anyone and she would have asked the same question.

'I don't do families,' I said. 'Nothing to do with children. Cushions some of the blows.' I poured hot water from an urn on to powdered coffee in my mug. 'Not all of them though.' I realised she was crying and sat down next to her on the low corduroy sofa. 'Are you new?' I asked, although she clearly was.

She looked across at me and sniffed. 'I'm Catherine,' she said. 'I started yesterday.' And she wiped her face with her arm, her tiny wrist peeking out from the end of her shirt sleeve. 'This was such a mistake,' she said and burst into tears afresh.

I moved closer to her. I am not prone to bouts of spontaneous affection, I never have been, but I reached my arm out to comfort her. She fitted so neatly beside me. There was something magical about the smell of her and the softness of her body, even in that miserable cream-coloured coffee room. Catherine, despite being a terrible social worker, was more worldly wise than me: in 1968, she already knew there was such a thing as a woman falling passionately and wholly for another woman. I, on the other hand, had no idea. It was a surprise that saved my life.

I used to dream, as a teenager, about the white light that destroyed Hiroshima. The photographs haunted me: the huge plume of cloud reaching the sky, swelling at the top with hundreds of thousands of souls. I would wake, bolt upright and gasping, with the image burned into my retina – a purple mushroom of murdered people.

After those awful dreams, I would walk along the landing to the bathroom and switch on the light, hoping that the yellow glow would equalise things. I could have knocked on my parents' door

– they would have hated to think of me alone and frightened – but, as I would eventually find out, that wasn't how things worked in our brittle normal: that wasn't what we did. I was too old for cocoa, for a hug. I was almost an adult; even staying on at school was an indulgence. Some of my friends were already married – all of them were working – and many of my parents' friends questioned or criticised my plan to go to university: what they saw as my 'chance to get up to mischief'.

My parents did things properly, to the letter. They followed the government instructions for our own nuclear shelter in the under-stairs cupboard, right down to the two lidded pails – one for in, one for out – that my mother topped up with fresh water every Friday evening.

Sometimes, when no one else was home, I would shut myself in the cupboard and go through the neat cardboard boxes stored for our nuclear winter. I sat in the dark but for the line of light that snuck in from the hall, marking out the trapezium shape of the door.

I knew my eyes would become accustomed to it, enough even to read the labels of the tins and packets. I had peeled the top off a packet of biscuits and ate them one by one, snapping them under my fingers to reveal the soft white line of icing inside. I packed the box back up and put them right at the bottom, but I knew I'd return – like a mouse in the dark – to finish the packet.

My parents had put together their attempt at survival, their apocalypse home, as a response to what they had been told would probably happen to the world. When my faithful patriotic parents were asked, by the government, to prepare for the worst, they found a stoic enthusiasm to do just that.

In another tin, high up on the shelf, my parents kept four five-pound notes that they had stockpiled to spend in the post-apocalyptic shops. They had enormous faith in Woolworth's re-opening dusted with nuclear snow, the ringing of tills muffled by the ash of bodies.

I didn't know then that I would steal those four five-pound notes one day, swap them for a twelve-hour bus ride to freedom, where drips and stripes of rain turned the whole landscape to a dark flat desert when the night drew in. I had never heard the phrase 'be careful what you wish for: you might get it'.

Chapter Three

I'm sitting in my living room, eating toast cut into triangles and watching the breakfast show. The make-up artist was right. On screen, I look like I've just returned from a particularly good and stress-free holiday. I shake off last night, dust James McConnell away from me. I have plenty to be grateful for.

Catherine and I were one of those families everyone misjudges from the outside: our friends assumed that I was the one who handled the logistics of life, that her artist's soul was the driving force. They were always wrong. I was the ideas girl: Catherine's imagination was swallowed whole by landscapes and pigment, replenished by admin.

She was the one who checked if we'd need a visa for our holiday, if the film I wanted to see was actually playing that evening. She was the one who made sure the sofa I'd chosen would fit into the sitting room without taking a door off. I pat the red upholstery, a size down from the one I'd bought but just as comfortable, just as much home.

On my TV the camera pans up and down our shelves of gleaming stock, pauses and focuses in on the tiny mermaid. My phone pings and beeps with texts and messages from people who care about me and I feel the pressure of him lessen already.

I lock the shop door behind me. I'm in an hour early but – if the phone and emails are anything to go by – today is going to be a monster: antiques dealers and boot-fair impresarios are emailing thick and fast, offering us money in exchange for taking all our stock off our hands.

I listen to a few to get the gist, then change the answerphone message accordingly. 'Thank you for calling the Mending Shop. The stock we keep is not for sale. We are a community asset and we exist solely to help those who need our support – either to meet a need, or to fix something broken. Thank you.' And then the long, indignant beep. I try to sound as snooty and unapproachable as possible.

Barbara, one of Catherine's oldest friends and someone I have entirely repurposed for my own, is the first person I think of when I identify the biggest problem we're going to have this morning.

Pre-retirement and in a different – less happy – life, Barbara was a headmaster.

She is at the shop within the hour but, even now, there is already a little group of people, some in desperate poverty and exactly the ones we'd hoped to reach, but others – pushy – with big bags and greedy eyes.

'You were marvellous in the interview,' Barbara says, locking the shop door behind her to keep them out. 'I've watched it twice and set my TV to record the repeat. I felt dazzling by association.'

She's such a dear.

'We need to sort real customers from people after some stuff to take to a boot fair,' I say. 'The main thing today' – I point at the door and the growing numbers – 'is going to be crowd control.'

'My forte,' says Barbara. 'I probably taught half of them.'

'And we have to look at the positive,' I tell myself as much as her. 'We wanted publicity, we wanted to spread the repurposing message. And it really did do that.'

We both look at the rows of people peering through the glass as if we're an exhibit.

'It did that all right, Judith.'

She opens the front door and her considerable shelf of bosom pokes out before her face does. 'Now, then . . .' I hear before I close the office door and turn my back on them.

I try to distract myself by playing back some of the preposterous messages. Now and then, I come across an offer of help and I jot down the numbers in a file for potential volunteers. I have almost returned to the muscle memory of normal life when there is a soft knock on the glass partition.

My first thought when I see James McConnell is that he is a bad penny, that – having reappeared – he's going to turn up over and over until he ruins my life for a second time. And then I see the small white envelope in his hand.

It takes my breath away.

He opens the door but there isn't enough room for him in the tiny office cubicle. 'I was awake when your email arrived. I've spent the rest of the morning looking for this.'

Now that it is restored to me, this picture won't live in a box or stuffed away in a drawer. This photograph will be where it always should have been: centre stage in my life.

My hand is shaking as I take the envelope. My face is burning and I am trying not to cry in front of James McConnell.

I unfold the white paper flap and take out the picture.

A group of young people stand at the top of a set of steps. Behind them, a large Edwardian villa looms up until the top of it is missing from the picture. To the right of the door is the open window we used to go in and out – we never had a key to the front door. I can smell the damp in that room as clearly as if I'm standing on the curled newspapers and fragments of threadbare carpet that covered the floor.

Jimmy McConnell is in the centre of the group. He is wearing a mismatched suit, and a thin tie – monochrome in the picture although I know it was knitted in brown wool and that it did the rounds weekly: each of the boys borrowing it for court appearances. He has one arm draped across my shoulders, like a fur stole along the top of my buttoned-up coat. I have an umbrella in my hands and I hold it in front of me, curled up and closed, touching the floor like a walking stick. I used to iron my hair straight through greaseproof paper and flick it under at the front, the mirror of the black ticks of kohl at the corners of my eyes.

There are other people I recognise: Kay; Paddy; Angus; sweet, kind Dougie. And on the other side of Jimmy to me, Polly Wright, her Titian hair drained of colour in the black and white image, but still tumbling wild around her face.

I want to be sick. Instead I sink down into my chair and whisper. 'This isn't the photograph, James. This isn't it.'

The phone on my desk keeps ringing.

'Are you going to answer that?' James asks. 'I could turn the ringer off for you, at least?'

'How could you do that?' I ask him.

'By pressing the silence swi—'

'I mean the photograph. How could you do that?'

He tries to close the door behind him but his left shoulder won't quite squeeze in. He sighs and there is an edge to the noise – as if he feels hard done by. 'You emailed me at four o'clock in the morning and asked me to bring the photo. I brought the photo. I'm sorry, the rest – whatever I've done wrong – is a mystery to me.'

'I meant the photo I sent you. I want it back. I've always wanted it back, but . . .' I let the thought trail away.

James presses his forehead with his finger, rubs it slowly across, the tip of his finger squashing the wrinkles into one another. 'This is another picture?' He releases his skin from under his finger. 'Where did you send it?'

I nod. 'To Aberdeen. To your mother's house.'

'Straight after Glasgow?' He drops the edge in his voice; it is something softer. A seventy-six-year-old man thinking about his mother. 'I wasn't there. I didn't get home for months.'

Barbara calls from the shop door. 'I need a loo break, Judith. Any chance?'

I look past James and out to the shop. The number of people at the door has dwindled now. Two of the volunteers have come in today and are at their benches, but neither of them are people who would want to handle the sudden and unlikely job of doorman in a shop where nothing is for sale.

I squeeze past James, trying not to touch him, and into the shop. Alan, the horologist, stops me on my way through.

'Judith, we've had a couple of envelopes stuffed with cash put through the door. And a cheque for five hundred pounds. Could someone take it all to the bank?' Alan looks just as I'd expect a watchmaker to look. The only difference between him and the clockmakers of fairy tales is that he wears proper half-moon glasses instead of a pince-nez. He is small and precise, very formal. His bench is a puzzle of cogs and springs, all sorts of innards that he puts back together to tick and whir into life. 'Aren't people kind?' he says.

'They are.' I smile at him. 'I'll pop to the bank when Barbara gets back.'

'I'll give you a lift,' James says, behind me. I want to tell him no, to shout at him to leave me alone and get out of my shop – my life – but it would be inappropriate to bellow, to spit words at him, in front of Alan. The contrast between him and Alan would be almost comic in any other situation. It's more than physical: I'm sure that Alan has never been arrested, has never left behind the tangle of broken lives, devastated hearts, that James has.

'I'm happy to help, it's fine.' James wasn't patronising as a young man, but he seems to have included it in his retirement skill set.

I am being offered assistance by the person who caused the most harm ever to befall me. Sometimes, the irony of life is ludicrous.

It was a priest who set everything in motion. My mother went to Mass every Sunday, twice on saints' days, and scrubbed the tiled floor of the nave every Wednesday. All of that was meant to save us.

Father Patrick and my mother had a deal: she baked and he visited, ate whatever treat she'd made him, blessed our house. Up close and out of the pulpit, he was a lot younger than my mum: dishy, even – despite his serious expression.

Our sitting room was 'open-plan'. I knew you had to say it in a special voice, with a tiny pause at the end for the person you were telling to express their admiration. I was sitting at the dining room table, doing maths homework and keeping half an eye on how much sponge cake was left.

'I've come to say goodbye,' Father Patrick said.

'You're not going to another parish?' My mother sounded like her heart would break. The priest before Father Patrick had been dull and mean. His sermons had gone on for hours and he refused, point blank, to make home visits, even for the dying. He was always the main topic of conversation at my mum's coffee mornings and the ladies had thought all their Christmases had come at once when

– and they all called him 'young' and 'handsome' every time they used his name – Father Patrick arrived.

'I'm taking on a calling outside of the cloth,' he said. His voice was sad, resigned.

'Does that mean you won't be a priest any more? Why not?' I had always thought of priests as just that: priests underneath their clothes; priests inside their bodies – Jesus and the Blessed Virgin rippled through them like the words in a stick of rock.

I came and sat next to my mother on the sofa, trying to pull my school skirt down to cover my knees while I was opposite the erstwhile priest.

Father Patrick told my mother about the occupation of the Faslane Naval Base. He was twitching with pent-up anger when he said that Prime Minister Mr Macmillan had invited the Americans and their nuclear warheads to Scotland, on to British soil; near to tears when he talked about the terror of a nuclear catastrophe.

'It's God's planet, Mrs Franklin,' he said, his brown eyes solemn. 'My job is to protect it and the people on it. It's what He called me to do.'

After that, I read and read. I went to the library, asked questions of my teachers. With every fact I found, every pamphlet about the inevitability of a Third World War, I became more committed, more sure, that I – like Father Patrick – could make a difference.

I joined CND, went to meetings every week in a draughty church hall.

'What's happening in Algeria is against every convention, it's an abuse of human rights. It's against God himself.' Father Patrick stood at the front of the hall every Tuesday, stripped of his dog collar but still delivering sermons. 'There are children living in that desert: families roasting under nuclear fallout.'

I made my first placard, carried it on my first march. We were protesting against nuclear tests in the Algerian desert. The white board said 'Send food, not atomic dust'.

It was 1963 and, aged seventeen, I believed I was the change I wanted to see in the world.

James is driving me to the bank – a sleek, silent journey with not a smear or speck of dirt inside the car – when I could have, would normally have, walked.

This part of James is the same as Jimmy, has never changed: the part that takes you by the metaphorical arm – lifts you and charms you – and before you know it you're doing exactly what he wanted and what you weren't sure about. And somehow you believe him, that it's for the best and that you're safer this way.

James pulls the car over right outside the bank door. His front wheels are on the yellow no-parking zigzag of a crossing and it makes the conformist in me uncomfortable.

'It's like a reverse bank heist,' he says. 'I'll keep the engine running.'

'There's no need,' I say. 'I can walk back in fifteen minutes.'

'Please.'

I wrestle with his 'please' while I'm in the bank but afterwards, as if under a spell, I pull on the chrome door handle and get back into the car.

'Thank you,' he says, the faintest trace of his old accent in the way he links the two words.

We glide up the High Street towards the Mending Shop at the far end. We are as silent as the car and, from the corner of my eye, I can see his jaw set as straight as mine.

'Thanks, then,' I say and go to undo my seat belt. We have pulled up twenty metres or so from the shop. The people have dispersed and Barbara is standing outside, chatting to the single person she is keeping in the street.

James's hand snakes across to cover mine before I can pull away. 'Don't. Please hang on.'

I shake myself free. My skin crawls.

'I will go, but you have to let me say what I came to say,' James says. 'You have to let me tell you the truth.'

His touching me has lit the fire: I can barely control my anger. 'You left me. You had an affair and abandoned me and that upended my entire fucking life. OK? Are you done?' I am hissing the story through my teeth.

'No.' His face is livid. He draws himself up to his full height in his seat, expands and inflates his chest to take up more room. 'No, I'm not done actually. I'm done with tossing and turning all night and going through my entire house looking for a picture I haven't seen in fifty-six years. And most of all—'

'I don't care, James.'

'It was chaos, that last day,' he says. 'When I was arrested. When we were scattered. There's so much I need to explain.'

I have my left hand on the door, my right moves across my body to the lever that will open it. My fingers curl around the black plastic, grasp tight.

James carries on as if I'm not half in, half out of his car. He carries on as if this is all about him. 'I've never stopped blaming myself, wishing I'd done things differently. I let you down.' He takes a breath, sighs loudly. 'But there's so much about me that you don't know, Jude.'

And then I see red. I snort – an exhalation through my nose, like a bull if a bull could laugh, could sneer. My breath feels like flame as it leaves my nose. I pull the door back towards me, it clicks shut and no one outside can hear us.

He keeps speaking. 'I can't bear to think of you – so far from home – trying to piece together everything that had happened. All alone.'

'I wasn't alone when you left, James.' If he knew me at all he would be terrified of the edge of ice that freezes my voice, crackling through to my insides and turning them solid with cold.

My face is a few centimetres from his, I can smell the toothpaste on his breath. I think of the secret Jimmy McConnell left me with, the one that put distance between me and anyone else for the rest of my life, that made every interaction with anyone I ever met – except Catherine – a lie.

And then I say it out loud. I cut the cords that have held me, tied me up in despair: ropes that have constricted and suffocated me for fifty-six years. They are words I wrote to him so many times – words I have sobbed into the dark for decades, each spectral confession quieter and quieter as the years passed.

'I was far from alone, Jimmy. I was pregnant.'

My first march was in London. More than thirty of us – a whole coach-load – met outside the church hall on the cold Saturday morning that February. The dawn was grey, reluctant, and we were surprised by the cold.

'Have you been to London before, Judith?' Father Patrick asked me. He had been the last to sit down after he'd ushered everyone on to the coach; the nearest empty space was beside me.

He was obviously a seasoned marcher. Where I was wearing my best shoes, a smartly ironed dress, a headscarf in case it turned to rain, he wore a thick jumper under a raincoat, strong boots.

'I've only seen it in films.' I wished so hard to be sophisticated enough to have been to London.

'Don't get lost, Judy,' my dad had said. 'When I used to do deliveries there in the war, you could go back and forward over those bridges for weeks: no one would find you.' He'd pinched my cheek like I was a toddler again. 'Make sure you don't forget your way home. Where would we be without her, Margaret?'

And my mum had looked so proud, because I was going to London, because I had a cause to care about and it was organised by a priest – the mark of all things perfect.

London was everything I'd imagined and more. Bright red buses and black taxis were an actual thing, and that surprised me – I'd believed they were just for picture books.

Our protest ended in Trafalgar Square. Pigeons gusted up in flurries whenever anyone moved and I shuddered, hearing my mother's warning: 'Rats with wings, rats with wings.'

I stood, side by side with Father Patrick – proud that he had taken me under his wing, befriended me. 'I'm not a priest any more,' he said when I called him 'Father', and his sadness was clear. 'I'm Paddy Gordon now, like I was at school.'

We had marched and shouted, sung until we were hoarse. We had jostled and jiggled our banners, heavy from hours of holding them up in one hand.

'This is turning into a sit-in,' said Paddy, sinking on to the ground and gesturing that I should do the same thing. 'We sit here until the police move us. It means they can't ignore us. They have to listen.'

There was a pillared stone gateway to one side of the square, impossibly tall and wide and covered with ornate carvings that celebrated a grand tradition of war. Below it, black police cars and vans began to stream through towards us. Up the slight slope on the other side of Trafalgar Square horses began to trot towards us. Their hooves were loud on the road, their riders wearing long black cloaks. I knew without being told that these were the real horsemen of the apocalypse.

Songs went up across the square. We sat, legs crossed, backs as straight and fierce as the lions around us. The people nearby sang a Bob Dylan song from last year's hit parade, and Paddy and I joined in with gusto.

'You will have to leave before the arrests start,' he said.

I hadn't imagined being arrested at all. My parents would go spare.

Paddy clicked his tongue at the grey pigeon that had landed on his hand. Its scaly feet scrunched into the contours of his palm. 'Your mother would never forgive me if I let you be arrested.'

The old and the very young – several retired people and me – were packed off back to the bus. The rest stayed to fight.

I was glad not to be sleeping in a police cell but I felt childlike, vulnerable. The old people were kind, offering me sandwiches and lukewarm tea from flasks. Rather than cry, I buried myself in a creased and second-hand copy of the newsletter Paddy and the committee had put together. In it, I read about Faslane in Scotland, about the occupation of the harbour, magical words like Skybolt, Polaris, Holy Loch.

I read Paddy's plea for help, his treatise that anyone who cared should be there – doing their bit. At the bottom was an address: where Paddy and the other protestors would be staying while they fought the good fight. The paper made no noise as I tore the bottom away.

Chapter Four

I watch James's face. I watch utter shock cross it like a summer storm, freeze his features like a new Ice Age, decades and centuries in a second. I see the confusion that spins through him.

His face follows his thoughts: colouring; fading; thundering. All in a single moment.

I watch as his mouth makes shapes, searches for a way to form words. His fingers clutch at the steering wheel, knuckles white.

'You knew.' I say it coldly. 'I told you.'

Now his mouth moves, up and down, his white teeth chatter. And then he shakes his head, side to side, a silent denial.

'I wrote to you over and over,' I say. 'Every single day.'

'What did you do . . . about it?' He sounds like a tiny mouse has crawled through his enormous body and spoken for him.

'It was 1966.' We both know that narrows the options.

I looked at all those options – such as they were – once upon a time. They all led to various versions of torture. The only one that offered any kind of liveable outcome was marrying him, Jimmy McConnell, and in letters that begged and wept, I told him so over and over. But he never answered.

'I can't count the number of times I wrote.' They are cold, short words, but he doesn't seem to understand them.

'You wrote to me? Where?' He looks punched.

'To Aberdeen. To your mum's.'

It is not part of history that James might not have read my letters. That is not the way I tell this story, the way I understand it.

His face is a glacier.

James shakes himself like a wet dog. He moves his legs up and down in the footwell of the car: one, two – as if he's trying to check that he's real.

'Fifty-five years ago.'

'Fifty-six,' I correct him.

He puts his head in his hands. I notice his long eyebrows again, the stray hairs peeling away wild.

I hold my breath, waiting for him to say something, for him to understand.

'Do I have a child who is fifty-six?'

Bile rises in my mouth and I swallow it down: it leaves prickles of sweat on my top lip, a needling discomfort in my throat.

'Did you have a baby?'

I nod, wordlessly. I have only ever talked about this with Catherine. In the story we knew, James abandoned me – walked away with another woman – and that has coloured everything I have ever believed about him, has tattooed him with shame.

James screws his eyes shut, his skin gathers by the sides of his eyes as if he is in pain. He does not know pain. 'A boy or a girl?'

I take a deep breath, spread my toes in my trainers and try to ground myself on the clean black mat that covers the car floor.

James makes a choking sound. 'A man or a woman?' His hands fly to his mouth as if to feel the shape of the words as they escape him.

'I can't do this here. You can come to my house.' The words will be the same wherever we say them but I crave the safety of

37

my own home. I open the door and, this time, he doesn't try to stop me.

'I'll see you there,' I say and snap the door shut behind us both.

I need to run. Not the fleet, ethereal running that Catherine managed so effortlessly, mine is a lumbering fall forward, a thudding repetition of feet at a quarter the speed that Catherine could move. But I understand its power, the feeling of flight, of escape: the cleansing fire in my chest, the conscious labouring of breath in and breath out.

Catherine started running in the eighties, in that first wave of the general public deciding they could run marathons. She was built for it, sleek as Hermes, light as a feather. I was her reluctant umpire, timing runs and waiting in car parks with flasks of hot tea, bottles of cold water. It took her ten years to get me to attempt a Scout's pace walk, jogging for fifty horrible metres, then walking for fifty till my breath came back. Rinse and repeat.

'I'm forty-three,' I remember huffing at her at the end of that first tortured run.

'And if you crack it now, you'll still be running when you're eighty-three.' She was adamant.

I grudgingly agreed to 5k – Catherine could be infuriatingly belligerent when she'd made up her mind. Barring injuries, I have stuck to my word and jogged a reluctant 5k – occasionally overtaking pedestrians – three times a week for thirty years.

Now I am running from Jimmy McConnell, running from memories, running from pain, and this release feels like Catherine's legacy of safety. It is a mile from the High Street to my house. The one-way system on the roads and the cut-throughs of the footpaths mean that I will get there before James, however sweating and breathless I will be.

I hear Catherine beside me. 'Lean in, chin out: breathe deeply and keep on putting one foot in front of the other.' The rhythm of my feet slows the beat of my heart, and the salt tears mingle with the sweat on my cheeks. 'Never look behind you, Judith,' whispers Catherine. 'Focus on what's ahead.'

Freedom, and more specifically Glasgow, didn't look like it had in my fantasies. The reality of freedom was cold and wet, seeping through my summer coat. I felt more lost and afraid than free.

The little strip of newsletter was fraying at its edges, the address was a blue bloom watermark and I pushed it deep into my pocket lest it be washed away completely. I knew it off by heart but I hadn't thought about the sheer size of a city centre, about the number of roads splaying out from the middle, any one of them leading to the boarding house.

The rain itself was different to the sort I'd known at home. This was a mist laden with moisture, a damp smoke that clung to every fibre, seeped into every pore. The houses on Leicester Close were no different to those on the council estate near my house, scratched pebble-dashed fronts and unruly gardens, all coloured by the incessant, cold drizzle. It would be weeks before I learnt the word 'dreich' to describe the weather, but once I had it, I used it every day.

I knocked on the door of the boarding house.

Father Patrick opened the door. He was wearing an ordinary white shirt unbuttoned at the neck to show a part of him that had always been hidden before. Faint tufts of black hair reached towards his throat and I felt uncomfortable looking at them – as if I'd caught him undressed. He was completely Paddy Gordon now.

'Judy. What are you doing here?' His surprise was real, his words tumbled over each other. 'You're soaking. Are you on your own?' He blinked as if to clear the mirage from his eyes. 'Do your parents know you're here?'

'Can I come in?'

'I can't let you in. Mr and Mrs Falkirk expressly forbid it. This is a men's boarding house.' He reached back inside the house, found his coat. 'I'll come with you. Where are you going?'

'I came looking for you. I've come to help.' I uncurled my fingers and showed him the strip of wet paper. 'You asked for help.'

Paddy stepped out into the rain. 'You can't mean you have nowhere to stay.'

'I thought I'd stay here. I've got money.' I thought of his sermon last Lent about the Judas tree and the shade from its branches that left the earth itself cold. I prayed a silent prayer that he wouldn't ask me where I'd got that sort of money.

He turned to face me, in the street now, his arms weighed down with my case and my bag. 'Judy, you must go home.'

'I can't. I won't.' I tugged my wet coat round me. 'I'm here to help. I read your article in the CND newsletter.'

'Paddy' Gordon looked like he might cry too. He inhaled and exhaled loudly. A puff of mist appeared on the cold air despite the fact it was June. 'This is no place for a girl, Judy, let alone at your age.'

His words stung me far worse than the rain and my blistered hand.

I lunged forward, grabbed my case from him. 'I'll find a boarding house myself. One that takes women. Thank you.'

'Wait. I know a place. There is somewhere. They might have a bed.'

Chapter Five

I have beaten James back to my house. Perhaps he has got lost, maybe he's decided to leave the whole situation alone.

My key is still in the door when his car pulls up in the road.

'Can I get you a drink?' The run has cleared my head. Catherine would be silently triumphant if the circumstances were altogether different.

'Water, thank you. A glass of water would be great.' He speaks rapidly, his accent seems stronger, perhaps disturbed by the silty dregs of the past.

'I'm having wine.' I open the fridge.

'Driving,' James says.

I pass him the water and notice his hand is trembling as he takes it.

He follows me into the studio and we sit opposite one another.

'I was a social worker for forty years,' I tell James. It is the second half of a conversation I've been having in my head. 'I'd finish work ruined sometimes, in pieces. And I'd come and sit in here and watch Catherine paint. Artists are supposed to be tortured,' I say as much to myself as him. 'But Catherine wasn't – at all. Her painting was about remembering to connect to the Earth, about peace, and all the places it can be found.' Catherine painted about the tiny size of happiness but that is too painful to say.

James listens. His hands are still shaking and he holds the glass in both of them, covering it from top to bottom.

'And she'd coax out details of my day – the things I could tell her. And we'd leave it in here, with the paint, to be cured. So that I didn't carry it with me, whatever it was – into the night.'

He is silent.

I can see that he is fishing for words.

'Where is she? He?' His voice catches at the end as if speaking took all of his power. 'Do they hate me?'

'She,' I say and worlds swim in the word.

'I have two daughters.' He stares at the glass. 'Three now. My girls have a sister.'

I wonder if he is searching for his wife inside him, if she is still the person he turns to – to tell news – just like I do with Catherine.

We can do this phrase by painful phrase, or I can take control: say it. 'She was put up for adoption when she was three weeks old.'

That is the whole story told.

That is my awful truth.

That is the shadow that has never left me.

Father Patrick and I walked through the grey lowlands' rain. We crossed a huge park, a glasshouse in the middle of it glittering under the sulphured street lamps and the bats beginning to flit across from tree to tree. That was where I promised him that I'd write to my parents first thing in the morning – and, if they so demanded, that I would come home immediately. None of it was true but I told myself that I wasn't lying to a priest, I was lying to Paddy Gordon.

'This is it,' Paddy said eventually. 'This is where the protestors stay when we've been moved on by the guards.'

The house was one of a long terrace. The road outside it swept upwards on a curved hill. It must have been very grand in its day. This was not its day. Just beyond the house, like punctuation in the long road, was a set of glass tram signals, each light popped out like monstrous teeth.

The house had stone steps running up to the front door and a bay window to the right of the steps. The sash window was open at the bottom, despite the rain and the cold evening damp. The curtain that hung there was a shroud of dark behind the glass, no discernible colour to brighten it.

Paddy Gordon got to the front door then turned to his right, put one foot on the windowsill. 'There's no key,' he said. 'Everyone comes in and out this way. It's nothing much, but it's safe and dry. There are good people here.' He looked apologetic.

I tried to swallow the tears, to kid myself that this was what I'd come for. I followed him through the window. There was no furniture inside. The wallpaper peeled up from the bottom and hung down in rags from the top. The carpet had long since worn to dust.

'What is this place?'

'It was an abandoned house. Some of the team have taken squatters' rights here.'

'A squat?' It was the kind of thing my father might have warned me about. 'It's not their house?'

'It isn't anyone's house as far as I know. Judy, don't make this worse than it is. You can't imagine how I feel bringing you here.' Beyond the dark sitting room, half-lit from the street lamp and full of flat shadows like ghosts along the walls, there were voices from inside the belly of the house.

Paddy stepped through the door and into the hallway, his coat flooded with light, and the raindrops shone like pearls on the gabardine. 'Anyone there? It's Paddy.' And then, when no one heard him, 'Hello?'

He walked along the hall; I followed him. There was a second door on the right – where a dining room might have been if this were a real home. Paddy knocked on the door and opened it without an answer. 'Is Jimmy here? Or Kay?' he asked of people I couldn't see. There was a scrambled reply and Paddy nodded his head, closed the door again. 'This way,' he said.

At the end of the corridor was a kitchen. A metal lamp hung low over the central circular table so that the three people round it were lit as if they were at a seance. Two girls looked up at me and one of them smiled. The other, red-haired girl dropped her gaze back to the poster she was painting, her interest in me faded instantly.

'This is Judy,' Father Patrick – Paddy – said. He was definitely Paddy in this dingy room, hardly any older than the others, wearing the same simple uniform of work trousers and button-through shirt. 'She needs somewhere to stay tonight.'

'Jude, actually,' I said, the last step of my reinvention.

On the far side of the room, half-shaded by the evening and the low lighting, a man stepped forward. He offered me his hand and I shook it, oddly formal in this bohemian setting.

'Hello, Jude. I'm Jimmy McConnell,' he said. 'Pleased to meet you.'

In Catherine's studio, James half-rises out of his chair – he thinks better of it and sinks back down. 'You didn't think I had a right to know? You didn't try to find me? Fuck, I would have done anything – anything.'

I think about those films where women beat their fragile hands against the strong chests of men as tall as James: I imagine how it would feel to take one slug at his jaw, crack my knuckles against the bone, or one desperate punch into his soft eye socket.

I consciously unclench my fists, try to follow the lines of the liquid hills in Catherine's painting behind James's head. This is why I had to run, why she had to paint, this is the boiling rage we doused by loving each other.

I look at him sitting in her green armchair. I speak slowly, deliberately. I do not want him to miss a word. 'I wrote to you every single day from that horrible place. Begging letters. I offered you everything – anything. Every single day until I left, until I was completely broken. You were my only hope of getting her out.' I am not frail, I would not patter against his chest with my pale fists. My hands are large and ruddy, my hands are able.

'I sent you her picture.' Now I have run out of words. I can't find the phrases I need to tell him that I sent him the only photograph I ever had of her. I sent it because she looked like him, exactly like him – those ghost-blue eyes. And I thought that seeing her might change his mind.

The colour of her eyes was still forming when the picture was taken: the limpid blue glowed from the centres as if someone was shining a torch from underneath fathoms of deep water. Even in the black and white shades of the photograph, you could see that emerging colour.

James is crumpling, folding into himself in the big armchair, shrinking in front of my eyes.

I should be glad, enjoy seeing some of the hollow pain transfer into him. But instead, it just accentuates my own.

I close my eyes and picture that photograph: the round cheeks, the soft pink lips, the lopsided corners of a mouth that had just learnt to smile.

'I did what I could, as soon as I could.' He clears his throat and looks past me into the garden. 'And I was racked with guilt. But I was in prison for six months after Faslane.'

I look at his leathered face and wonder how many of those lines were etched while he was in there.

'And as soon as I got out, I went looking for you. I went through the phone directories in the library. And then I . . .'

'It was too late,' I say. 'You were too late.' The pain is excruciating, needles of what might have been force open scars that only barely held before. My hands cover my solar plexus, try to stop me from spilling. 'Where were my letters? My photograph?'

He puts his head in his hands. 'My mother must have kept those letters from me,' he says, loud in the calm studio. 'And I can't tell you how much that hurts.'

'I presume your mother's dead now?' I do have friends, my age, whose parents are in robust nonagenarian health.

'She died in her sixties. A long time ago.' He thinks for a moment. 'Could I have a glass of something after all?' He holds out his hand and I can see the trembling. 'It might help.'

In the kitchen, I fill my wine glass again, fetch a fresh one for James. I wonder if he cleared his mother's house when she died.

'My sister and I went through my mother's photographs.' It is the first thing he says when I go back in: great minds. 'There weren't many. I don't remember there being any we . . .' His voice falters. 'Any we didn't recognise.'

'She looked exactly like you.'

'My daughters do too. My other daughters.' He takes a large gulp of his wine. 'They'll be delighted. Devastated. Both, both things.'

I nod. I would feel the same if I saw her now: overwhelmed with gratitude to see her grown shape, her adult self; devastated at the embodiment of everything I've missed.

'Where is she?' he asks. 'How long ago did you find her?' He stands up and walks towards the garden. 'Or did she find you?'

I pause, wrong-footed by his question.

He takes a picture from his wallet. 'My girls. The other two.' He risks a smile. 'They're forty-five and forty-three. A bit younger.'

I reach out to take the picture. I don't want to look but something is dragging me to it, a magnetic compulsion that cannot – will not – end well. The picture is old, creased with tenderness. Two young girls are sprawled on a yellowed lawn. Beside them a large golden dog has rolled on to his back, pale belly up. I cannot resist the pull of looking in their faces.

My memories of that darkest time are snapshots of scenery or colour. I don't remember how I walked from one place to another, where my footsteps fell. I can picture the pale cream lino of municipal corridors, silvered carpet rods, the grey chipped doorways: I know where I slept, where I ate – but I can't put me in the rooms, I can't see me.

I can see her face though, the way her sparse hair framed it, the tiny nascent eyebrows barely there, her rounded perfect nose.

These girls have that same face. I sink down into the chair, short of breath. This is the closest I have been to her in fifty-six years, the nearest idea of what she grew into, who she became. If I had seen this photograph years ago, I would have known which child to watch in the park, which girl to follow in the supermarket, which pram to peer into in case it held my baby.

All the times I thought I saw her, all the times I thought I'd been close, those children had looked nothing like her: these two are her doppelgangers. These two are her sisters.

Without asking, James steps out into the garden. The blue metal bistro table and chairs are on the patio outside the studio. He sits down, planting his feet solidly, wide apart. 'My mother's betrayal . . .' He shakes his head, leans down – his face covered by his hands.

There are wrinkles where his hands meet his wrists and I'm suddenly aware of how old he is.

'How could she do that?' His fingers are spread in his white hair, sparse tufts of it poke through like lamb's wool caught on a barbed-wire fence. 'I thought you hated me.'

'I hated you more than anyone I've ever known.' It is the time for truth. 'In the end.'

I think about how long it took to add my loss to who I am, to accept everything that happened for the history it has become. Catherine let me cry, helped me grieve for all the things that were or that might have been. She and I buried the hatred and now James has dug it up, disturbed and altered it.

He is waiting for me to speak, still staring at the cracked concrete of the patio, focusing on the tiny succulents forcing their way through the thin fissures.

The silence between us is so amplified I imagine I can hear the footfall of the black ant scaling his shoelaces.

'Not that it's relevant now, but you know there was never anything between me and Polly Wright back then, don't you?' He still doesn't look up. 'She was an odd girl, and – it transpired – quite dangerous, but there was never anything like that between her and me.' He raises his head, almost makes eye contact. 'Fifty-five years later, I'd tell you if there was anything in it.'

'Fifty-six,' I say, automatically, because I never lose count of how long ago it happened – how recent it was. And then the floodgates open: bricks and barriers crumble; walls crack and oceans pour away.

Chapter Six

I'm in the shop at 6 a.m. I was awake for the second night in a row. I think of that Macbeth quote we learned at school, of how James McConnell has murdered sleep. My eyes are swollen although I have done my best to ease them with cold-water compresses.

I cried solidly, without speaking, for what must have been at least twenty minutes.

James was kind, like the boy I loved rather than how I've imagined his frozen heart, his callous attitude, over the last fifty-six years. He squatted down on his heels by my chair, put his arm round my shoulders. He asked permission first. I don't remember answering him, but I suppose I must have. He made no attempt to take the picture of his girls back from me and I saw it this morning when I came into the sitting room, just where I left it on the arm of my chair. Two of his daughters under the same sun as the first.

He didn't ask any more questions, just let me cry. Eventually he said, with an air of calm, 'I'm going to go. My dog walker will have left some hours ago. I need to sort my dog out. I need to think a bit too, actually, by myself.'

I nodded, without looking at him, focusing on my feet, hazy through the tears.

'Can I make you a cup of tea before I go? Anything?' he said.

My 'No, thank you', was feeble, was all I could manage.

'I'll be back tomorrow. We'll talk. We can make this all . . . We can try and be OK.'

And he was gone.

I put a record on the second he left – nothing to do with him or our history: a tune Catherine and I had heard in France, a lyrical dream of close evenings, cobbled streets. A memory of warmth. I thought the music might chase away enough demons to let me sleep, but that will have to be another night.

Yesterday, before this chaos arrived in my life, I had started on a long string of beads that an old lady brought in.

She was terribly agitated. 'They're worth nothing,' she said, 'but they belonged to my sister.'

The beads are plastic, translucent like round, boiled sweets. I swear I can see the memories twinkling inside them.

'I got on my hands and knees when it snapped,' the old woman said. 'I think I got them all but I wouldn't know how to start to restring them. And a jeweller won't want to do them, they're not much more than a cracker toy.'

'But they are to you,' I'd said to her and smiled. 'I'll have them finished by tomorrow. Come and get them and have a coffee with us.' We measured the length they'd been, discussed whether they might be better than they originally were by being two inches longer, and she went away happy.

Now they're on my desk, pink, blue, orange, yellow, green, repeated over and over in that order, and I'm glad of the distraction. They are shades of heathers and vivid beach stones – Catherine's colours – and threading them is an absolute pleasure, almost like

50

she brought me this task that requires utter concentration but zero thought.

I'm almost done when there's a quiet knock on the door. I am ready for James to appear at any time so I don't spook, don't start.

When I look up, it's the same old lady, the one whose necklace is in my hands at this very second. I glance at the clock on the wall. The big hand moves to ten past six with a staccato click.

'Good morning,' I say and open the door. 'You're an early riser' – I glance at the tag on her beads – 'Mrs Johnson.' I can see straightaway that her jacket is a dressing gown; her summer sandals, slippers.

'I've come for my coffee,' she says and smiles. 'You said to pop by for coffee.'

'I absolutely did,' I say. 'And biscuits. We have biscuits. Do you want to sit here while I put the coffee machine on? Is it warm out?' I ask her. 'Are many people up yet?'

'The whole world's waking up.' She points at the window. 'It's a lovely day.'

I nod. 'I believe it is,' I say.

'I can't come later – my son's taking me out for lunch. I couldn't let him down.' She takes out her phone and shows me the text message. It's lovely, so simple yet intimate: *Lunch at 1 tomorrow, Mum. Don't forget. We'll pick you up. x*

She accepts the coffee from me, and her hand is shaky as she adds half a teaspoon of sugar. 'I get a little forgetful. Confused.'

She looks at me and I can see the core of her – the version of her that hasn't come out in her dressing gown – still alight behind her eyes.

I continue to thread the beads and we chat, Mrs Johnson – Gwyn – and I. We are the same age, we discover, born in the exact same month, not quite two weeks between us. Her recall of the past is sharp and we talk about attitudes, about how awkward our parents were when they saw musicians of colour on the television, in our record collections, about how embarrassed and frustrated we were by their awful racism, and how powerless we felt to change anything.

'We thought we'd got all the answers, didn't we? And when people give me that "if you remember the sixties you weren't really there" nonsense? All I remember is no one ever listening to what I had to say. The absolute rules of it all.' Gwyn looks at her feet. 'I've come out in my slippers, haven't I?'

I don't mention the floral dressing gown. 'We all do stuff like that from time to time. Especially when we're stressed about not forgetting something else. There's only so much the brain can hold on to at once.' How I wish that were true of me today, that my short-term memory shelf were shorter. 'Try this on for size.'

I clip the re-strung necklace round her neck. The pastel beads – the orange of cough candy, the pale yellow of pineapple cubes – lie against her dressing gown and pick out perfectly the petals and blooms of the pansies and hollyhocks in the fabric.

'I've come out in my dressing gown too, haven't I?' The true cruelty of old age: the lucidity returning, gasping through the moments of confusion like a witness.

'It's still so early. No one's up but us and I can walk you home. We're invisible, so don't worry about what people think. No one can see a pair of old women, no matter what we wear. It's so liberating. I might go topless.'

Gwyn manages a laugh.

I thank my lucky stars that, although I feel my losses every day, I still have my physical strength and my mental health. The creeping anonymity of old age weighs heavier on some of us than others: Catherine embraced it from fifty. 'I've become entirely transparent,' she said. 'So this is the time to start queue-jumping, shoplifting, streaking. All the things we weren't supposed to do when people could still see us.'

It is a privilege to be here, running this shop, and able to help Gwyn. It kicks me up my metaphorical backside.

'Let's finish our coffee first. In peace. Then I'll decide what to flash as I walk you home.'

Gwyn smiles, content in her dressing gown and slippers now that she isn't lonely on top of all her other worries.

And I am grateful for her company, glad of the distraction.

Two and a half hours later, James phones at nine on the dot.

'Did you make it in to work?'

I don't tell him I've had coffee with a lost old lady, walked a new friend home to her house, started mending a set of nativity costumes that once belonged to the local primary school. 'Just about.'

There is a wide space of silence filled with all the things we need to say.

'I wondered if I could come down later on.'

'Of course.' I am going to fill in the details but I can do nothing about his anger – the fury he feels towards his mother is feeble in the path of mine.

'I haven't got any dog care. Could I bring him? He's very gentle, very good. He's an old fella too.'

'I love dogs.' There is an echo that whistles 'I loved you too once'. Neither of us can hear it but we both know it is there.

'I wondered if we might go for a walk? I think better outdoors.'

I have never forgotten that about him. James managed people well; his size and his gentleness were a powerful combination for running meetings, motivating groups. But outside, he came into his own, like a general mobilising troops. Outside, he was even bolder: he possessed a fearless calm that everyone admired.

'James?' I speak before he has a chance. 'Would you mind coming a little later? I have a commitment this morning. I'll be back by half two.' I have a desperate need to be me. To stick to the life I have built, place both my feet on the ground and stop it swaying.

I loved art classes when I was at school. But I spent fifty years living with one of the most celebrated artists of a generation and after that I daren't so much as doodle on the telephone pad. Catherine was never a teacher: it was beyond her to effuse about something terrible, even when it had been drawn by the woman she loved. It took every ounce of courage to walk through the door of the adult education centre and sign up after she had died.

Catherine only ever did one life-drawing: an unmitigated disaster, never spoken of again. The rest of her life was spent with her beautiful landscapes. It made the choice an obvious one. The classroom is the colour of cigarette smoke. We sit round the edges on plastic chairs, and in the middle is a raised dais for the models.

We haven't seen this model before: skin tightly pulled across gaunt features, a bald head – glossy and shining. The strip lights make her pate look wet, slippery. Her long hairless legs are sleek, white bones shining through. Her chest is tattooed with scars: two puckered wide stripes of red just below where her breasts once were. This is a body that has been attacked, this is a body that has suffered.

She has an impact on all of us, I can tell, as she strikes her first pose. We do rapid sketches first. Five quick poses for a few minutes each. We warm up our hands and eyes, our materials, by drawing these preliminary poses in all their transience.

I have been drawing with this group for three terms now; I know them all well but I don't know what lies beneath their clothes or under their skin. I don't know if they're single or married or parents or . . . and that is what I need today.

She's easy to draw, this woman. She's easy because she's all angles and lines. I zigzag jagged colours as the contours of her body, the length of her thighs, the strength of her shoulders. When I've acknowledged all the woman's history with my oranges and reds, I scratch the light into her with white chalk. Her long pose is a standing one. She thrusts her hips forward and holds her palms flat on her buttocks. She pushes her elbows back like wings. 'Here I am,' her pose says. 'I am real and visceral and tangible. And I . . . am not dead.' As I draw her life, her courage, it seeps up my arm and I remember that I haven't lost my own.

I knew I belonged with the people in the squat. The feeling that had ripped through me at my first demonstration, the breath of all of us as one united entity: that was what I had come for.

These people knew things. These people had stood, face to face, with American soldiers and told them to go home; they had been dragged – physically – from the naval base and spent countless nights in cold prison cells.

I became someone new, someone bolder. At the time, I thought I'd become someone very grown up.

The squat was dirty in a way that I hadn't known was possible. The smell of a hundred years of cooking clung to the corners of the kitchen. All the cooking had to be done on a blackened old stove in the corner, stoked and stacked with any bits of wood we could find and the occasional, glorious bag of coal.

The lavatory was at the back of the kitchen, freezing all year round and utterly grim. The dark-blue door that separated it from the house was cracked and peeling and couldn't be trusted not to trap you inside until someone kicked it from the outside to make it open. To this day, I credit my cast-iron bladder to my desperation not to use that loo any more than I had to.

The two girls were called Kay and Polly. I never took to Polly, right from the beginning. She was a cold girl, serious and aloof. Kay had a quiet kindness that made me feel at home. It fell to the three of us to try and clean the kitchen floor one day. We were warriors and freedom fighters, but the idea that women were better at cleaning was ground into all of us – not just the men.

It took us the best part of a day. I had found a nail brush in the bathroom upstairs and scrubbed at the black tiles until a brick red started to appear from under the tar.

'Oh, my God, look,' I called to the other two, rubbing at the floor with suds and cloths.

'That's disgusting,' said Polly.

Kay wrinkled up her nose. 'I honestly thought it was black, that the whole floor was black. That's awful.'

It took us hours. Once we'd realised it could be cleaned, we had to carry on.

'At least we're warm,' Kay said.

We fed as much wood as we could into the monstrous range, which would only heat enough water for a few inches in the bottom of the cold iron bath. Each one of us would have to use it in turn, topping it up with a kettleful of hot water.

'This is like the bloody Stone Age,' Polly said as we drew straws to see who got to go first.

I got third bath.

'She fixed that,' Kay whispered when Polly had gone into the bathroom.

'I've got it worst. I've got both your cast-offs.' I raised my eyebrows at her and we laughed.

'She's after spending more time with Jimmy McConnell while we're still up here.' Kay obviously wasn't a fan either.

'Oh.' I blushed to the roots of my hair. And then blushed more at the surprise of that. 'Are they a couple?'

Kay shook her head, lowered her voice. 'Polly wishes. He isn't into that kind of thing. He's very focused, dedicated.'

My face continued to burn, betraying something I denied even to myself.

'Jude? You've gone awful pink. Are you soft on him? Jude!' Her eyes were wide in the dark corridor.

The bathroom door opened and Polly came out wrapped in a towel. Her long legs shone white, not a blemish on her skin. 'All yours, Kay. I kept it clean, I promise.' She dug a bony elbow into Kay's arm. 'And you need to boil another kettle, Jude.'

By the time I got downstairs, the Aga was stoked and there were six people sitting around the kitchen table. Their body heat had made the small room almost homely.

'Take my seat, Jude,' Jimmy said, standing up from his chair. 'You'll catch your death over there with wet hair. And I'm too warm anyway.'

He didn't look too warm in his big sweater but I gratefully accepted the seat. In front of me, the two girls, Paddy, Jimmy, and two men I had seen coming and going but had never spoken to sat around the table. There was a bottle of spirits on the mat in the middle, brown glass with a cheaply printed label. From the smell in the air, I assumed it was whisky.

This wasn't how I'd pictured adulthood, but here it was: third-hand bathwater and trying to keep warm in a filthy kitchen. It would make my mother weep. I smiled to myself, feeling a million miles from home and very grown up.

'We were talking about today's raid,' Paddy said. 'About how Jimmy saved the day.'

'Saved my backside more like,' said one of the two men, his face a network of freckles animated by laughter. 'I thought I'd had it when the guard let the old dog go.'

Jimmy shook his head. 'I'm just not scared of dogs, Angus, that's all.'

'Well, I bloody am.' Angus laughed till he started coughing and wiped his mouth with a rag he pulled from his trouser pocket.

Jimmy stood behind Angus, put one hand on his shoulder and patted him. 'But it shows things are getting serious. That maybe we should call off the big raid. Maybe people are going to start getting hurt.'

'Enough politics,' said Polly loudly. She patted the stool beside her, gestured for Jimmy to sit down.

I wondered if he really paused for a moment – or if it was wishful thinking on my part.

Jimmy reached backwards between his knees to pull the stool underneath him.

Polly placed her hand territorially over his arm and squeezed his wrist. Her hair was so vivid that a line of light shone across it when she moved, the same tawny spark that glinted in her eyes. 'Can we talk about something else?'

'What else?' said Jimmy. He stretched his arm across the table to get his glass and her hand slipped back on to the table. 'There isn't any "else". Everything is politics.'

'Oh, Jimmy, please.' Polly rolled her eyes.

'Everything,' said Paddy, his voice quiet and serious. 'From the country you were born in, to your education, to the clothes you wear on your back. It's all politics.'

'I'll prove it.' Jimmy sprang up from the stool.

I could hear his enthusiastic footsteps as he bounded up the stairs. He made as much noise, if not more, coming back down.

When he came back into the dim brown kitchen, Jimmy was holding a guitar. He sat back on the stool, crossed his long legs. 'What shall we play?'

One of the quiet men, his name was Dougie, leaned over to the dresser, wrestled the drawer open and took out two spoons. He laced them through his fingers, bowl backs together. The dents flashed as he clacked them against each other. I had heard people play the spoons before, but never like this. This was a subtle art, a percussion of lace and filigree.

'"This Land is Your Land".' Jimmy's accent was thick when he said it, his vowels knitted like a warm shawl. My parents – in another world – sang this song at Christmas with aunties and uncles and sherry. We even sang it at Sunday school.

'Politics,' Jimmy said, and nodded his head to Polly in a told-you-so way. It wasn't a warm gesture. 'Like all folk music: songs of the people, songs they didn't have to ask their masters if they could sing. Freedom and a way to express it.'

I was afraid to join in at first but Paddy's deep voice, the one that had led our hymns every Sunday at home, gave me confidence. I sang along with most of it, but every now and again I stopped: in the pause I listened to the melody of my new life, the rhythm of Dougie's percussion, the sweet voices of the girls – even Polly. In those short moments, my hair still damp on the nape of my neck, I felt actively happy for the first time since I'd taken the five-pound notes from the tin under the stairs.

Chapter Seven

I meet him in the car park.

I chose this walk deliberately. Catherine and I were particularly fond of it. Its paths are wide and will give James and me space to walk without being too close to one another. The views swoop from the downs over the sea and out to the horizon, slopes of green leading to the dazzling ceaseless twitch of waves. It will be a good route for talking, for perspective. The soft, hopeful grass will give our tears somewhere to fall.

'You made good time,' I say as if we are strangers. 'Whereabouts in London are you?' We are strangers.

'Maida Vale. My wife and I moved to Kilburn in the early seventies, when that was the only place anyone non-English could go. And then upgraded when the girls were . . . you know, when we had the girls.'

The dog breaks the awkwardness. He is fat and shaggy. A golden retriever so old his coat has faded, the glow of his fur reduced to the colour of cornstalks. He is enthusiastic and excited to meet a new person.

'He's lovely,' I say, my hands on his soft ears. 'What's he called?'

'Dougal. He's the last Dougal in a long line. We figured we would only call the new dog by the old dog's name anyway, so he's Dougal the Fourth.'

The first part of the walk is wooded and thick, the brambles reaching out to pinch us on the path. I walk in front of James, in silence, Dougal in front of me. When the green eaves above us widen and allow James to catch up beside me it becomes apparent that one of us should speak.

'I presume you've never looked for her?'

It is a reasonable line to start on.

'It's complicated.'

He doesn't speak. Our footfalls on the springy turf and the sound of brackens and twigs against our arms isn't enough to fill the silence.

'I looked on the Adoption Contact Register,' I say.

He holds a branch back so that I can walk under it. Shouts at Dougal for eating something on the path. 'On what?'

I pick words that will make this easier for him. 'Adoption reunion isn't as easy as you think. It isn't the trope of happy-ever-after or long-lost family that you see on the TV.' I don't tell him how deep those portrayals, misty-eyed medical dramas, mistaken identity romances, cut me. 'I was a social worker and I saw this stuff from the raw end.'

James snaps a twig from the top of a long cow parsley, almost as tall as he is. He breaks it into tiny pieces as he walks, looking only at the stem in his fingers.

I wait for him to make eye contact. When he does, I tell him: 'Fewer than one in ten adoption reunions ends happily. The other nine are life-changingly awful for all the parties involved.'

We are striding out across the soft grass. To our right a field of barley waves and moves, soft against the light summer wind, shh-ing as loudly as the sea. 'Many adoptees from the fifties and sixties were never told. Didn't know that their parents weren't their biological family. And imagine that? Imagine that, when a stranger comes crashing into your identity. Imagine the effect on your mental health. On your parents.'

James puts his hands in his pockets. He is nodding at what I've said. The creases under his eyes are deeper than yesterday, like his skin is filling up with sorrow.

Walking was a good idea, the views, the salt breeze; they are playing their part. It is helping put the trauma of yesterday behind me, for a moment.

'What happened to me happened to half a million women in England and Wales over two decades.' I swallow hard, outrage making my teeth clench together. 'Not counting Ireland, or Scotland. Imagine that. Five hundred thousand people. Not people, women.' I stop still and the breeze blows warm behind me, a silhouetted caress as it puffs past.

'I can't begin . . .'

I shake my head. 'Don't.'

We walk on. I concentrate on the ground: heel, toe, heel, toe – steadying myself with the rhythm. 'Any relative could join the Adopted Children's Contact Register.' A flint edges out of the mud by my foot, sharp-edged. 'Your daughters could.' Those words are still fragile in my mouth and heart. 'Then, if there was a match, social services would step in as intermediary, limit the fallout. I left a letter too, in her adoption file. So that she knew . . .'

I stop for a moment. In the distance I see another couple our age. They have a dog too. They look like us: dressed for a walk, familiar with one another – but we have a lifetime of reasons to never be like them.

'The letter would be given to her by social services if she ever asked to make contact with me – us.'

His voice is small in the huge sky. 'Was my name in there? Did you talk about me?'

'I wrote your name and where you came from.' I take a breath and exhale slowly. 'It said that I'd loved you but that you weren't around, that you couldn't – didn't – help. Whichever.' It is an arrow that glances his skin: an unintentional shot.

'I'm so sorry.' His voice cracks.

I shake my head at him. That is not what this conversation is going to be. This is about me. We can deal with his losses when he understands properly – when I have spoken my piece.

'She was born in an unmarried mothers' home, run by Catholic nuns.' I look at him, to make sure he is processing the scale of this tragedy.

'Can we stop? Sit for a moment? I . . . It's a lot to manage.'

I have had a lot of practice saying these words. I can talk lucidly – now – because Catherine listened to decades of it: in fragments and single words; in philosophical projections where I wondered about the possibility of erasing all the separated years – of rebranding my child; in tirades of fanatical anger.

There is a small copse of trees, planted rather than naturally occurring. One of them lies on its side, presumably felled by lightning when it was the tallest thing for miles around. James sits down on the faded trunk and I sit a little way away from him.

'I'm so fucking sorry,' he says. 'I would never have let any of it happen. Never.'

'What's important here, James – what's missing from every newspaper report, every television show – is the law. In Britain, in 1967 – right up until the Children's Act of 1975, actually – it was illegal for an adopted child to trace their parents. And' – I make sure he is looking at me, that he understands the importance of this – 'it was impossible for a parent to trace their child.'

'But—'

I stop him. I learnt long ago that there are no buts. 'When we had our children taken away from us, it meant we knew that we would never ever see them again. Never.'

He has tears on his cheeks, they flatten in the warm breeze and the salt turns his skin matt underneath them. I can see the tracks they have made.

'The nuns told us that we had to think of it like the "veil Jesus Christ had drawn between life and death". Literally. That they were gone for good – because they were.'

And I remember when that changed: when the doors of contact, of tracing parents or children, swung open. I read about it, as it happened, in social work journals.

I vividly remember the day it became law, the cold November morning, the smell of fireworks and bonfires still in the air. By then she was nine years old. She had belonged to her family for nine years. For almost all of her life. 'And there were no demos for us, James. No banners or leaflets about the unmarried mothers' homes, no songs of protest. Just thousands and thousands of women, each one absolutely alone. No one marched for us, there were no sit-ins outside those miserable prisons. Not one.'

I'm glad James has brought Dougal. The dog is immune to these words: he is enchanted by the smells and the sounds of the fields, thrilled by the wheeling seagulls above his silky head. He wags and woofs and runs. Watching him is a joy.

'I'm sorry.' James has stretched his legs out in front of him and he is leaning forward over them, his head hanging down and his face hidden. 'I didn't know. I mean, I didn't know any of it.'

'There have been attempts over the years to bring it to Parliament, to get an apology. It gets thrown out every time.' I shrug.

'Anyway.' I stand up, stretch my arms and stamp my feet. I gesture towards the edge of the downs, the start of the glittering sea. 'The long and the short is that no one has ever asked for the letter, never applied for the file. And there are only two reasons for that, given that she's almost fifty-six. Either she doesn't want to meet me, or she doesn't know she's adopted. Both of those leave my hands totally tied.'

Dougal heads off in front of us and the sun glitters on his tail. It's a beautiful day – the air is clean and we can see for miles.

'Did you tell your daughters?' I ask him as we walk.

James doesn't break his stride. 'They're both in Australia. I was too shot last night, I'm going to call them this evening.'

'That's good.' Is it good? Is it going to make them happy?

'Judith.' There is a warning note in his voice. Dougal hears it and turns round: checks obediently that he isn't the worry. 'I didn't know any of this last night. I thought it was as simple as those programmes on TV. And . . .'

'And?'

'I had one of those DNA kits, an ancestry website thing. The girls bought it for me a couple of Christmases ago. But a lot has happened since then and I never got round to doing it.'

I assume he means his wife's death.

'I sent it off this morning.'

Chapter Eight

Ruby

This is exactly what my mum said would happen. The exact reason she never tried to find her birth family. I've really fucked up here and now I don't know what to do. And Dad is going to go ballistic.

The worst week in years started quietly, with a meeting with my MA supervisor. If I can't come up with a question for my thesis, I have to join her research. If I finish the rest of my assignments, get on top of everything, I will have a clear space to sort it all out. Would have had.

But I've blown that right out of the water.

I was procrastinating, in my flat. I'd been on the phone to my dad and he'd done one of his lectures-dressed-as-jokes. This one was the 'undergraduates think they know everything, masters students realise they don't know everything, PhD students realise they know nothing at all' – he's said it before, more than once, but either he's forgotten or he doesn't care that he's boring me. Bit of both, probably.

I love this little flat – it's the size of a handkerchief but it's the first place I've ever lived where the bathroom is mine alone, where I can leave cups in the sink and not disgust anybody. Dad bangs on about the rent but Mum paid a big chunk upfront so, as long as I keep my job, I can make it work.

My finger was on the mouse, hovering over a link to go into the uni library, when my email pinged. 'YourGeneCheck.com.' They've sent a fair bit of spam since I signed up a year ago, and even threw up some second cousins once removed although when I told my dad, he knew exactly who they were, where they lived, and said my grandma probably still sent them Christmas cards like she does to half the population of Hong Kong.

I clicked on it.

'Match', it said on the subject line, and I felt a little frisson of excitement. And then on the line below and such a shock it made my heart race, it said, 'Most likely relationship: half-sibling/grandparent.'

I've always known my mum was adopted. She was nine weeks old when her parents got her. There are no photos of her before that age, which I always found a bit weird but that didn't bother her, and in so many after that, she looked like a fairer version of me – ice-blue eyes like mine: her hair far lighter but just as straight.

Her parents hadn't meant for her to be an only child, they'd expected to adopt at least another two kids as easily as they'd got her, but the Abortion Act was passed in 1967 and the supply chain – my mum's words, not mine – dried up. And then, she says, she was the apple of their eye, the one almost-perfect replacement for the baby they couldn't have and – although they were great friends – the burden on her was heavy. She had to do everything only children do for their non-existent siblings – sports; qualifications; marry well – but, on top of all that, she had to be everything their child-who-didn't-exist might have been too. It made her go a bit easier on me, until I was in my teens, anyway.

So Mum grew up playing the piano, studied to be an architect, played hockey for the county, and turned herself into the perfect daughter-in-law for my other grandmother – who had absurdly high expectations, considering her son is my dad.

I was about twelve when I really got a bee in my bonnet about the whole birth parents thing. About what if her parents were really famous or rich.

'My mum is a brilliant granny to you,' she said. 'The absolute best a granny can be.' And it was true. 'But we've had a lot of pressure on us over the years, and being a mother to me was hard for her. We do not need the trauma of the other stuff, setting fires we've spent a lifetime putting out.' And then she smiled, tweaked my nose and put her finger across my lips – standard. 'And that, my dear little friend, is that.'

I'm almost afraid to click on the details, but I'm compelled to do it. He has a completed profile. James McConnell. Seventy-six. Retired television executive. Most likely relationship grandfather then, I'd imagine.

There is a photograph of him kneeling down beside a big yellow golden retriever and there, next to that, is the box that says 'contact'.

Most likely relationship grandfather.

I rock back in my chair and exhale. There is a cheese plant beside my desk that is nearly as tall as I am. I have nurtured it since I was a teenager, dusting its wide leaves and testing the soil to make sure it's just right. In return it grows and grows, curving over my desk like a jungle canopy.

Most likely relationship grandfather.

I google him. There are a surprising number of people called James McConnell in the television industry. I click on to images, looking for clues.

The chair at my desk has arms on it. I grip them tightly. There, staring back from my screen, from the wrong face – a large, lined face – are my mother's blue eyes, my eyes.

I have no clue what to do next. This is uncharted territory.

I am going to have to go and tell her.

It's only a twenty-minute walk from my flat to Mum. It's one of the reasons I like the location. It's good to stay close, to have her on hand.

I pass the church, the primary school, the little coffee shop – I walk the wide diagonal path across the park, the short cut. It's a beautiful day, birds are shrieking almost as loudly as the children in the big concrete paddling pool. There was a pool like that where I grew up and I remember walking in it, terrified as it came up past my waist. It wouldn't reach my knees now. Some things get less scary as you get older.

The gates are tall and old. Victorian, I imagine. They have a taste of those books I did for A level, all thunderous moorlands and boats crashing on to Gothic cliffs.

I spend the rest of the journey rehearsing what I'm going to say. I feel like a child when I realise it all begins with, 'I didn't really mean . . .' or 'I didn't think it would matter if . . .'

I am almost all the way there before I turn round.

Chapter Nine

JUDITH

I dream about a bird with wide black wings: it swoops above me dropping letters in white envelopes. They rain down on me, sharp, the paper corners cutting my face and hands. In my dream I can't tell whether the envelopes are feathers or droppings, whether the bird is shedding them as the seasons change or firing its shit at me, deliberately.

James McConnell has murdered sleep indeed.

I wake, wet with sweat, tangled in my white duvet cover. This is one of those moments where my hand shoots across the bed to grab a part of Catherine, whatever is nearest – a hand, a shoulder, a hip. There is nothing there but wrinkled linen.

'We need to talk,' I say out loud to her. I get out of bed and do what Catherine would do: change the air in the room – whether I was ready or not. I strip the sheets off the bed and heap them on to the floor. Then, still naked from sleep, I throw open the bedroom windows so that the world bursts in, soaks me with chill early sunshine, bathes my fretful skin. I look down at the garden as it wakes, cobwebs dripping with dew, hedges and shrubs trimmed with pearls of morning. I am glad I don't have neighbours who can see into my house: even so, I will pull a T-shirt on to go and make coffee.

For all my tortured sleep, I'm as excited about what James has done as I am nervous. The two parts of me pull away from each other: my mind is alive with possibilities, a crackling static of What Ifs.

Jimmy was always impetuous: one of those people who pounces on life and counts the options and the odds, the costs and opportunities, afterwards. It made his silence all the more difficult to bear, all the more unlikely. The hardest thing in all of this is adjusting to James's side. Literally upending and rebalancing my own truth. This is where I need Catherine, to talk me down, to remind me that you can have your own truth till you're blue in the face but if that isn't the same as The Truth – the single truth that applies to everyone – it means nothing. Despite the awkwardness, the polar opposites, of having my two lovers in the same headspace, I need Catherine to convince me that Jimmy McConnell was a victim of circumstance, of his mother, of the system. That he didn't do the things I've always believed he did, that he isn't that person.

I have to separate the strands of the history I assumed from the few bare threads I know are fact. Back then, Jimmy McConnell had broad shoulders. Jimmy McConnell was brave and dependable. Jimmy McConnell would have run – sprinted – across hot coals to do The Right Thing.

It made what happened afterwards even harder.

I'd been at the squat a month or so when Angus brought the guy from London in. We were a real mixed bunch: half-Scottish, some English, the odd one or two – Paddy Gordon included – were Irish. Peter was southern, posh – he was different to us in every way.

'This is Pete,' Angus said, coming into the kitchen. 'Anyone mind if he sleeps here for a few nights?' They were both dirty and wet. Angus pressed himself against the Aga and steam rose from his coat.

'It's fine by me,' said Kay, and I nodded my agreement.

Pete wore a shaggy sheepskin coat: damp, it smelt like a dead goat. He laid it across the back of a kitchen chair and Kay and I made faces at each other.

He had long blond hair, down way past his ears and curling out across his shirt collar. He wore skin-tight jeans with kicks at the bottom, flaring out over dirty tan desert boots. None of us were part of that tribe – his clothes, his coat, were part of the new American import of fashion. It wasn't for us – it was new, it was untidy, but most of all, we couldn't afford it.

Kay and I shared skirts, borrowed each other's tops, and owned four jumpers between us. Polly kept to her own stuff – ours was too big for her. The boys all wore smart clothes, even to wriggle through the mud. The trousers they wore for demos or marches were the same ones they wore to work. Their jackets were button-through bum-freezers, sharp lines and neat hems – or old men's donkey jackets like their fathers had worn on the shipyards. If any one of us had had two pennies to rub together, we would have spent them on trying to warm up our house.

Pete stood out like a peacock in our brown kitchen.

Angus made tea in the big metal teapot and, for once, we even had milk. The spout had a big dent in the end and splattered drops of tea on the table as he poured.

'Jimmy, this is Pete. He's from London, he's been up at the camp.' Angus gestured across the table to where Pete had put his tobacco pouch on the table.

'How do you do?' Jimmy said, stretching his big hand over to shake Pete's. He had been at work, fitting shifts in a factory around his stints at the base. 'Sorry,' Jimmy said, staring at his hand. 'I'm still covered in grease. I've been fixing rivets for twelve hours.'

Pete waved it away. 'It's fine, man. Thanks for letting me crash.' Pete was a large man, emerging from a gangly boy. His nose was wide and long, his jaw jutting forward and square at the corners. He was big enough to assume he'd get pretty much what he wanted in any situation. It must have been a surprise to him to meet Jimmy.

Kay and I smirked at one another: we weren't quite up to 'man' yet. The boys we knew called people 'lad' or 'fella' – 'man' belonged to another kind of person altogether.

'Did I see you in a phone box earlier, man, down by the post office?' Pete said. 'I opened the door and . . .'

Jimmy shook his head. 'No' me. I've come straight from work, just now. I've not stopped.'

Pete unzipped his tobacco pouch, laid out papers and lighter on the kitchen table. His hands were below the edge of the table.

I heard the wheel of his lighter spin but I couldn't see what he was doing.

'Fucking hell.' Jimmy jumped up. 'What are you doing?'

Pete looked up. He wasn't particularly fazed but the rest of us were startled to hear Jimmy raise his voice like that. 'Rolling a joint.'

'We don't have drugs in this house.' Jimmy was almost roaring. 'You need to get out now.'

Angus was mumbling beside him, nodding agreement with Jimmy. 'Christ, Pete. Not in our house.'

Pete leant back in his chair, and the stinking coat stirred like a waking sheep as he moved. 'It's a squat, yeah? First time I've . . . Hey!'

Jimmy leant forward and grabbed the lump of hash from his fingers. He strode down the corridor and into the front room we used as an entrance hall.

'He'll be fucking that through yon window.' Angus nodded his head towards Pete, pointed after Jimmy.

'What?' Pete was gathering his belongings. 'What did he say?' he asked us, the vowels of his Queen's English long and incongruous.

'Your hashish,' I said. Kay was smirking beside me. 'He's gone to throw it out of the window.'

Kay was fully laughing by the time Pete skittered down the hall, dragging his stinking coat behind him like a reluctant dog.

'I say! I say!' he shouted after Jimmy. He sounded like a schoolteacher.

Jimmy was visibly rattled when he came back in. We'd caught the tail end of the shouting but no discernible words. He thumped down on to a kitchen chair that shuddered under his weight.

'I'm sorry, pal. I had no idea.' Angus was genuinely sorry. His huge mass of red hair bobbed about as he talked. 'He'd no' done that at the camp.'

'Just so we're all clear.' Jimmy looked round at every one of us in turn, his gaze pausing just long enough to connect with our innermost thoughts. 'This isn't that kind of place. We're in enough danger as it is, there's no point adding to it.'

Later, when Angus had returned to the camp, and Kay and Dougie with him, I was sitting in the kitchen reading when Jimmy came downstairs. I had never been in a room alone with him before and the familiar awkwardness of thinking about him prickled in my hair follicles. I fought down the rising heat.

'Sorry,' he said, 'I didn't mean to disturb you.' He picked up the kettle, weighed it in his hand and moved it across to the hotplate.

I lowered my book to my lap. 'You're not.' And then I summoned all my courage, opened a conversation. 'What you said earlier, about danger. Do you mean on the base?' In the mid-sixties, a drug conviction – even just from being on the premises – would see any one of us being banned from ever teaching, holding any kind of office.

'And here. We're under surveillance by Special Branch. They drop people in all the time, plain clothes.'

'You think that guy – Pete – was Special Branch.'

Jimmy shrugged. 'It would be easy for them. Plant some drugs here: get him to sell us some. Then raid us.'

We knew of plenty of people who'd been raided by Special Branch, many who'd been framed or been roughed up while their possessions were trashed.

Jimmy pointed to the teapot and I nodded. I slid my bookmark into place and closed the pages.

'But now there's another enemy. It's all very hush-hush, we're still finding stuff out, but there's a new Terrorism Squad. Worse than Special Branch. And we're of' – he enunciated his words in pure English, his worst of insults – '*special interest* to them.'

'We're not terrorists.' I could imagine my father's face, how he would rage at anyone connected with that word. I swept him and my mother from my mind, brushed them back into the old world with a phantom promise to write. 'The government are the bloody terrorists. How dare they?'

The kettle blew out clouds of steam, the valve that made it whistle long gone. Water spat and danced on the hotplate.

'They think we are.' Jimmy shrugged his shoulders. 'They think that what they're doing is unassailably right and that anyone who gets in the way is a terrorist.'

The cloud that had haunted my dreams at home billowed in my mind, the flash, the flattened cities. Nagasaki. Hiroshima. Millions of casualties. 'They . . . I . . .' I couldn't put my frustration into words without crying.

Jimmy sighed. 'And a terrorism conviction comes with a long prison sentence. A record for life.'

That belonged to the future, something I barely imagined. I was nineteen years old; it was another country.

'I worry about you.' It was his turn to colour up: it was like watching a bear tremble.

I pushed the book away. 'Do you worry about Dougie or Angus?' I felt my prickling skin take on a different bloom, this time matching my mood. 'Or can they manage because they're men?'

Jimmy moved suddenly, as if he couldn't work out where to place his clumsy hands, his long arms. 'No.' His voice was loud but faltering. 'No, that's not it. It's – you're so young.'

The twin sins of using my age and my gender against me had been committed. I stood up, ready to leave him there and stomp back to my bedroom with my book. 'For one thing, I've been cutting fences, moving pegs, egging trucks, with everyone else. All the things you've done, Mr Big-Yin. And secondly, why aren't you worried about Kay?' I was pretty much the same height as him, squared up, only I was standing and he was sitting down. 'And then, third, you're barely older than me. Not exactly mature.'

He grabbed my arm, softly, but his fingers closed round the cuff of my jumper. 'I don't worry about Kay in the same way.' There was a silence between us and we both fought for breath in it. 'Because I don't feel the same way about Kay as I do about you.' He looked angry.

I sat back down. The chair legs scraped on the greasy floor.

'Sorry.' He took a huge slurp from his cup. 'Christ, that was hot.' He looked up, his hand held to his burnt lips, his blue eyes wide. His fringe was sticking up slightly, the rest of his light-brown hair was slicked down: it made him look shocked.

Outside, the evening had closed in quickly. The last moments of the day lit the chimney pots with a peacock blue.

'I'm being an idiot,' he said, and I realised that I hadn't spoken.

I looked at him, then at the floor. I squeezed my eyes shut to stop what was coming, but I couldn't, the laughter rose inside me like a flood, bubbled from my throat like freedom. I stood, stepped towards Jimmy. My arms lifted themselves like a silent-movie somnambulist and I walked, laughing fit to bust, straight at him.

It took him a few seconds of puzzled inertia and then the roar of his laughter raised the hairs on my skin as he threw his arms around me, squashing the breath from my lungs.

Jimmy McConnell had a single bed. We went up to his room rather than risk being caught by the others in the kitchen while we were still working ourselves out, still swapping details of how long we'd liked each other, and how many times we'd tried – and failed – to say something. His room was on the top floor. It was small – in the same exhausted condition as the rest of the house, but clean and neat. He had an old wardrobe and a bookcase made of planks and bricks. The floor was bare boards, the curtain a thin towel tacked to the pelmet.

I sat on the edge of the bed, trailing my finger along the spines of his books to see what I had and hadn't read.

'I loved this.' I picked up the book, stroked its red leather cover. 'I read it at school.'

'It's my ma's. She gave it to me.' He took the book out of my hand, put it back on the shelf. 'She doesn't have many books. It's very precious.' He smiled, and there was love in his face, in his thoughts of home.

I didn't know what to say to that.

He obviously felt the awkwardness of the silence. 'I send my wages back to Aberdeen. For my ma and my sister. It's all they have really – my daddy died. My ma does bits and bobs, but.'

It hadn't occurred to me that someone might be poorer than us. That people who weren't fighting for a cause – choosing to live this way – might have to rely on the generosity of others, on handouts. I had never met anyone who had more money than their parents.

I put my finger on Jimmy McConnell's lips and whispered, 'Shhh.' The guilt of what I knew I was about to do, what I was desperate to experience, was enough on its own – without remembering that I had stolen from my own parents in order to do it.

Afterwards, content and complete – surprised by how easy it had been to slip into adulthood – we curled into each other. Jimmy pulled the blanket round us, felt my back to make sure it covered me against the cold room.

We were in awe of sex in the 1960s, terrified of its risks, of its never-go-back threats. At my Catholic girls' school, in my magazines, there were constant reminders that the cost would be so high, we had to be sure that we'd found The One. I looked at the outline of Jimmy McConnell, sketched by the moonlight beside me. I loved everything about him: his heart-on-the-sleeve way of looking at every experience; the conscience that he wore like a huge velvet robe. He was vast and unusual and bewitching.

'You OK?' he asked me, his voice soft in the dark.

I exhaled. I didn't know what to say – what might give me away as the inexperienced little girl I was, or what might make me sound loose, too easy.

'Judith?'

'I'm fine. Great.'

'I'm sorry my bed's so tiny. It doesn't help that I'm such a giant.' He squeezed me tighter and I curled into the space between his arms.

'You should have chosen someone smaller.' I pictured Polly Wright, her wild red curls, her petite frame. 'And I am definitely not that girl.'

At that moment, and for comfortable months afterwards, I had absolutely no desire to be anyone but me, or with anybody but Jimmy. We worked hard. The girls found jobs in places with duplicating machines: I worked in the library; Kay in an office. We were never sure where Polly Wright worked and imagined that she had rich parents. After Jimmy and I became an item, Polly rarely spoke to me; if she did, it was just nosiness or little digs. I didn't miss her for a moment.

Any spare time we had we spent at the base. Things were moving fast there, tracts of land had been churned up, sliced away like wounds.

We'd not been particularly scared of the Ministry of Defence in the past. Their security had been a selection of angry middle-aged men with Govan accents and the dog that Jimmy had discovered wagged its tail and jumped up at you with its tongue out if you stood your ground. Now, attacks on the tents by bulldozers were becoming commonplace and the squat was filling up with people who had nowhere else to go and who didn't feel safe to close their eyes near the base.

The times were changing as the worst of winter rolled in towards us. The squat became more serious, more of an operations HQ. The horrible old toilet at the back of the kitchen suffered from the extra footfall: Kay and I would make great efforts to go to work in the mornings before we had our first wee, hoping and holding through the cold streets rather than risk going in there.

Our efforts to delay the submarine base, to be a thorn in their side, were no longer enough. The harbours were cast: concrete cliffs at the top of the loch, devoid of birds or other wildlife, monstrous in their straight black dominance of the landscape. High metal

79

fences – strengthened with steel and topped with razor wire – replaced the haphazard protection that had ringed the site when I first arrived. We were strengthening our efforts, handing out more leaflets, writing furiously to newspapers and politicians – but we were losing.

The inner circle of the planning committee was Jimmy, Paddy, and Polly. I didn't like it – hated coming downstairs to find her and him head to head, fingertips almost touching across the map laid out on the kitchen table – but it was part of the sacrifice for that once-beautiful landscape, for our safety.

Jimmy called a meeting. It was held in the sitting room – most of us sat on the bare floor, a few of the older men stood against the walls around the edge, leaning their backs against the torn wallpaper.

'Thanks for being here, for coming at such short notice.' Paddy started the meeting. 'The first warheads are imminent. The harbours are almost ready for them and our fight is at a crucial stage.'

Jimmy stood next to him, his right-hand man. 'It is important to keep all this secret as long as possible, nothing discussed here must leave this room. We have one more reconnaissance raid, we need to make a series of measurements that are perfectly accurate, and then . . .' He stood a little straighter, cleared his throat. 'It's the big one. All hands on deck, prepare to stay chained to the harbour, the jetties, the gates, for as long as it takes. There will, without doubt, be injuries, casualties even.'

'We're expecting Special Branch, the Glasgow Constabulary, the Military Police, and the contractors themselves,' Paddy said. 'It's going to be a dangerous place to be. Those of you with families or dependants need to think long and hard about what you're going to do. The likelihood is that we'll finish either in prison or in hospital, but we can generate an enormous amount of attention. We're coordinating this with journalists, with peace groups across Britain and the States. We have three separate demonstrations in America that will happen at the same time and' – he made his voice sound solemn, the gravity of his priesthood days – 'there will be an attack on the American Embassy in London.'

A ripple of surprise went round the small room.

'No one will be hurt,' Paddy continued. 'It's being carefully set up to make sure of that.'

I glanced at Kay and she shrugged her shoulders, wrinkled her nose so that her freckles clustered and crinkled: she had no more idea what was going on than me. 'Where's Polly?' I whispered.

'Visiting her family. Back tomorrow, I think.' Kay put her finger over her lips and Jimmy continued speaking.

'Nothing like this has ever happened before.' Jimmy looked around the room, made eye contact with every person. 'You will be part of an international protest. The eyes of the world will be on us. We will stick – strictly – to the principles of non-violent direct action, but there will be action – illegal and direct.' He gestured across the room and two older men I'd never met looked up, nodded.

'Stewart and Don are from Scots Against War.' We all looked towards them. They looked like a pair of old dads, stumbling out of a factory shift, or like Jimmy might have interrupted them on their evening walk to the pub.

'They are also explosives experts,' Jimmy said to a silent room. 'At the end of this month, on the day of our sit-in, the first warheads are to be delivered into Gare Loch. There will be nuclear bombs on submarines, sliding silently into our river, past your families – asleep in your homes. And we can't let that happen.'

One of the two men lit a cigarette and the fizz of the match made me jump.

The room was so quiet I heard the man let the cigarette smoke back out of his mouth and it hovered like a ghost in front of him.

Paddy spoke. 'We can't let those Polaris missiles dock in Faslane. Non-violent direct action remains our priority – there will be no violence and no human beings hurt in any of this. Many of us here are led by our belief in Jesus Christ and in peace.'

I forgot – most of the time – that Paddy's motivation came from a higher place than mine. Even dressed in civvies – dark-grey trousers and an almost matching suit jacket – he still had a presence, a serenity, that he had brought with him from back then.

'We are taking this action as a last resort. A reaction to the betrayal of Downing Street, and to their ignoring the lessons of the past. Jimmy?' He gestured to Jimmy to take over and a fizzle of pride ran through me.

Jimmy stood silent for a moment, his lighthouse beam gaze making sure that every person, every living thing, was listening. 'We have been left with no choice but to use direct action. We are going to blow up the road that runs through the glen to the end of the loch.'

Chapter Ten

Ruby

I'm putting off going to see Mum, I know I am, but I might as well find out everything I can first. Get hung for a sheep as a lamb.

I make a list – a Dad thing – and I try, for ages, not to let 'text girls, drinks tonight' creep any further up the to-do ladder than it already has.

Apart from a catch-up with the girls, everything else on my list is so enormous I get a headache just thinking it, so it makes absolute sense to call the girls first and get to the list proper tomorrow. There are six of us in the text group: so little effort for so much distraction. It's a no-brainer.

We meet outside Red Willow if the weather is nice enough, any Tuesday, any Thursday – two-for-one on cocktails. There are more seats outside than in and those that want to can smoke without offending too many people. I spent so much stupid time fighting with my parents about smoking when I was young and now, when I totally could if I wanted to, I couldn't care less about it. It still adds to the feel of summer though, smelling cigarettes somewhere on the breeze when you go out for a drink.

It takes less than fifteen minutes to walk to the pub. I practise telling the girls all the way there, rearrange the words into maximum drama. This is a rehearsal for telling my mum, the only difference is that at the end of telling them I won't feel terrible, or guilty, or childish.

Dad has always been the quiet parent, and Mum the shouty one. So much so, in fact, that my teenage years have left a bit of a scar on everyone. Especially me, if I'm honest, but I try not to share that. There was one day worse than any other – so bad I'll never forgive myself – but it's never talked about now. I wonder if I'm the only one of us who carries it everywhere.

People always say that thing about quiet parents – 'Ooh, doesn't that make it worse when they do, actually, shout?' – but I wouldn't know. That's not my dad, it's not how he does things. In the thick of it all, I came home one day and most of the plant pots on the patio were broken, soil everywhere, so I know he – once – smashed some stuff up too. But he never shouts.

I suppose stopping being a teenager has made me, some might say, marginally less angry. Unless, of course, I think about my mum and me and all the tears and all the raging, how most of my memories of the last few years are just us screaming like crazy people at each other.

The pub is quite quiet when I arrive. I am the first there and I rearrange a bit of outdoor furniture, pull two tables together and nab six chairs. I've got a cardigan I can loop over the back of one and I put my bag on another to make it look like I'm not on my own.

My masters is better than my degree for my social life: on my degree, everyone went home to their mums whenever they had a deadline. Their mothers sent parcels of home-cooked food or envelopes of cash with funny cards or cute notes. With the masters, people are older, they talk less about their parents – I assume more of them manage without. Dad tried – he tried really hard and I appreciate that he did – but there seems to be a difference in the way dads do things. For my dad, the angry years involved lots of long, long walks that, ergo, meant mine involved a lot of cooking for myself and trading amusing stories with the cat.

The girls start to wander in after a few minutes: there were no awkward moments where someone needed our chairs and I had to defend them, but Emma buys my first drink anyway for getting such a good table.

Laughter was what I needed to make me forget – and I'm with the right people: Sophie's disastrous last date; Candice and Marta's horror of a landlord. Each time I think about telling my story, I lose the impetus, can't find the words. Even by last orders, sloshed, I haven't managed to spit it out, turn it into a tall tale. I know why. It's impossible to tell the whole story – describe James, all of that – without talking about my mum.

Sometimes I wonder if I chose my friendship group because none of them ever mention their parents.

I get up late and already tired. The worst thing about a studio apartment is that you can't hide from anything, even with a hangover. My clothes from last night are in a heap on the floor and the midnight feast I made when I got in is a car crash in my kitchen.

The computer is open on my desk. I did drunken internet searching last night, stayed up far too long looking for more information about The Mystery Grandfather. I found a couple of documentaries his company made that I've actually watched – that blows my mind. A stack of textbooks sits next to the laptop like a threat. I've scoured them, and the library resources, but I can't find that one sentence, that one simple idea that my tutor says will bring my masters' question springing to life like it was always there.

I ruffle the long green and white leaves of my spider plant like a pet in case it's hiding something, some snippet of vital information. A tiny baby version drops on to my desk and I press it into the soil – I can never bear to let them die, just one of the reasons this flat has more plants than surfaces. I get a glass of water and share it with the plant.

I press the dial button on my mobile.

'Hello, are you ringing to tell me you've found a sparkling essay question? One that tells us everything anyone's ever needed to know about Global Environmental Politics and Society?'

I know what he's doing – he always says things like this to prove he's been listening.

'Maybe not.'

'Damn it.' His voice is kind. He's an academic, he knows how this all feels. 'Maybe I could come and take you out for lunch. A change of scenery can work wonders. Tomorrow?'

He's standing in the kitchen: I can hear the metallic creak of him moving a saucepan on to the cooker.

'What are you cooking?' This always gives me a few minutes to zone out. There is a calming buzz of recipe and chef and ingredients in my ear. It lasts a while, sounds delicious. It sounds like home.

'Do you know, Dad, maybe I'll come to you. Stay over.'

'What a treat,' he says. His voice goes slightly higher with happiness and I remember how much I miss him. 'I'll cook us something nice.'

My dad comes from a long line of people who demonstrate caring through cooking. I am the perfect recipient for this as I am deeply committed to showing compassion through eating.

The smells from the kitchen are glorious. They're also evidence that my dad has been doing 'heritage cooking', as my mum used to call it, where he conjures up generations of my grandfather's side of the family before him – the Li side – by cooking Asian food they'd never recognise from recipes written by British and American chefs. I'm being mean: it's a lifetime's work and a project I never tire of. Given what I've come to tell him – and how he'll feel about that – my dad's Crispy Lai Wong Bau, although fluffy and sweet, are irony at its very finest.

If I came in blindfolded, I'd still recognise every single thing about this kitchen. I'd know the apron my dad wears – black, with 'Nice buns' written on it in white letters, I imagine my mum bought it for him, given that it's 'humour'. I'd know without looking how it strains, slightly, across his tummy. And I'd know the sound of the same bashed-up saucepans that have been crashed and rattled in this kitchen for the twenty-odd years they lived here together, even before I was born. Even the spatulas, the fish slices, the wooden spoons, are the same. I like the continuity.

'It's terrible timing, Ruby,' says my dad when I tell him about the old man, about my 'grandfather'. 'This is typical of you to launch into another project when you're paralysed with the importance of the one you're on.'

On a scale of impetuous, I am not my mother. She ranks a full one hundred and Dad, dear old soul, has always been a one. Two at Christmas. I'm in the middle – I'm not as foolhardy as Mum but I'm not as slow as a tortoise like my dad is.

He has a punnet of enoki mushrooms on the work surface and I put my palm on top of it, like I'm patting hundreds of miniature children on their heads. 'Be fair, Nick . . .'

'Stop that.' He hates it when I call him by his name.

'How was I to know *a*, that there'd be any kind of result, and *b*, that it would be the same week as bloody Jacqueline turns down my masters' question?' I nip one of the mushrooms off with my fingers and eat it raw.

He moves the punnet nearer to the chopping board, implying that he will chop off my fingers if I take another one. 'I don't know why you even did it. Why do you need to know?'

'What? Are you kidding me?'

'You know all Mum's reasons. I don't know why that isn't enough.' He starts punishing the vegetables on my behalf. He has a huge steel cleaver with a bamboo handle: it rains down on the peppers and the mushrooms tremble.

'You are literally the person who did the whole DNA thing first,' I remind him. 'You're the only reason I know about it.' I feel like I did as a teenager: that rising pressure of frustration – Dad was the king of generating it, Mum the queen of watching it blow. The crosser he gets, the more slowly he speaks. I don't know how Mum didn't spend their married life throwing things at him.

He sighs, thuds a red pepper into two pieces, and then four, and then tiny strips of almost-perfect symmetry. 'I was looking at my DNA. Working out where my father's family came from, given the vast diaspora of Asia, particularly China, over centuries. It's not the same.'

You wouldn't know my dad is only half-Chinese in the same way you wouldn't know I was a quarter Chinese at all. He takes every feature from my granddad's side, his straight dark hair, his deep-brown eyes. I'm the opposite: my genes are from my dad's mum – tall and white and easily sunburnt – and my mum, solid and strong. Mum, slightly apologetic for it: 'I wouldn't blow over in a storm.' Me, saying sorry to no one: 'Thick thighs save lives.'

I have my mum's eyes, the colour and the shape. I know now, from my Google search, that my mum's eyes are direct from James McConnell, retired exec, Rideout Productions. Old people keep an absurd amount of information about themselves online and James's email address is stored in my phone.

I look in the fridge for wine and raise my eyebrows at my dad. He nods the relief of a thirsty man in a desert and I pour two big glasses. We clink them together before we drink and looking in his eyes as we do it makes me remember that we're all each other has and that, despite the fact he's a massive spod, I really do love him.

There are Szechuan peppercorns in a pan, it's my favourite flavour: although he's very cautious about everything else, Dad never holds back on spices.

My eyes start watering. 'So,' I say, when I stop coughing. 'You're allowed to be fascinated by your roots thousands of years ago – that's completely normal and to be expected – but I'm not allowed to find out about people who are, literally' – I stretch out the word – 'the same age as Grandma and Granddad.'

'They might be,' he says, 'or they might be much older. They might have died.'

'But this guy here, if he's dead, he forgot to tell his website,' I remind my dad, tapping my phone with my finger.

Dad drops cubes of smoked tofu into the sauce and my mouth waters. He is multitasking now, skipping dextrously from work surface to wok, sink to pan. He is in his element and, to be fair, if I want this fabulous lunch, I need to let him finish making it.

My mouth is on fire, popping and fizzing with sweetness and pepper. The mapo tofu is that kind of pain that forces you to go back for another mouthful, another hit. There are spring onion pancakes and rich brown noodles. There is glutinous rice and egg foo yung. I eat until I can't fit anything more in – although I know he will have made me Crispy Lai Wong Bau: little deep-fried doughnuts with a sweet yellow centre. They will have to wait till we're watching a film in front of the fire later on.

'Are there doggy bags for me to take home?'

'Always.' He tops up our glasses. 'Now. Just two things I want to say about your little problem.'

I am too full to object, even if he's going to lecture me. I trace a finger around the red edge of the mapo tofu bowl, lick it.

'You must promise me you're not going to spend all your time worrying about this and ignoring your studies. You have a huge amount on this year.'

I wave my hand at him. 'Yada, yada. And?' He always delivers on a two-pronged attack, even if it takes ages.

'And what are you going to say to him? What are you going to say about Mum? He might not even know she exists and then . . .' He doesn't need to finish the sentence for either of us.

In the end, Dad is true to form – and I'm really grateful. We adjourn to the sitting room, telly on, a fresh bottle of wine cold from the fridge – although he moves on to red – and he pretty much writes the email for me. This is the quality Mum valued in him: for every push there must be a pull, for every inquisitive adventurer, there must be a spod with a way with words who knows just how to do everything without causing offence.

I send the email – Dad's email – through the contact system on the genealogy website, then we sit side by side on the sofa, eating the little doughnuts and reciting the dialogue of the film.

'We'll probably never even hear back from them,' says Dad.

Chapter Eleven

JUDITH

Each time my phone rings, I jump – wondering if it is James, wondering if he has news. I arrange to meet Barbara for coffee in the little café near the shop to take my mind off it. 'Let me buy you a cake,' I say when I call her: she has kept the shop going for me for the last few days. 'It's the least I can do.'

'I take it this is all down to our mystery visitor?' is the first thing she says when she sees me.

'This?' I am sitting at the table for two with my coffee cup in my hand. I was, until I spoke, blowing softly across the foam on the top of it, trying to dislodge one of those silly pictures that baristas paint in foamy milk, the ones that always look like vulvas. 'By "this" do you mean the state of complete physical and mental exhaustion painted across my face like a tattoo?'

She sits down. 'I meant the delicious chance to meet for coffee actually. And you promising to pay, which you hardly ever do.' She smiles as she says it, it's not true. 'A blast from the past, I presume?'

I nod. It has been five days since James McConnell exploded back into my life, and thirty-six hours without contact from him. The level of devastation, of change, is almost equal to five days after Catherine had died. The state of not-knowing that I had learnt to live with can never return. It is a reverse Pandora's Box: I had kept hope in there deliberately.

'We've all got a past at our age,' Barbara says and raises her eyebrows at me. 'I wouldn't trust anyone who didn't.'

One of the things I like most about Barbara is that she never digs: finds out enough to know what she should or shouldn't say, and then stops.

'Alan told me his little skeleton the other day,' she says and stops, sitting back and clearly waiting for questions.

'Alan? Our horologist Alan?'

'The very same.' She puts both hands on the table, leans forward enthusiastically. 'He invented some kind of synthesiser.' She splays her fingers out as if she's playing the piano. 'He was the synth player in a sixties group: all the way to the top of the charts.'

I think about his neat self, the way he stands as if he's tightly wound. He is the last person I could imagine in a pop band, draped with groupies. 'Which band?'

She lets out a loud and disgruntled *harumph*. 'He won't tell me. Says those years are behind him. I've spent hours online. "Chart band, 1960s, Alan" not the narrowest of searches. Makes him a bit sexy though, don't you think?'

'I do not think. No.' I'm laughing now.

'Suit yourself. Anyway, no one missed you while you were gallivanting,' she says.

'No one?'

She waves at the waitress, points at my coffee. 'No. The shop runs far more smoothly under my ruthless efficiency.'

'Thank you.' My gratitude is real. 'Any news?'

She shakes her head. 'Nada.' Her coffee arrives and she thanks the waitress, opens a sachet of sugar. 'But I have been talking to the treasurer.' Barbara sits on the Mending Shop committee, like most of Catherine's old friends. 'That roving TV reporter couldn't have come at a better time for us, you know. Things are tight. The Mending Shop could really do with some extra donations.' Barbara sticks her teaspoon into the coffee, stirs it round then puts it between her lips to clean it off. 'Make sure we're still a shop next year. And for a good few years after that.'

'I could always sell something.'

'You can't.' Barbara knows what I'm going to say. 'You've sold all Catherine's paintings that she meant to pay for this. If you sell any more, they'll have to start coming off your own walls.' She sighs and puts her coffee cup heavily on to its saucer.

'It feels a bit selfish. I don't need them.'

Barbara cocks her head to one side, looks at me like a beady old hen. 'This is so typical of you. Why do you have to give everything away?' She sighs through the word 'everything'.

'I'm just not that into money.' I'm smart enough to know that's because we've always had some, Catherine and I. Before she became famous, I was a senior social worker. Back then, social workers were paid their worth – and a decent pension. 'Also, you know . . .' I am fishing for the right words.

Barbara makes her teacher face. 'Spit it out.'

'It's been a lifesaver, the shop. The something to do, something to build.' I am speaking in hesitant phrases but she doesn't interrupt. 'But I wonder if I'm ready to do a bit more me, and a bit less other people. Does that sound awful, selfish?'

Barbara smiles. 'You know that phrase, that thing about "if you're unhappy in a relationship, you can guarantee the other person is too?"' she says.

I know exactly what she's getting at.

'It's been a long time coming. And it's what Catherine wanted – she made no secret of that: she never wanted you to stay for a lifetime.' Barbara dabs at an imaginary fluff on her décolletage, deliberately avoiding my eyes – letting me have a moment alone despite her presence.

'I want to get more involved,' she says. 'Not just help out here and there. Retirement is quite dull with only internet dating sites for company – I'm worth more.' She leans towards me. 'And I've got some big ideas that could really see the charity grow. Financially, there are lots of things we can do – things that are good, that work with our ethos. You get to climb off your stepping stone, and I get to be *in charge* – which we all know is my favourite thing.' She spreads her arms, palms upwards, to declare the obviousness of what she's saying.

I'm surprised how relieved I feel at the thought of someone else running the shop. I've never really forgotten, over the years, that it was Catherine's dream rather than mine.

Barbara is still going. 'We can run training courses, apprentice-ships, liaise with local—'

My phone rings and I swear my heart shudders in my chest.

Barbara's neatly pencilled eyebrows rise, a near-perfect arc across her forehead. 'Our friend again?'

I nod. 'James,' I say instead of hello.

'I'm on my way down. I'll be about an hour, maybe an hour twenty. OK?'

'Fine.' I press the button on the phone to cut him off. This is it. My hands are shaking. I think back to what he said, trying to discern the timbre of his voice.

'Do you need help?' Barbara asks. 'Is everything all right?'

'Just skeletons climbing out of closets.' I try and smile.

'Wretched things.' Barbara is digging in her bag. 'I do wish they wouldn't. Or do we wish they would?'

'If I knew the answer to that.'

Barbara finds what she's looking for in the bottom of the large tan handbag. She puts the little mermaid snow globe in front of me. 'In case you need a friend,' she says. 'Rob put her back together last night and now she has a whole new chance at life.' Barbara looks at me: she knows something is changing.

The glitter is still swirling from its journey to the table. The water, the faintest of blues – almost petrol – is full right to the top, not the smallest bubble of air left to choke her. The mermaid basks on the rock that once imprisoned her, slick with water and ready to swim away with any tide that comes. I pick it up. I can't see a mend or a plug, you'd never know that she was once dried and marooned. I shake the globe and watch the flurries that surround her, frenzied at first and then gentle, slowing and sparkling as they make their way on to her hair, the rock, catch in the top of the seashell bra that covers her modesty.

'Thank you so much.' A line of glitter marks where the mermaid's tail curls round under her: it looks perfect against her green scales. 'I love her.'

Barbara nods. 'I'll skip the cake today. But you owe me.' She stands, leans forward and kisses the top of my head. 'Call me if you need me. Any time.'

And then I have nothing else to do but to pay for our coffees and walk home. The streets are busy, it is a beautiful sunny day, and I pass people I know. I wonder if I look different, if I look like someone who no longer knows what the rules are, what the real truth is. My only certainty is that enough has changed to make James drive back down again today.

He reads me the email. Dougal is leaning in a heap against my legs and I curl my fingers into his fur.

'Her name is Ruby Cooper-Li,' James says.

My voice is a tiny hollow, a dry, flaked thing. 'Whose name?'

'Sorry, sorry.' He clears his throat.

The seconds slice through me.

'Our granddaughter. Our granddaughter's name is Ruby Cooper-Li. Spelt L-I.'

It doesn't matter that I don't know what to say – there is no way I could speak. A band tightens around my head, my breath is on fire. I have a granddaughter.

'Dear James,' he reads and the clock behind him ticks loudly as the minute-hand moves.

I don't really hear the rest. I feel that it is cautious and beautifully worded. I know that it lays out her and James's most likely relationship. I understand the cleverness of the sentences, the agility of saying so much without saying much at all. The part where she presents, for us to check, that her mother was born on the 16th September 1966 trickles warm as blood through my body, becoming everything I ever have been, refloating me like the mermaid.

Afterwards, James is silent. The clock ticks. Dougal shifts on the floor in front of me and his claws click against the tiles.

My breath is a tight scratching.

James takes two steps forward, wraps me in his arms, against his chest. It is such an instinctive, guileless move. 'What exquisite pain,' he says, and we don't speak again for the longest time.

We move, like people made of cotton wool, around the kitchen. I am making a sandwich for us both. We have agreed to take Dougal for a walk after lunch. My work surfaces are still made of polished concrete and it is still Tuesday; bread still sheds crumbs as it is cut. James and I know so little about each other's adult selves, and now we know so little about reality.

We don't talk about Ruby Cooper-Li, about her email, about her possibilities. We don't discuss the things she told us – that she is twenty-two years old, a masters student at a London university. If we did talk, we would marvel that she studies Environmental Policy and James would add – half-joking, half-breaking – 'They used to call Barlinnie jail "Glasgow University" in the sixties.' We might, if we discussed her, imagine what she looks like, who she favours. I would wonder if she looks like my mother. James would wonder whether he can ever forgive his. Potentially, there might be a debate about what we might be called: whether our old names should be resurrected by the connection – Granny Jude and Grandpa Jimmy.

But we don't talk about Ruby Cooper-Li because we can't picture her mother: because we realise, with this chatty informative email, that we still know nothing about our own daughter. Not her name, not her hair colour, not her marital status. We don't know what she has been through, how she grew up, what she likes to eat. We have been denied every one of these things.

But now we know she has a daughter. Now we know she 'is'.

Chapter Twelve

There was one last raid planned for the base before the big one, a last checking of details and measurements. No one in the squat had thought past the explosion – we avoided calling it a bomb, but that's what it was – when our work would, to all intents and purposes, be finished.

I had, in the last few days, realised what I would be doing after the raid – and for the rest of my life. A surprise – a shock – at first, but one that felt so right.

When Jimmy and I had got together – back when we first started having sex – Kay had come with me to the chemist's. We'd rehearsed the lines, giggling and blushing: I knew them off by heart.

'Wait,' Kay had said as we stood outside the shop. 'You'll need this.' She wriggled the ring off her middle finger. It had a small black stone, flattened and polished and set in a thin silver mount. She held the ring out.

I looked at her. 'What for?'

Kay clicked her tongue at my stupidity. 'For this finger, if you want to come out of there with a Dutch cap.' She squeezed it on to my ring finger, spinning the stone round so that only the silver band showed and the detail was inside my curled fist.

'Does this mean we're married?' I asked her and kissed her on the cheek.

'Forsaking all others.' She opened the door of the chemist's shop and pushed me in.

When I came out, I had a small cardboard packet inside a plain paper bag. Inside that, I showed Kay when we got home, was the brown rubber disc that would save me. I'd paid extra for a pale-pink case, like a make-up compact. The man in the chemist's had explained how to use the diaphragm, without ever once using the words cervix, sperm, or vagina: a miracle.

All these months later and despite all that, or possibly because of it, the truth had dawned on me. I tried to be rational about it, to think about the ways our lives would change, what we would do for money, where we would live – ours wasn't the kind of squat you could raise a child in. I tried to be sensible, calm, adult, but all of those things were smothered by my sheer joy.

Even with the cordite smell of a shotgun wedding hanging in the air, my parents would be disappointed. It would take them a long time to move from the Christmas and birthday cards we were stiltedly sending one another to welcoming a baby with open arms, one who had certainly been conceived out of wedlock.

My university place was a whole other life away, it belonged to someone else.

I didn't tell Jimmy on the first day that I knew. I wasn't being coy or playing games: I knew he would catch me up in his arms, spin me round, and smile that huge split-face grin that he couldn't help when he was truly happy. We'd talked about the possibility of accidents: one had to – contraception in the sixties was a wing and a prayer.

'Let's do something tonight,' he said when he got in from work. He was still greasy from the factory, his hands blackened with oil. 'I won't be long at the base and then we can sit and have supper together when I get back. Slope off if everyone's downstairs?'

'Why don't I come with you?'

He didn't answer but his eyes flicked, involuntarily, at something behind me. I knew before I even turned round that it would be Polly Wright.

He held his breath for a moment, puffed out his grease-streaked cheeks. 'I need someone who can run. Run in the dark.'

If it had been a week ago, I would have still felt tired, mysteriously lethargic. Now I was full of beans, and bravado. 'I was pretty good at cross-country at school.'

He sat down on a kitchen chair, tipped his tired head back and closed his eyes. 'You'd be on your own. I'd be in the van at the gate.' He patted his lap, pulled me down to sit on his knee.

'You're filthy,' I said but sat there anyway. I put my arms round his neck even though I could see dirt on the cuffs of my sweater already. 'What time are we leaving?'

'There's no need, Judith.' Polly's voice was its usual frozen sweetness. 'I already said I'd go, Jimmy. Remember? You asked me the other night.'

I felt Jimmy's fingers tighten on my waist.

'Jimmy?' She tapped her fingers on the table, as if to wake him.

'You're right, I did.' He muffled his face in my sweater. I heard the quiet 'For fuck's sake'. Out of character.

'I'm fine to do it, Polly. I'd like to do it actually.' I bent down, made a show of lacing up my boots.

Polly wound a ringlet of her perfect hair round one finger – her eyes widened as she tugged on it. Her hair was always shining: it thrived on the lack of washing in the exact opposite way to mine. Mine got straighter – heavier and darker – as the week wore on and my Sunday night bath got further away.

'Did I hear you say you were having a little supper, Judith? If I go to the base with Jimmy, it'll give you a chance to cook something nice.'

I was speechless. I could hear Jimmy's breath in my ear, steady, passive. He didn't know that there were two of me to speak up for but – my eyes welled with tears and humiliation.

'Crumbs, Judith.' Polly stretched out a hand towards me. Her fingernails were polished, shaped. 'I had no idea it was so important to you. Jimmy, perhaps you should take Judith after all?'

Her words were acid that prickled on my cheeks. I stood up. 'Don't worry about it. I'll see you later,' I said to Jimmy and, without looking at her, I went out of the back into the cold scullery.

'Why do you have to do that?' I heard him say, but I wrenched open the toilet door so I wouldn't hear any more. I sat there, in my slacks and in the dark, until the legs of his chair scraped across the floor and I knew that they'd left.

A door being smashed from its hinges by a battering ram doesn't make a noise as such. It is a sensation. The bricks and mortar – the fabric of the house – vibrate around it. When the sound does come, it is deep and primal and terrible. It is the scream of a splintering house.

Our bed moved, stuttered. That was what woke me. And then the lights – blue flashes and white beams that cut through the night to our top-floor window.

Booms rang through the house like lost ghosts.

'Jimmy?' I said into the patchy darkness.

He moved in an instant. 'Get dressed, quickly. Then stay here.' He stood on one leg, pulling on his trousers, his chest bare: the beams lit the edge of his body.

'Stay here,' he repeated. He had pulled his shirt on, still open, the cuffs flying out like wide white hands. He pushed the door shut behind him and his feet were loud on the stairs.

There were shouts throughout the house now. Screams.

I dressed as quickly as I could: my chequered slacks, the button at the side undone where the flat front wouldn't stretch across me; a black roll-neck jumper, pulled down as far as it would go to protect the tiny swell. I had been angry with Jimmy last night – I hadn't cooked or waited up for him. I hadn't told him. Now, something was going wrong and that missed opportunity was all I could think of.

There was another crash, and voices spilled into the house – strangers. I could hear Dougie and Archie, who'd been sleeping in the front bedroom, nearest the permanently locked door, swearing and shouting. The house was alive in the dark. Crash followed crash: voices I knew were swallowed by barked instructions.

I opened the bedroom door. A man in a suit was running down our landing. I flattened myself against the wall.

'Stay right there,' he shouted. Behind him, more footsteps thundered up the bare wooden stairs, more banging. Four policemen shoved past me, searched the two attic rooms.

Jimmy's voice, desperate, a floor or two below me. 'Let me go. Don't go near my girlfriend. I swear, if you touch my girlfriend.' I heard dull thuds – one, two, three – and a cry of pain, Jimmy's voice. 'Let go.' Another scuffle.

I flung the door back open and ran down both flights of stairs two at a time. Below, Dougie and Angus lay on the hall floor – their hands caught behind their backs and stretched face-down like sporting trophies. Angus looked at me, his face covered in blood, a cut tearing his eyebrow in two.

Two men in suits and raincoats stood behind Dougie and pulled him up by the back of his arms.

'Get the fuck off me.' Dougie spat on to the floor and the larger of the two men cracked his hand across the back of his head. They dragged him and Angus to standing.

102

'You're under arrest. You'd do well to shut the fuck up.' The suited man moved his knee upwards into the back of Dougie's thigh. Dougie crumpled, still suspended by them holding his arms behind his back.

I jumped the banister at the end of the stairs. 'Jimmy!' I screamed through the bedlam.

'Get out of the way,' a fat man with grey hair yelled. He raised his arm and pushed me backwards across my chest.

I looped one arm into the banister to stay upright. The other went instinctively to my belly.

'Jimmy's gone,' Angus shouted at me. 'They got him first.'

Two of the suited men started dragging Dougie through the splintered door, the side of his face purple with bruises already. I saw my chance and, head down, barrelled past them and out of the house.

'Jimmy!' I screamed it down the wide stone steps.

'Lady constables needed here,' a policeman directly in front of me shouted. He grabbed my arm and twisted it behind my back, pushed me down the steps, into the dark. Flashes of headlights, torches lit one side of his face, shone off the peak of his hat. 'Stay still,' he hissed and I could hear how tightly his teeth were gritted. The pain in my arm shot through my body. I curved into myself, doing everything I could to keep the baby safe.

His leather gloves squeezed – too tight – against my wrist.

In the road, a black car waited, its doors open. I looked through the gap between the policeman's arm and his body. Behind me, two uniformed men pushed Jimmy into the car. The air split with his scream as they slammed the door, deliberately, on his leg.

'Jimmy!' I bellowed with every breath left in my body, louder than the sirens filling the streets, louder than Dougie and Angus fighting their way – handcuffed and wounded – to the vans.

I was pulled sharply backwards. My feet slipped from under me and I sat down, hard, on the bottom step. A woman, close to my ear, spoke coldly through the chaos. 'You're under arrest for offences covered by Section One of the Official Secrets Act.'

I turned my face towards her, trying to make sense of her words.

The woman, wearing the same short coat as I had bought myself a month ago, said, 'You have the right to remain silent but anything you do say may be used in evidence against you. Now, you can walk to the van, or we can drag you.' She nodded towards Dougie lying on the ground, four men leaning over him, their ties dangling down like bell pulls. 'Which will it be?'

I struggled to my feet and walked beside the woman to the smallest of the three vans. There were two small cages in the back, barely bigger than something you'd keep a dog in. I looked up at the house and the last of the shouting.

'He's a fucking priest!' screamed Angus as they carried Paddy Gordon out, his clothes torn and filthy, his face a mass of blood and bruises, one arm hanging, limp, broken.

I closed my eyes as I was folded into the van. The doors clanged shut and it was black. It smelt of metal and cruelty.

'The only thing you need to remember about any of this,' Polly Wright's voice spat out from the darkness of the other cage, 'is that you don't know Jimmy McConnell at all. You have no idea who he is.'

I jammed my fingers into my ears so that I wouldn't hear anything else she said.

We'd been arrested by Special Branch, but I was held at the local police station. I had no idea where the others were or what was going on, and no one would tell me. I'd watched the sunrise move across the tiny window and vanish, eventually, into an orange ghost in the opposite corner. My loo was a bucket on the floor and my bed a plank. There was one filthy grey blanket and the cell was freezing. All night, murderous sounds screeched down the hallway, crept under the door with the cold. People howled and barked.

By the time the door swung open, I was hoarse from crying. I felt like I'd forgotten how to speak.

'You're not being charged.' The same woman who had snapped the handcuffs round my wrists stood in the corridor, neat in a skirt and blouse, her cardigan open at the front – for all the world like a schoolteacher or a matron or someone's mum. She sneered at me. 'And do you know why you're not being charged?'

My tongue was dead inside my head, lifeless on the bottom of my mouth. I couldn't speak if I had wanted to.

'Because you're not important enough. Because you're just a silly wee girl playing a game.'

I touched the bruising round my wrists. My whole face hurt. 'Where is Jimmy? Where is my boyfriend?'

The woman shook her head. 'Could be anywhere. My money's on Barlinnie. But wherever, he's not coming out for a good long while.' I took the words like a punch. I'd seen the outside of Barlinnie jail, heard stories of the day-to-day cruelty, the conditions.

'And you are leaving Scotland. For good.'

'I haven't got any money.' I didn't have anything: no coat; no food; no hope. 'And I've nowhere to go.'

'Unless you want to spend a long time in jail yourself, you'll go back to where you came from. We will issue you a travel permit and that's it. You've one chance.'

I got back on the same bus I'd arrived on, ten months sadder, and with two uniformed policemen standing by the door to make sure I didn't get off.

The bus took me as far as Manchester. Back at the Glasgow bus station one of the policemen had given me a dried cheese sandwich wrapped in paper. I didn't know if it was his lunch or standard issue but I ate it quickly and washed it down with a cup of cold tea. Afterwards it made me retch.

It was no surprise that it took over an hour to hitch a lift out of Manchester, back in the direction of what had once been home. I was filthy dirty, dropping with tiredness.

I knocked on the clean stippled glass of the front door, conscious of my chipped nail varnish, the bruises round my wrists.

My mother opened the door, comfortingly familiar in her apron, her hair neat and carefully curled.

I imagined the tiny curve of my belly had grown in the last three days, a baby as defiant as me, as its father. I pushed my stomach forward, made a statement of us. With my cold hands either side, I stretched the wet fabric of my coat tight across my belly.

Her eyes travelled down my body, stopping below my waist. My mother stared, a silent greeting made of the thinnest and most dangerous ice.

'Go to your room,' she said. 'And for the love of Mary, do not let your father see that.'

Chapter Thirteen

'James, would you feel awkward staying here on your own for a bit?' I don't give him time to answer. 'I really need to go for a run. I do three a week, come rain or shine. And I'm running out of days this week.' We have been sitting, talking in circles, for hours.

'If you wouldn't mind me having a key, I'll take Dougal down to the seafront. I could do with some fresh air.'

Dougal's tail thumps in response to his name.

The hypnosis of the run starts before I leave the house: the relief to be returning to routine, to certainty, starts as soon as I take my clothes from the drawer. I pull off my top, undo my bra. I leave it, off-white and strung out like a tapeworm, on the floor. I fasten my sports bra – one, and then a second over it – as I do every time I run. Mechanical actions that bring me peace. I pull on the same T-shirt. Black shorts, whatever the weather, over blue-white legs. I tie the laces in my trainers, my breathing shorter while I do it, bent forward. I am remade.

In my running routine, I walk for five painful minutes to wake my hips and knees and ankles, slowly while the cartilage loosens and the muscles tighten. As I stretch, life returns to my extremities, adrenalin kicks in and masks the aches, and then I can run. The first few hundred metres are painful in places as I warm up – sometimes I take painkillers before I leave to quieten them. But today is warm and easy and I fall into my slow, steady stride in minutes. I want to head for the cover of the woods as soon as possible – James and I spent the biggest chunk of the day staring at each other, immobile as cats in the street; now the afternoon sun is high in the sky and I risk sunburn on my shoulders.

I have to watch my feet carefully on this rough track of roots and broken branches – there was a sudden summer storm a few days ago and the path is littered with fragments. Watching my feet makes me feel young again: I am watching the same feet that ran when I was a child, fearless feet that leapt into new experiences, devoured life and possibilities. This rhythm of sandy path and dried leaves has the power to transport me, to shave the years away.

My childhood was note-perfect – holidays and ice cream and birthdays and Christmas. It made it all the sadder that, as a family, we never recovered the ground we lost. My parents never got to fall in love with Catherine – which was a very easy thing to do – because I never introduced them, never trusted them enough to welcome her.

It's easy to think they would have turned us away – to accuse them – but they never got a chance to prove otherwise. In reality, I think my parents would have done what most people of their generation did – think it was a lovely idea that the two ladies had bought a house together, in the absence of managing to find husbands; that we were company for one another, like having a cat.

Despite the brief storm, the path is dry: there have even been tiny fires further down the coast. I am careful how I run on the shifting sand. Only change one thing at once, Catherine used to say: pace or distance or terrain. If you change two on the same day, you will get injured – one and you'll be fine. I have swapped the smooth pavements for this trip back in time to school cross-country, to playing with my friends in the fields behind my first house, so I move carefully on the uneven ground.

I pass a couple walking their dog. The dog is stocky and white, with one black patch over his eye. He follows me for a short while and his owners call out, embarrassed at his enthusiasm. I smile and wave back at them: anonymity, normality.

There is a great deal for me to process – although none of it is new, I have thought about every aspect of this, every permutation, a million times. I started decades ago to wonder about grandchildren, about whether I had any. Even if she'd got pregnant very young, mistimed pregnancies don't have the same consequences now. It took little more than a decade from the concealment and torture of forced adoptions for society to recognise that not all parents are married, not all parents are straight or non-disabled. That not all parents are the same.

Nowadays single parents can go to college, retrain as anything they want. Nowadays a pregnant woman has options, can have a safe and legal termination if that's what suits her best at that point in her life. 'Best for baby' means something entirely different nowadays, although people, often men, still wave placards outside abortion clinics – all over the world – exercising control over bodies that do not belong to them. Women haven't changed, and babies haven't changed, and yet the process of recent history seems barbaric to us now.

I half-jump over a tree root, impress myself with my landing, the closest thing to flying in my own body.

When I was young, people believed that a baby had a right to two parents, a man and a woman – that anything else was a failure, was less than a child deserved. I will have to find words for my granddaughter to explain all these things. To put into a modern context ideas that sound as if they come from the Dark Ages, but feel like yesterday to me.

I run out of the forest: the sun is warmer than I had expected after the cool shade and I take the most direct route home.

'Cathartic?' James asks when I come back into the garden after my shower.

'I don't like to talk about how good running is in the house – in case Catherine can hear me.' I instantly regret saying it, then remember that he is widowed too, that he has these same conversations with someone he can no longer see. 'The running was hundred per cent her idea. I pretended to hate it for decades.' I slide my feet into my flip-flops. 'That's not true: I did truly hate it for decades. I promised her I'd do it till I'm eighty-three. Seven years left and then I'm done.'

James smiles. 'Rather you than me.' Words Catherine would have seen as a challenge.

He has his laptop on the garden table. 'I started a reply to Ruby,' he says. 'But I thought about everything you said.' When he had finished reading Ruby's email to me this morning, I had to stop James from replying instantly and signing it 'Grandpa'.

'Softly, softly, catchee monkey,' I said. 'You don't know them. We literally know nothing about them.'

When I read his contact email, it seems that warning has fallen on deaf ears.

Two words stand out more than any others on the page.

'We're her mother's *mother* and *father*, James.' It hurts to say it, now as much as then. 'We're not her *mum* and *dad*.'

Mum and Dad are words that recognise sleepless nights over biology, childhood illnesses over genes. Mum and Dad are words we were never given the chance to earn.

My mother moved me around the house like I was a huge piece of furniture: too ugly to want, too enormous to get rid of. She hid me in corners and coats and huge nylon dresses that she must have got from a magazine: sent away for them so that the local shopkeepers wouldn't know she was ordering outside of her size.

My father knew, and he couldn't look at me. All his dreams had withered into what I was now: pale and unwashed, living – uninvited – on the edges of his life.

I knew what the plan was. When I woke up, the second morning, a tarnished ring – that would leave green marks in a band round my finger, indelible for months – had been placed on my bedside table by a silent night-time visitor. I waited till my dad had gone to work to leave my room, the pattern of most days.

'I don't need your pretend ring,' I said to my mother.

She was drying the frying pan that she'd cooked my father's breakfast in. The cloth was blue and dazzling white and she rubbed without breaking her rhythm, without acknowledging that I had spoken. I only knew I still existed when she glanced at my hand to see if I'd put the ring on.

'I need some money for stamps. Please. I'll do anything.'

The frying pan made a bang as she slid it into the cupboard. She balled the tea towel up in her hand and used it to push bread-crumbs into a heap, then swept the heap into her other, waiting hand.

'You could have a legitimate grandchild if you just let me write.'

Her hand flew to her mouth. 'It isn't though, is it, Judith? My grandchild – my first grandchild – is a . . .' She couldn't say it. Instead she folded and refolded the cloth, stretching it across the work surface, folding, straightening, folding again.

'I need to write to him. He loves me. He does.' In the hallway, the silent telephone, the still letterbox. In my head, Polly Wright's last words: 'You don't know Jimmy McConnell at all. You have no idea who he is.'

In my mother's kitchen, I sounded like a child who believes in Father Christmas. 'Jimmy will come and he will rescue us.'

She pushed past me, went into the dining room to take her anger out on the non-existent dust, the imaginary clutter. 'This isn't a fairy tale,' she said from the hallway. She reached into the cupboard for her dustpan and brush, although the only untidiness was me and I wouldn't fit in it. 'I want things to be good for you. I want the same for you now as I wanted when you were a baby – happiness, love, a good husband. You need to put this behind you when it's over.' She attacked a small section of the parquet flooring. 'You need to start again: a clean slate and a happy life. Please, Judith.'

Later, I lay in the bath, hoping that I could see the small bump moving, catching my breath every time I felt that fish flicker of him or her coming to life. I held my hands above my belly like a blessing, and whispered that it would be all right.

Once night fell and my parents were asleep, I slid outside in my nightie and shook sixpence out of the envelope my mother had left for the milkman. It would buy two second-class stamps. It was a crime that wouldn't go unnoticed, but I had to get word to Jimmy. I had taken pages from the back of my mum's shopping list pad, envelopes from her bureau, and I scribbled messages of desperation: letters of love and hope, of the promises we'd made to each other so many times.

'You don't know Jimmy McConnell at all. You have no idea who he is.'

In the morning, I made a plea for a walk. 'I haven't been outside this house in six weeks. I'm going mad.' I had to post the letter before the milkman realised that his bill hadn't been fully paid, before my very last line of communication had been severed. My mother agreed if I promised to keep to the edge of the woods behind our house and didn't go near the town, I could go out. I had to promise I wouldn't tell my dad, and my mother tied me into her biggest, thickest coat.

Within a couple of days, I knew the milkman had sent a new bill. My mother had blooms of mascara under her eyes, her blue eye shadow that made her feel so happy in the mornings had smudged at the sides so that she looked as if her head were going mouldy.

My father was quiet, monosyllabic, but I caught him looking at me with such sorrow. The tension was so thick, I wouldn't have been surprised if he'd announced they were having me shot. Instead:

'We have managed to find you a job,' was how my mother began the announcement.

A purposeful pause.

'And it comes with a room.'

I looked at my father in his armchair, newspaper folded across his lap. His knuckles were white on the chair arms.

'Father Dominic helped set it up. He knows a place.'

My mother was holding one of her hands in the other: wringing them was the only way to describe the way her fingers writhed and gripped and slid. She spoke lightly, quickly, as if there wasn't enough air in the world for what she had to say. 'And Daddy and I thought I could drive you. Tomorrow.'

Panic pounded through me but I didn't know what to say, how to stop this monster who was wearing my mother's clothes, had put my mother's fashionable curled wig over their own hair.

'Your mother will help you pack.' And I didn't know then that they would be the last words my father ever spoke to me.

My mother made sandwiches for the drive. They were wrapped in greaseproof, not quite closed and drying in the warm air of the car's hopeless heater. The car was full of hard-boiled egg smell. She packed a tartan Thermos of tea and two apples, dull orange russets.

We left home in silence save for the rhythmic squeak of the wipers on the screen.

I wanted to be sick: the smell of the sandwiches, the hypnotic wipers, the stinking car heater blowing past my face. I couldn't stop crying.

We drove closer and closer to the city. As the houses became grander and more urban, my tears fell heavier. The buildings grew thicker round us, and at every roundabout, every street corner – the house fronts slicked wet with rain – it reminded me more and more of Glasgow.

I realised how very happy we had been.

My mother passed me a handkerchief. It had been up her sleeve and smelt of her perfume. She used to dab at my face with it when I was a child, licking the linen first: I hated the smell of breath it left on my skin. This time, I wanted to keep her handkerchief, hide it so I could take something familiar with me.

'We can't go home.' She read my mind. 'The arrangements are made. All made.' Her hands were at a perfect ten to two on the wheel, just as she had been taught in the Wrens.

The baby jogged a rhythm against my diaphragm and I wondered if it knew how sad I was. Instinctively, I hugged my arms across the curve of my distended belly.

'Don't do that.' My mother moved one hand from the steering wheel to brush mine away. 'You're only making it worse for yourself.

It's best like this. We will all be back to normal soon. Daddy will stop worrying himself sick. And no one needs to ever know.'

'And me?'

My mother pushed down the left indicator and we waited through its loud tick, tick, tick, until we pulled in to the side of the road.

She turned to face me in her seat, her slim waist twisted towards me, her feet still on the pedals of the car. 'Listen to me, my girl.'

It was the final transformation into the creature who had been squatting her body.

'Think, for one minute, about what this does to Daddy and me. I carried you.' She gripped the steering wheel like it would start to move without her. 'This is my first grandchild. I will never see it, never touch it. I think about that night and day and I will be thinking about it for years after you've gone off again to save us all from what-you-know-best-about. While you're doing good-ness-knows-what with goodness-knows-whom, I will be at home wondering where this . . . this . . . Wondering what happened to my family.' She couldn't bring herself to say the word 'baby'.

'I won't swan off. I'll stay at home. We can pretend, we can say it's yours and Daddy's.'

'I'm sick of the damned pretending.'

My mother swearing shocked me into silence.

'Every day the neighbours look at you more and more care-fully; each week people ask me why you're not coming to Mass. They talk about it behind my back, you silly cat.' Her driving gloves were tight and shining under her taut grip. The windscreen was misted with her anger.

'And everyone knows, Judith. They know that you have taken all the wonderful chances God gave you and thrown them away in one silly childish moment.' The teeth of the gears screeched as she forced the car back on to the road.

My face was hot, I felt faint. 'Mummy, please, pull over. Please stop.'

I managed to open the car door and tip my head down towards the verge before I was sick. I heaved and gasped until I was as empty as the future. Drool mingled with my tears and I let it hang there.

'Sit back in your seat. We're late.'

I wiped the corners of my mouth with her white handkerchief and dropped it, sodden, into the glove compartment of the door.

We stopped outside a large red-brick house. A silver plaque on the gatepost read, 'The South Liverpool Maternity Home'. It was in a leafy green suburb, opposite a huge expanse of parkland, studded with trees, light dappling beneath them.

'When you come out, Judith, Uncle George has found a nursing job for you in London.' My mother was almost whispering. 'You'll go straight there.'

She didn't have to look back to see if I went in through the gates, she knew there was absolutely nowhere else for me to go.

Chapter Fourteen

RUBY

I watched my inbox like a hawk all day.

They didn't answer until I'd gone to make pasta. A watched kettle never boils, Dad says. Except it does and it did and they – 'they', not 'him' – wrote.

Insane. I keep reading it. Over and over. I read it so hard that there is spaghetti sauce down my top.

I thought about replying straight away, sat with my fingers on the keys and my little finger tapping on the edge of my keyboard, but I started sensible and I'm going to try and stick to sensible. Don't jump to conclusions, keep calm: essentially, try and channel Dad rather than Mum.

And then I kept picking up my phone, looking at the screen and thinking of sharing it with Dad. But it's not his news. So I pull on a clean T-shirt and my flip-flops, grab a can of pop from the fridge to drink while I'm there, and I go and tell Mum.

We talked long and hard about whether to bury Mum or to cremate her. She wouldn't decide, said it wasn't going to be her anyway by then and we mustn't think that it was.

So I don't think that she is here, in this Victorian park with the birds and the squirrels and the foxes that pour themselves over the wall if I stay till dusk. But when I come here, I can slip into the right place – the right mood – to feel her with me, in me. It's like yoga or meditation or something: I sit here, by her stone, and I know I'm using part of her to think, that I'm using the molecules of her that are in the molecules of me. And now, I suppose, I'm using the molecules of James and the molecules of Judith. There are parts of all of us that are the same. Blows my mind.

It's quiet today. The kids came out of school hours ago so there's no one hiding by the mausoleums to smoke or snog or – would never have happened in my day – just sit and eat ice creams. In the distance an old lady – on her knees and her hands full of flowers – tends and fiddles, no doubt talking in the same not-quite-silent way as I am.

I walk along the row, swinging my bag and trying to fit nonchalance over the terrible guilt. I stop at my mother's stone.

Penelope Joanne Cooper-Li

16th September 1966 – 5th June 2017

Wife to Nick and mother to Ruby

Loved by everyone who ever knew her.

'Hello,' I say, and I sit down on the soft grass. Dad and I planted dark-yellow marigolds in front of her headstone and they have curled and dried into an orange tangle, a few desperate heads still shining. 'I think I've cocked up.'

I sit down beside my mum, my legs out in front of me. It's the end of summer and my knees are brown. Maybe one year my whole legs will go brown but, for now and every other year so far, it's just my knees. 'Why is that?' I ask my mum.

'Definitely from my side,' she says.

I snap open the can of Coke I brought with me and toast her, picture her eyes meeting mine. 'Well, now we know who "your side" is. We actually do.'

Even if anyone could hear me talking, they wouldn't think it odd. It's what we all do here: the roses and the honeysuckle, the jays and the crows, they all ignore us, carry on just growing and being.

This thing is huge: so much bigger than I thought when I did it. It has ripples on its ripples. There's actually something uncomfortable about realising there is more to you, more to your mother, than you knew.

'Shall I just read you their email? Yep, "their". It's from his email address but it's written by both of them. Your actual parents.'

I was always more bothered by the adoption idea than my mum. 'That's because it isn't your wheelhouse,' she'd say. 'Because you're thinking about the people we don't know as if they were Granny and Granddad. And they're not. They're strangers to us. We don't know them.'

And I'd argue and say that we could get to know them. And Mum would say, 'It's not the same. It's not my history. My history is with my parents, with how I grew up, that's who I am.'

'But maybe you just don't know. Maybe you'd feel different if you looked like someone.'

'I look like you. And that's enough for me.' And there it would end. Every time.

I think of James's blue eyes in the picture on Google, of the photo they sent me of the crowd of people outside the house they lived in back then, black and white and like something from a film. The woman at the top of the steps who looks so like my mum.

My mum died when I was seventeen – at the very height of my efforts at teenage rebellion. We clashed night and day till almost the end. Dad says that I'll get over it, that I'll realise 'when I'm older' that fighting with teenagers isn't real fighting, that those ranting rages don't matter to anyone in the 'fullness of time'. He says that similar people always fight like cat and dog. He says all that, but whenever I try and really talk about it, about the worst of it, he shuts me down.

I'm too close to the arguments Mum and I had for her last five years, Dad in between us like a ping-pong net. I'll never be able to forget the day she was diagnosed – or to forgive myself.

And I never got a chance to say sorry.

It is late afternoon, quiet and lazy here. The sun can't be bothered to burn us any more so it sinks down to the hedge, trickles along the skyline – although it'll be hours until it's dark.

'So this is it,' I tell her. 'This is what they said:

Dear Ruby,

We are so delighted to hear from you. It has come completely out of the blue and we're a little short of words, but we are both truly thrilled.

We are Judith Franklin (retired social worker) and James McConnell (I used to run a television production company). We met in 1965 when we were both members of the Scottish Committee of 100, campaigning against nuclear warheads being stationed in Scotland. We attach a photograph of us (we are the two in the middle) outside the house we lived in at the time.

We would very much like to meet you and any other members of your family who are interested in making contact. We are writing from the south coast but can easily be in London – or anywhere else that would suit you.

Do let us know: we all have a lot to talk about. We are so thrilled to hear from you.

With very best wishes

Judith and James.'

When I've read it to her, I let out the longest sigh. 'They mean you really, don't they, Mum? Not actually me.'

My mum's cancer came out of nowhere: snuck up on us all. It wasn't related to genes or diet or lifestyle. It didn't have a treatment or options or questions. It wasn't fair at all. And now it isn't in the past either – now I've got to find a way to say it all again, make two more people feel like Dad and me and all our friends and relatives do. The gift that keeps on giving.

'Oh, bloody hell, Mum,' I say. 'I can't think about anything else. I have to find a way to do it. I know Dad would tell them for me but I'm trying to be a grown-up. Maybe this is something that you and I could do together?'

Before I go home, I tidy the little yellow marigolds that bloom eight months out of twelve on top of her grave. I tell her that I miss her, even though she already knows that because I tell her every day.

Chapter Fifteen

Judith

I leave James at my house and go back to the shop to distract myself. I've tried to find room in my head to think about the shop, about Barbara, but it's a hurricane in there. Occasionally I smooth down the sides of my hair, certain that the tempest inside will have blown up tufts around my ears.

'I could do with you here, Catherine,' I whisper as I walk round the shelves of mended things waiting to be collected, wondering how it would feel to be one of them – to be whole again.

I used to believe that I had to pack every day with Good Deeds, with things that made me feel alive. That urgency is certainly lessening with the years – perhaps I've served my time.

The last customer of the day is here for a collection. I didn't take her item in so it's lovely to unpack it for her and see what it is at the same time as I see her reaction.

'Thank you so much for doing this,' she says. 'It was completely unusable before.'

'I hope it restores a few happy memories,' I say as I take it out of the box, piece by gentle piece.

It's a bone-china tea service. The note that the restorer – Parminder does all the ceramics – has left on the top tells me what he needs the customer to know. Each piece is white with a delicate rose and gold motif running all the way around. It is so thin that the china is almost blue.

'Our restorer has added a bit of a description,' I say. 'Do you know it's bone china? That it has bone-meal ground into the clay to make it lighter?'

'Sounds about right.' The woman in is her forties, friendly. She raises her eyebrows at me. 'It belonged to my aunt – I wouldn't be surprised if the rotten old cow hadn't ground the bones herself.'

The surprise manifests itself in a grin and I cover my mouth with my hand in an attempt at good manners.

'I want to use it daily – just to annoy her, now she's dead.' The woman shrugs and her dark curls bob up and down. 'She hated children – my brothers and me especially – and never shared a single thing. I'm going to get this out at home and have my loud and happy family make memories with it. It's what she wouldn't have wanted.' She gently puts the teapot back into the bubble wrap. 'Thank you ever so much. I feel like she's made up for so many missed Christmases and birthdays.'

She hums as we put the box of crockery back together. 'Happy Birthday' is in there, along with the odd traditional carol.

'Happy Christmas,' I say, even though it's summertime, and she laughs as she leaves.

I wander around the empty shop, wondering how many other of our objects are grudge-fixes: the battered tuba, waiting for its dull dents to be straightened and its mouthpiece replaced; the leather cage of boules missing a round wooden jack and team of players; the four fur coats with torn pockets that we almost didn't take until the Environment Agency assured us that vintage fur was better used than thrown away.

There's a pair of leather golf gloves on the 'Textiles: ready' shelf and I neatly fold back three of the fingers on one of them, tucking the thumb in behind it. The glove's statement middle finger makes me smile and I wonder if anyone will notice, will wonder who would do such a thing.

Everywhere I look, the shelves are groaning with objects; they are stacked up along the walls, and sit – waiting for a home – on the end of the benches. Barbara's not wrong – we have grown to a size where we need to expand, or fold up. I haven't the energy for the expansion but it would be so sad to see all this work, all these brilliant new habits, go to waste.

I stop by Alan's bench while he's not here, peer into his tangle of springs and wires and watches, fascinated as ever by his trade and even more impressed now I have a window into his past. It looks like the harmless workings of several kitchen clocks but who knows what they really might be – perhaps Alan is building the renaissance of prog-rock.

There is a box full of watch faces on the bench – round glass discs like see-through shells. I'd love to run my fingers through them but I don't trust them to be clean enough. There isn't a speck of grease or dirt near here.

I wonder if Alan knows what Barbara's plans for him are. Perhaps she has a plan for every one of us.

I know – with an absolute certainty – that Catherine would be both pleased and impressed by the gentleness with which Barbara is stepping up, that her shop will be in good hands.

Dougal has squashed himself around the metal legs of the garden table in order to catch any falling food. It doesn't look very comfortable but he has definitely decided it's his place to be.

James and Dougal are going to stay here tonight. I wanted them to stay. I hadn't thought about it before James asked but it made total sense. If Ruby gets in touch – when, I hope, she does – I want us to be together: not least so I can control what James writes back.

It's not lost on me that James and I are acting out the alternate reality. Maybe somewhere we are a real version of these people: an old couple, tired of talking, sitting watching the sun go down on another day; an old couple waiting for an email from their granddaughter.

Inside this peach old lady skin, there is a constant panic that won't leave me, an intense kinetic energy in my muscles. I recognise it for the buzz of adrenalin, and even after my run, it's still there. In an effort to suppress it, I have poured a very large glass of wine for each of us.

Some things about James haven't changed in fifty years. He still makes arrangements in his head and runs away with his own version of their outcomes, valid or not. It used to be charming but then, I used to be in love with him.

It's difficult to know what to talk about. I know now that he spent six months in Barlinnie prison when we left the squat. I know that when he came out, he couldn't get a job because of his criminal record: he gravitated to the more bohemian world of television but the BBC didn't hire ex-cons unless they'd been to Oxford.

I don't have to be told that what he went through was no bed of roses: a different bed of roses to the one I was left in but more than prickly in itself.

We all lost. Every one of us.

I searched the social media sites for Ruby's name straightaway. She was there on a couple of them but her profiles were secure: absolutely no clues for us bar a profile picture on one that proved she could swim. I couldn't find anyone else with the same surname. I presume, from that, that one of her parents is Cooper and the other Li – each surname on its own too ubiquitous to stand out.

'I just want to meet her.' He says it every now and again, punctuation to the day and into the evening: sometimes in a sentence, sometimes stand-alone. I don't ask whether he means Ruby or her faceless mother.

The whole thing paralyses me with fear. I've seen this, watched over it occasionally through work. I've seen so many outcomes, so few of them happy. James's other two daughters are known entities: he taught them to ride bicycles; he watched them grow; he knows their politics, their religious beliefs, their values. Will he understand that she is a different person, as a result of being raised by different people?

I have lit two candles on the patio as the day ebbs and darkens. The flames stutter and wave in the honeysuckle scent of the evening.

'What happened after you went home, Judith?' The question comes out of nowhere. We have had a whole day of avoiding difficult topics.

I am still remodelling the past, trying to rebrand him. And I am terrified to speak of the future.

Our conversations are like a game show where we move from square to square. Every time we land on a subject the floor lights up neon and a deafening quack of 'AWKWARD' rings silently round the room. We jump again: repeat.

Over the day, the conversations slowed to the banal, to a place of safety. I would prefer to stay there. I stay silent, sipping my wine, so quiet that every sound in the garden hums through me.

'Where was she born?'

It was my most private night. My most alone night. The idea of describing a situation where he was so completely missing – telling it to him – feels like a rock in my throat. I stand and walk a few steps away from him. Dougal swishes his tail in an apology for not bothering to follow me.

I look around the shapes of the garden, the way Catherine sculpted shrubs to sit neatly with trees. The green drapes of her prized weeping willow move gently and I imagine her voice in the scuttle of the leaves. My movement destroys the balance of the air, the two tiny candles struggle then go out, a half-second's gap between them.

'Do you remember how everything changed? After the time in the squat?'

He looks up at me. He is sitting with his feet planted wide, his forearms resting on the table. It reminds me of being a child, of saying that it wasn't my elbows on the table. The sound of my mother's gentle 'shoo' – the one she didn't mean.

'Everything. Music. Demos. The way people lived.'

'Because of psychedelics? Drugs?' he says.

'Maybe.' Not for Catherine and me: it was the time where off-duty social workers had to think about calling the police if they even smelt marijuana at a party. At the very least, we had to leave immediately.

'You?' I ask him.

He waves his hand a little, it means 'maybe'. 'Too late for us.'

I remember music becoming more political, demonstrations more violent, the news ever more surreal. Mine and James's generation were already lost to real life by the time Hendrix arrived. When the US culture came, the drugs and the hippies, we were already grown-ups.

'I feel like I stopped.' I see a branch covered in curled-up leaves, a rubble of aphids clinging to it. It snaps off easily, dry in my fingers. 'Like I ended after she was born.'

I hear the creak of the wine bottle being lifted from the metal garden table, the 'tink' of its neck against the rim of a glass, then a second.

'What happened to Paddy Gordon?' I ask. 'I tried to write to him too, but my mother's priest wouldn't pass on where he'd gone.'

'Paddy was a good man.' There is something in his voice that says that perhaps, in comparison, he himself was not. 'He went to Peterhead when I was in Barlinnie.' His accent returns with the memory, Peter-heed, he says. 'They split us all up. Peterhead made Barlinnie look like a hotel. I don't know what happened to Paddy after that, but he wouldn't have been the same man.'

'Maybe we all stopped.' I lift my wine glass to my mouth, pause. 'To Paddy,' I say and move my glass towards James.

'To the lot of us,' he says and drinks.

I spent my first few days in the unmarried mothers' home in silence. I wasn't trying to be difficult or rude: I simply had no words. The words I did have had no power – I had learnt that. I vanished, not entirely intentionally, within myself – a tiny world of two – and watched the outside bustle round us.

There were twelve pregnant women in the home on the day I arrived. I had expected them all to be my age, but – at twenty – I was one of the youngest. Some of them didn't look pregnant at all, others stretched to bursting through second-hand dresses which were three sizes too big all over, barely holding on the front. Most wore the same yoke of despair as I did.

The outside of the building was grand: it had once been an opulent family home. The inside was nothing but echoes; tiled corridors that made our shoes shhh; institutional yellow walls below the picture rails, off-white above. Nuns, in grey tunics that matched the atmosphere, gliding among us, checking on the condition of the growing babies. My room was simple – there were three beds in it although I was the only occupant. The other two were neatly made, white sheets turned down over brown wool blankets, waiting for the next girls. I heard people refer to them as cells: I've been in a cell, I wanted to say, and it isn't like this – it doesn't have a door you're allowed to open and close yourself.

The front door of the home wasn't locked – we weren't held behind bars. There was no point in holding anyone against their will when society had already done that.

On the third night, I woke to the sound of crying coming from one of the other beds. I listened for a bit but it didn't stop.

'Hello?' I said into the dark. 'Are you all right?'

The noise became muffled, she was crying into her pillow. I could just make out a shape huddled under the sheets.

'It's not so bad here.' I had no idea what it was like, but I wanted her to feel better than I did. I had spent three days sitting on the edge of my bed, passing rosary beads I couldn't rely on through my fingers because there was nothing else left to try. I did pray, when the nuns marched our little crocodile of shame to Mass. I prayed in the mornings, at lunchtime, I prayed all night. And Jimmy didn't come.

'I've come from here.' Her voice was clearer and I watched the shape sit upright. 'I've been here for five months and now I've . . .' She made a noise I'd never heard before. A lowing. A howl. A noise that came from the very centre of her. 'I've left him.' Her voice rose and rose, almost screaming. 'I've left him in the hozzie. He's . . . he's . . .' Her crying drowned out any words.

I worried about the nuns, whether we would get into trouble. I put my cold feet on to the floor and leant across to her bed. I found her shoulder beneath the scratchy blanket. 'Shhh. It's OK. You're safe here. And he's safe.' I didn't believe what I was saying. Inside I was screaming with her at the injustice, at the failure of humanity, at the sheer crime of separating this girl from her baby. I still held out a glimmer of hope, I still thought that someone would help me before it came to this, that Jimmy would write.

'My mam didn't come.' The words were tiny amongst the billowing sobs. 'I wanted my mam but she didn't come.'

I sat back down on my bed, frozen with the reality, with the understanding that this would be me: this cow; this wolf; this broken animal caught and bleeding in the trap.

When I woke in the morning, she was gone.

Sometimes, over the months that I stayed, boyfriends did arrive at the door, pledging to take care of their girl and their baby. They would be ushered, quietly, into Sister Anne's study and a discussion would take place. None of us knew what was said, but there were rumours that money changed hands, that girls could only be rescued if their boyfriends paid a ransom for them. No one came to throw the tables over in this temple.

What my mum had said was true: I was here to work – the board and lodgings came with a job. Each woman was given a brass 'wedding' ring in order to be fit for the outside world to look at, and sent off into whatever service would pay for our keep. I worked as a secretary, tucked in the stuffy backroom of a dairy, typing invoices. With every bill I wrote out, I thought about the sixpence that had got me here and the two desperate letters it paid for.

My pay packet only left me a few shillings each week, once the Home had taken its share. I was working five full days – swollen ankles, aching back – for less than I'd earned on my paper round when I was fourteen. We were supposed to spend what we had left over on a layette for the baby: on wool to knit blankets and hats; on fabric and cotton to sew tiny rompers.

'Mother and Father will be very touched if Baby arrives with some clothes,' Sister Anne would say. Her front teeth had a gap between them; it made her look benign. Perhaps she thought she was: she was only following orders. 'And you'll know that you sent Baby off properly dressed and properly cared for.'

Every penny I had went on stationery. I stole envelopes from the office at work, filled them with sheets of paper and snuck them out inside my clothes, squashed – rustling – across my enormous baby bump.

I bought stamps each week in the post office. 'Husband working away, is he, love?' the woman behind the counter asked too often. She knew full well I was one of Those Women.

My letters to Jimmy – I never missed a day – became more and more desperate, begging him: words blurred, the ink smeared with tears. Nothing I could do would stop the baby exploding out of me: already elbows and knees stuck out from the bump, turning my skin translucent with the pressure. The baby would get out and, when he or she was out, there would be nothing I could do – without Jimmy – to keep them safe.

On the rarest of occasions, it was the parents who gave in. I was in the dining room once when it happened, vacantly staring out of the window and spooning soup into my mouth. The girl I was sitting next to looked out and saw her mum and dad walking down the drive. She threw her spoon on the floor and ran.

The rest of us lined up to watch her leave, our breath clouding the glass and softening the pain. The mother walked with one arm around the girl's shoulders, wrapping her in apologies, and promising her the future we – most of us – wanted. The father took care of the car door, tucking her inside like an egg surrounded by shell.

No one spoke for a long time afterwards but I know we all prayed harder that night.

We had health checks every week from nuns who had our best interests at heart. Two weeks before The Big Day, each woman got an appointment, one on one, with Sister Anne.

I knocked on the heavy oak door of her office and then sat in one of the chairs lined up opposite. There were windows along the corridor and it seemed fitting that, while I waited, I watched the first leaf of autumn – bold and orange – leap from the biggest sycamore.

'Thank you for waiting.' Sister Anne smiled and a pattern of miniatures deltas appeared, silver, in her skin. She gestured to the chair in front of her desk and I sat down.

'You're remarkably agile, Judith. Lots of girls are barely able to move at your stage. You've handled this very well: a model pregnancy.'

A model pregnancy would be one without the nightmares: the swooping black shapes who gouged out my insides as soon as my eyes closed, the ghost of an empty cot that made me wake up screaming as my dream hand pressed itself against the still-warm mattress. The worst, that came almost every night – and that I wasn't to know then would go on for years – was a tall cat, in long leather boots, who wheeled the pram away. The marmalade cat whistled a wobbling tune and, as he walked, a long pheasant feather wiggled in his green hat. I could never quite see the cat's face.

'We've enjoyed having you here, Judith,' she said as if I'd been to a finishing school. 'You've been an example to the others.'

I wished with all my heart that I'd been a different kind of example, that I'd organised people into a cabal who formed a ring fence of motherhood, a rebellion of women who walked out and took the jewels they carried with them.

'I know it seems hard now.' She pointed to the teapot on the side, nodded her head to see if I'd like a cup.

'No, thank you.' We were not friends, this was not a tea party. The baby woke up, circled inside me. I patted her instinctively.

Sister Anne poured herself a cup of tea. She spoke with her back to me. 'You are very close to your delivery now and there are some things to think about. Our babies . . .'

Within me, the baby curled and flicked, furious. My baby, not our baby.

'. . . Some girls choose never to see the infant. It can be much easier for them that way. It's something you might want to think about.'

I wouldn't have to see my baby to know her or him, I knew every atom, every inch of them as they swam and spun in me. 'I have given it some thought.'

Sister Anne looked at me. Her eyes widened slightly under the straight edge of her veil. The starched white band of the cap underneath it was as clean as a halo.

'The girls talk,' I said. The girls did talk, the ones who still wanted to when they came back with slack skin, with soured burning breasts and empty arms. They talked about the money – that every couple who collected a baby handed over a cheque made out to the Home; they talked about the births and the despair; they talked about the gnawing hunger in their souls. My face burned hot and a wave of nausea bubbled through me. I swallowed it down. 'I would like to stay in the hospital as long as I can. With my baby. I would like to feed her,' and then, for effect and looking her right in her eyes: 'as God intended me to.'

I saw the tip of Sister Anne's tongue poke pink through the gap in her teeth. She sat back, the ends of her fingers touching each other: here's a church and here's a steeple.

133

'A lot of institutions encourage girls . . .' She looked down at the desk, straightened the handle of her tea cup in its saucer. 'A lot of institutions require girls to feed naturally. They feel that women' – she went to huge lengths to avoid the word 'mothers' – 'learn their lesson more effectively if they establish a bond with Baby, by keeping it beside them for the duration of their stay. Whether it cries or not. They feel they are less likely to see those girls back in the same bother again.'

My baby attempted one of the circles it could easily make a few months ago: bony toes kicked into my stomach.

Sister Anne stood up and walked to the window. 'We hope that the kindness we've shown you has taught you a more valuable lesson. I can't promise exactly what will happen at the hospital – that will all depend on the way in which you deliver. But, if you do want to see Baby for a little while, even feed it yourself, that can be arranged.'

I gave her a half-smile, grateful for these crumbs in the same breath as being furious that they lay, scattered, around my feet.

'But expect it to be hard, Judith. And expect this to make it harder.' She turned back to face me. 'Afterwards, you will come back here and get better. It may take a few weeks to recover in body and mind, but recover you will – and you will find, once you've left here and taken up your nurse's assistant position, that you never want to think of this time again.' She pressed her palms together over her chest, fingertips touching. 'It will be a new start for you, in God's good grace. In His compassion He will grant you a clean slate.'

Chapter Sixteen

My labour began as it does in legends. The baby and me, still a unit in the dark, tiny pains rippling through me. My waters broke gently and warm across my legs: I'd spoken to enough of the other girls not to be afraid. This was still an era where some pregnant women went into hospital so ignorant that they didn't know where or how their baby would come out, and I was grateful for my education – from school and from the last four months.

By the time the taxi dropped me at the hospital, I was starting to feel a little more realistic. The hospital was a long red-brick building, just across the park from the Home and probably from the same architect's stable. The midwife was impressed with my progress. 'You've missed the ante-natal ward entirely, dear,' she said. 'We can go straight to a delivery room.'

The delivery room was the palest green, like a cross section of leaf held up against the light. The floor was yellow parquet with the same smell of polish as my old school. Next to the bed was a slim cabinet and on it, a bell. 'Ring if you need us,' the midwife said and left.

I tried to slip away in my mind, to concentrate on the past and summon Jimmy by the power of my thoughts, but the pain gathered momentum and – every few minutes – obliterated everything but the fear.

When the midwife came back an hour later, I was crying.

'What's the matter?' she asked, stroking my arm. 'Why didn't you press the bell?'

'I didn't like to,' I said. 'I was waiting for the baby to come before I pressed it.' I held my breath as another contraction swept through me.

She timed the tensing with the silver watch pinned to her uniform. 'You're doing so well. I don't think Baby will be long now. Dry your eyes.' She looked at me. 'It isn't just the pain though, is it?'

'I don't want to be on my own.' I sobbed. Months of sadness and loss flowed now that the dam had been breached. 'I want to be here with Jimmy, I don't want to lose my baby. I can't . . .' It was too huge for words.

The midwife leaned in, put her kind arms around me: the first human contact I had had since leaving Scotland. 'Everyone is alone in here, dear. You're the only person who can do this and that's a great leveller. No husbands, not even if they really want to come in – we don't hold with it. So even if things were different, your fella wouldn't be here now. This is a place for women.' She tucked the sheet in around my legs; I imagined that room would be cold all year round. 'Let's see what happens when Baby arrives. Don't worry about anything until then.'

The pains twisted and worsened. Instead of crying, I rang the bell.

The midwife smiled as if she was pleased to see me, as if I'd done the right thing. 'This is going to be a fast one,' she said after she'd examined me. 'Hold on to your hat.'

I needed to know. 'Is it going to get worse than this?' I could barely speak.

'Fast ones tend to be hard: shorter but tough.' Her face was all sympathy and I was so glad she was there. 'A bit of pethidine will help you cope.'

An hour later, everything is changed. My body is no longer my own, no longer human. I rock, I low, I howl. I can no longer tell where I begin and end, how I fit in this room or it inside me.

The midwife stands next to me, she says words but I don't know what they mean or why she says them. She grips my hand, makes the noises one would make to coax a little animal to come nearer. Shhhh. Sssssss. There.

I see her hand move as she pats mine but my skin has lost all feeling; it is stretched to bursting, it is on fire.

The cat with the feather in his hat stands at the end of my bed, leaning in with his hot fish breath and showing me his teeth. His claws stretch around the handle of the pram and he smiles at it, at the crisp white blanket he has laid out in the bottom of it, ready for my baby.

Another explosion of pain and stars shatters over me. I am sprinkled with red-hot pepper. The dust enters every pore of me. It mingles with my blood.

I hear a chime. A ping. A man with white hair and wild eyebrows lifts a tray to his eyes.

The cat sticks out his tongue; he makes sure I can see it. I hear the roughness of it pass his teeth. He strokes his long claws in the bed of the pram and purrs.

I hear a voice that sounds like Jimmy's. It breaks through the waves of pain.

'She's dead.' He wails, split apart.

Another contraction. And this time it is my turn to split in two. I can feel the functioning of my organs. I am so aware of my anatomy that I can pinpoint with my finger where her head is stuck as it crowns through my cervix.

'She's gone.' The old man lays his hands on my shoulders. Looks at me with eyes I know, will know.

'We are too late,' says the old man.

'Now!' shouts the midwife.

I grunt and push and scream and the baby slips – wet and hot – out of me and into waiting hands and she is gone.

'We've lost her twice,' says James.

James repeats and repeats the words. He tries to hold the iPad in front of my face so that I can read the email for myself, but I am beyond that.

I go inside, into my bedroom. I sit on the end of my bed. My running clothes are on the chair where I left them earlier.

This is why Catherine taught me to run. So that one day, when I needed it, I had the means to escape, to get to her.

I open the front door. I do not answer James, who calls out to ask where I am going. I walk down the path. There is silence in my head, a limitless terrifying silence. The dialogue that has run silently between her and me for her whole life has stopped. The internal chatter of souls that takes place without words is gone. In its place is a vast deserted universe that I inhabit alone. Without her.

I start to run.

I don't start gently. The aim of this run is very different to any I have done before.

I ignore the screaming of my joints, the pulses of painful breath as I draw in too much, too fast. I shift up a gear as the fences and trees of my road fall away from me. The pavement is uneven and throws me slightly sideways: I right myself and I run.

I run faster than I have ever run before and I turn on to the quietest streets so that no one will save me.

It has started to rain: fat summer raindrops that I would normally welcome. I shake them from my cheeks and keep my lips firmly together so they don't moisten my dry mouth.

The pain in my legs is not enough. I run faster. I concentrate on balance, on achieving my goal. I fill my mind with breathing, with the noise of my screaming lungs, the pulse that rages in my ears like timpani.

I turn on to the pavement alongside the main road. Two carriageways of cars thunder past me; two of the cars beep in quick succession. One a toot, one a long warning blast. I ignore them and run faster.

I cross the bridge over the bypass and head right towards the country park and its winding trails through the woodlands. The trees wave and whisper: they will witness but they won't interfere.

There is a long ash road through the centre of the parkland; trails run off from it on each side, a maze of impossible pathways in an enchanted forest. I pick one that runs downhill, increase my speed. I can barely breathe, hardly see, but still I run. My legs pulse with pain but hold firm.

And then I feel it, the oblivion I am running for, the prize. A pain sits, like solidifying lead, in my chest. I quicken my stride, close to collapse but pushing myself upright. There is only one way to get through this heartache. I run and run, the pain grows and grows.

This is what it was like when she was born, in those last moments before her life began – when pain overwhelmed my thoughts, my speech. I am back there. My body has turned to molten metal; the pulse in my ears is one long noise. I am choking down vomit and coughing acid.

The fire in my chest grows and my eyes start to fail. I thunder through, staggering and gasping, my thighs wet and rubbing, the joints in my ankles barely holding. I hit the ground hard and the tiny grit embeds itself in my cheek. I feel each stone. I try to claw myself upright but the pain reaches a point where I know I am bursting. This is what I ran for: this is the end. This is where I will find Catherine and, I believe with all my heart, she will be holding my baby.

I close my eyes and welcome it.

Chapter Seventeen

When I open my eyes, I am sitting on a bench.

'What happened then?'

I turn my head towards the voice. I am surprised to find that I am not alone. The sun is still shining and the birds are calling an end to the day. It is peaceful. The park in front of me is calm and green and, with this huge expanse of tailored lawn, pretty much what I thought heaven might look like.

'Once she was born, then what?' It is Gwyn Johnson. The set of beads I threaded for her are round her neck. She is still wearing a floral dressing gown but, this time, she has wellington boots on her feet instead of slippers. 'Did you take her back to the Home? To the nuns?'

I wonder if Gwyn has died too.

I shake my head. 'No. They let me stay. The midwives let me stay.' This is not heaven. This is the park near my house, gentle in the late afternoon. There are people in the distance but no one near enough to disturb us; two old ladies sitting on a park bench.

'Why?' I ask Gwyn. 'Why are *you* here?'

I look down at my feet: my trainers are dusty and a dried line of dark-red blood snakes down my calf. The edges of the blood spider out into scratches in my skin. There is a gash across my knee.

Gwyn looks at my legs too. 'Your face is worse,' she says. Her handbag is on her knee and she opens it, takes out a mirror so quickly that the whole bag must be organised in immaculate compartments. She passes it to me.

I look like a boxer. I'm not alarmed – or even bothered. My heart does not quicken at the sight of my puffed and purple eye, the tic-tac-toe of gravel stuck to my cheek. My skin is flaccid and white: I look dead. I take a breath in, feel the bruises in my lungs. Parts of me are alive.

Gwyn reaches out a hand, picks a twig from my face. I feel a pop as the tiniest of thorns that held it in place gives up its dominion in my flesh.

'I thought I would take her back to the Home with me,' I say. 'I don't know why, I knew no one else had. But I let myself believe.'

Gwyn flicks a fragment of grit from my leg. She punctuates the conversation with these tiny grooming movements, a primal instinct of soothing, of reaching out.

'We spent the first two days just staring at each other. Enchanted. She didn't cry and I didn't speak. There were about twenty beds on the ward – all those babies crying and wailing, barely a moment's peace in the rest of the room.'

A young man whizzes past on a mountain bike. Gwyn and I maintain our invisibility shield and he doesn't even glance at us.

'I got these big grey canvas screens – they were all lined up at the end of the ward – and I put them round my bed, like a little room. And we stayed there and stared at each other.'

Gwyn nods. 'I had my son somewhere similar. He was a fretful baby though. I didn't really know what to do with him.' She smiles into the past.

'I had to come out in the end. I had to eat, I had to wee.' I remember the gap at the end of the screens getting fractionally wider each time I pushed the clear plastic cot through it to take

142

her to the loo with me. I couldn't leave her on her own, not for one minute. I didn't know who would come for her – how she would leave. Presumably that's why I invented the fiction that we'd leave together, that we'd go back to my little cell in the Home and that a cot would have replaced the other bed. We would only need to stay there long enough for me to find some childcare, and then a job.

Or for Jimmy to come.

'I still believed in him.' The slight breeze stings as it blows against my face, but it carries the summer birdsong too – a double-edged sword. 'Every time the big doors at the end of the ward swung open, my heart leapt and I'd look up. I honestly believed it would be Jimmy. Every single time. I thought he'd run through the ward, desperate, and he'd stop at us – at her – and he'd see what I saw and . . .'

Gwyn nods. 'Shall I fetch us a cup of tea?'

I know roughly where I am: the tea hut is about half a mile away. 'Maybe we should go and get one together, Gwyn? In a while.'

'That's a good idea.' She dips into her handbag with the same efficiency. This time she pulls out sweets, hard minty candies like the sort my dad used to keep in the glove box of his car.

'No, thanks,' I say – I think my face is too swollen to chew. 'Gwyn . . . how are we here? I mean, you and me on a bench?'

'Oh, you poor old thing,' she says. She pats my knee and I wince. Feeling is returning to the nerves and my skin stings all over. 'You had taken a bit of a tumble. Over there.' She points to the bottom of the long grassy slope but I don't remember being near there.

'How did you find me?'

'You ran past me, I think.' She pauses for a minute. 'Yes, that's right. You ran past me and you didn't look very well. So I followed you.' She nods to herself, confirming the memory. 'And then we walked together for a bit until we decided to sit down. I expect that's what we did.'

I am covered in dried blood, dust; I am bruised and battered. Gwyn isn't at all fazed by it. We go back to the companionable silence for a while: she is happy to have company, I am trying to piece this afternoon together – fill in the gap between when I left James and when I started talking to Gwyn. In the back of my mind, the thud-thud-thud of loss continues.

'But he didn't know you were there?' she asks. She seems to know every detail of my story – only I can have told it to her. 'He didn't know you were in the hospital?'

I shake my head. 'I carried on writing. The midwives were so kind. They brought me paper and envelopes. They gave me stamps from their own purses. And Jimmy's mother threw them all away.' It is still something my brain can't process. I have an image in my head of the wee wifey, the woman I have never seen – will never see – tearing open the envelopes meant for her son, unfolding the paper. Did she think of her own babies as she made her decision? Did she trace the contours of their faces with her memories, lift each hair from their heads and feel its gossamer weight, watch it fall? Did she remember the pearl shell shape of their tiny ears, at the way the pink light shone through them, as she tore the letters into ragged pieces and fed them to the fire?

I stayed for three weeks. The staff let me stretch into three weeks of wonder, three weeks where we shut out the outside world and concentrated on memorising every pattern and scent of each other. When the rest of the ward was sleeping, in the rare pauses in the dark before one of the twenty babies woke, I would whisper to her. With my words, I gave her every birthday party, every nursery rhyme and song, that I thought she would ever need. With my fingers I stroked her skin and traced all the holidays, the sunshine, the salty sea swims, that she would have without me, that we had to imagine while we could. With my breasts I gave her every strength I had, I fed her bones and brain, the cells of her skin, fortified every microscopic armour that I could to protect her. With my heart I wished every good thing for her: to find love; to find peace; to be happy.

The other mothers were kind, thoughtful. When they realised what was going to happen to my little baby, they held their own slightly closer, squeezed them more fervently. One girl sent her husband over to my side of the room.

'My missus asked me to take your picture.' He lifted the camera in his hand. 'I develop them at home, in our back room. She thought you might like a photograph.'

I looked across the room at his wife, pale and tiny in the hospital bed. The frames of the beds were gunmetal grey and they rose over each of us like bars. She smiled at me, nodded encouragement.

'Thank you,' I whispered at her.

She read the shape of my lips and smiled.

'And, when her husband came back – bless him – with his beautiful little portrait of her and me together, I knew that's what I needed to get Jimmy to come.' My voice rolls down the wide field in front of us, tumbles – unheard – through the grass. 'I knew he wouldn't be able to resist her face. That seeing his eyes stare back at him would be enough. The ward sister posted it for me on her way home.'

Gwyn is staring into the distance. I follow her eye-line and see a yellow dog, tail like a banner, running through the long grass. Behind him, far away, a man with white hair strides, Scout's pace, across the field.

I know it's James, even at this distance. If I could, I would get up – run away – but I am broken into too many pieces.

'How did he get here?' I ask Gwyn.

James stops every now and again. He has black binoculars that he raises to his face and scans around. Despite the binoculars, it is Dougal who spots me first and bounds through the long grass. James struggles after him.

'I wonder if you asked me to call him.' Gwyn lifts her hand to show me that she has my mobile phone.

'Did I?'

'Probably, dear,' she says. 'Detail's not my strong suit.'

James is stumbling and out of breath by the time he reaches us.

Dougal is looking for something behind the bench I'm sitting on and has no further interest in me past a brief tail wag.

'Judith, Christ. I've been looking for you for hours.' James stands bent over, hands on his thighs and panting for breath. Once he can speak he takes his phone from his pocket. 'I'm calling an ambulance.'

'Don't.' I feel suddenly sheepish. 'I don't need an ambulance.'

'For fuck's sake,' he says, and I feel Gwyn flinch slightly beside me. 'You can't see yourself. You need an ambulance.'

It sparks an anger in me, perhaps on Gwyn's behalf. 'How do you propose it gets here? I'd need an air ambulance and even you would agree that's a total waste of fucking time.' My turn.

Gwyn looks at me, her mouth an 'O' of surprise.

'Sorry, Gwyn,' I say.

'This is no good.' James runs his hand through his hair. 'Your leg is bleeding. We do need to get you to a hospital. Your face . . .' He trails off and I imagine my boxer's face, the bruises and the grazes.

I look down at my leg. I can't see properly out of one eye but, with the other, I can see now that there is a flap of skin open across my knee: bubbles of subcutaneous fat are visible underneath it, pearlescent as frog spawn.

'She wanted to die,' Gwyn says in the same voice she probably uses to read out her shopping list. 'She told me.' And then, proudly, 'I remember that.'

My eyes fill with tears when she says that. Nothing has changed. I have still survived all of those I love and, whichever way you look at it, that doesn't leave much to live for. I try to hold back my sadness but it erupts as a cough, a painful gasp.

The bench has a green film of lichen on it, damp despite the summer. I curl my fingers around the slats each side of me. I am going to try and stand up. I inch myself to the edge, putting the weight on my left leg, and lean forward.

James dives in to catch me as my leg gives way. He leaves his arms round me and settles me back to the bench.

I realise, now that my face is buried between his shoulder and his face, that I am shaking all over.

His hands meet across my back and he squeezes me into him. 'I'm so sorry, I'm so sorry,' he whispers into my ear.

We organise ourselves, the three old people at the top of the slope, eventually. Gwyn promises to stay put next to me and James will go and get the car. He thinks he can drive across the parkland – if he does it slowly – and leave the car at the bottom. Then we only have to get down this slope.

James wanted to leave something to keep me warm. It is still summer, even if the temperature is dropping with the afternoon sun, but he was only wearing jeans and a T-shirt. He has gone back to get the car half-naked: his chest a mass of wiry white hair. When he turned to go, I saw that the hair grows on his shoulders and slightly down his back and thought, with renewed realism, how very old we are.

I am wearing his T-shirt over my clothes: it smells of aftershave and sunshine and sweat.

We drop Gwyn at hers on the way back through town.

'And, Judith, if you want to leave the Mending Shop, you should do it,' Gwyn says through the window to me.

I am half-lying on the back seat. 'Did I say I wanted to?' I ask her.

'Desperately, you said. Do it. Your friend – Catherine – she won't mind.'

'She wasn't my friend,' I say, brandishing Catherine above my head. 'She was my lover.'

'Well, she wouldn't want you to be unhappy.' And Gwyn turns away, starts walking up her path.

James waits at the kerb until she's safely inside. As soon as her door closes, he exhales loudly, stares straight ahead. The car glides on, silent.

'I'm going to run you a bath and call your doctor. Where's the number?'

'It's fine, I'll call.'

I'm sitting on the sofa, lying back on a pile of cushions James put behind me. My leg is up on the arm of the chair. Under the bright overhead light, it looks awful. I'm not sure that I can't see an ivory piece of kneecap at the bottom of the pink.

Our local doctor's surgery was wonderful when Catherine was ill. Their care meant she was able to stay here at home right till the end. The number is still in my phone.

'Sweet tea,' James says, bringing me a mug. 'For the shock.'

'I don't think I should drink it,' I say. 'In case.' I point to my knee. My finger still trembles as I stretch it out.

James sits down beside me. 'It's my fault. I shouldn't have started digging.' He puts his hand to his eyes, finger and thumb stretching across his face. 'We wouldn't be going through this now if I'd waited.'

I close my eyes. I don't want to look at him, to have to consider him. I want to be alone with this new version of my grief, in the house that has already heard all the stories, every angle of it.

'It's not your fault, James. It was only natural to want to know. I don't blame you.' Perhaps I do: I haven't had long enough to think about it. The whole of the inside of me is hollow – I am utterly empty.

On the bookcase to the left there is a photograph of Catherine and me. The frame is white and it highlights our tans, our wide smiles. We were hiking in northern Spain, leaving impossibly early in the mornings to watch the fat sun crown the mountains, and walking on until we hid from the sun in the next *agriturismo*. I didn't think about her then – Penny, her name is Penny. I didn't take her with me on that journey, I'm sure I didn't. There were days, weeks – maybe even months – as the decades wore on, where I didn't hold her front and centre, where she sat quietly in my heart as a companion.

That's what makes this grief so strange. It is a loss of a loss: the compounding of a negative space. I am both completely different and exactly the same.

The doctor gives me painkillers, stays longer than she should to talk to me, to make sure that I'm no more traumatised than I was before I knew. I wonder if she is suspicious as to who James is, what his role might be in my accident. The doctor knows that two women loved each other for a lifetime in this house.

She gives me the choice of having my knee stitched here or in A&E, no choice as far as I'm concerned.

I watch her face as she runs the long, curved needle through the sides of the gash.

She asks tentative questions, comments on how strange it is to learn something new about someone she's known so long, been through so much with. It makes us instantly different, and exactly the same. It doesn't change either of us.

The doctor asks if she should send a home help round and James offers, straightaway, to do the job.

'I can stay. I have no reason to get back. I'll get some supper on.'

He doesn't leave me a choice.

I wonder if I should explain the definite parameters of mine and James's relationship to the GP, but I don't have the energy, the words, even if I ought to.

I want to hide from him – lock myself in the bathroom – but my leg is too sore, I can't bend it enough to get into the bath.

James brings a bowl, warm cloths, and starts to wash the dust and grit from my arms and legs as I lie on the sofa. The softness of it makes me cry.

I am glad James stayed last night. It was the simplest of decisions for the most difficult of days.

I slept that kind of sleep where your mind saves you, shuts down and cuts off to allow you a few hours of respite. I'm not sure whether it's the throbbing in my leg that wakes me – as every stitch tries to pull itself free of the swollen flesh – or the tapping on my bedroom door.

'Come in, James,' I say because there doesn't seem any point in not.

'I've brought your painkillers. I didn't know if you'd prefer tea or coffee.' He puts the packets down on my bedside table. He takes up a lot of space in this room that's not used to him in it.

He goes to make me a coffee and I take as many of the painkillers as the instructions allow. I hope they can work for my soul as well as my body.

James brings his own coffee up with mine. He hovers by the door, unsure of propriety.

I pull the duvet up to my armpits and pat the bed covers beside me. 'Feel free.'

James sits as far away from me as he can and swings his legs on to the bed. He is wearing a pale-pink T-shirt that I lent him, pretty much the only thing I could think of that would fit.

'How do you feel?' I need to acknowledge that he is injured too.

James blows across the top of his drink, makes an issue of it to distract from looking at me. 'I'm OK. I'll be OK.' He picks a strand of cotton from his jeans. 'I still haven't told my girls, and now I don't know what to say.' His hands are shaking slightly. 'Can we reply to Ruby today?'

I nod.

'Something to look forward to,' he says.

My face smarts as I swallow the coffee. It misses the side of my mouth, slides past my swollen cheek, and lands on the bedclothes. James and I both go to rub the stain at the same time and jump as our fingers collide.

'Sorry,' we both say.

And then it's awkward: James sitting on Catherine's side of the bed, leaning against her pillows, his head about eighteen inches higher than hers would have been; the whistling silence of loss moves between us, and neither of us knows how to tackle it.

'Have you looked in the mirror?' he asks.

'I deliberately left the bathroom light off when I went to the loo.' Catherine used to wake at the slightest light; I am practised in moving around our en-suite in the dark.

'Maybe don't look.' He smiles at me and I can see his younger self inside the fading skin. 'I'm going to nip out and get some breakfast – and some proper dog food for our friend. And then I'll bring my laptop in here and we can write to Ruby. OK? I really think you should stay in bed today.'

I shrug. It seems silly – weak – to stay in bed, but the stone of grief that sits inside me is comfortable here.

When I close my eyes, the pressure of emotion inside my head is overwhelming, so I pick up my phone to check up on the world's news. I have messages from Barbara.

> *Are you all right? Let me know that skeletons not rattling too loudly. Have sent two emails viz shop. No rush. Bx.*

I open my emails. There are two about Barbara's plans: one from her and one from the local authority. I can't read them today – I am not ready to need a future.

I sink back on to the pillows, my eye smarting and my knee throbbing.

It is time to give myself a talking to. The beauty of knowing someone as well as I knew Catherine is that you can channel them with ease, predict the tone of voice they'd use, the pitch and tone of their delivery. I close my eyes and bathe in Catherine's common sense.

At the end of her lecture I open the other email in the inbox – the one Ruby sent us, forwarded to me by James – and I wonder if there might be some sort of future, after all.

I manage a shower of sorts, going through the indignity of leaving one leg outside the cubicle, before James gets back and offers to help or something equally dreadful. I put on shorts and a T-shirt then sit back on my bed. I hear Dougal come in before I hear James. It turns out – although it's taken me seventy-five years to realise – that the sheer enthusiasm of a dog is enormously liberating. Dougal's clattering claws and wildly swishing tail are the good that I need in my life right now.

Dougal left the door ajar but James taps on it anyway. He has a tray of coffee and pastries. He goes to shoo Dougal out.

'Oh, no, let him stay. Please.' I pat the side of the bed so that Dougal comes all the way round and leans up against it. 'He's keeping me going.'

'Don't let him on the bed then,' James says. 'Even if he asks. He's not allowed.'

James and I eat in silence. It hurts my face to chew but I had next to nothing to eat yesterday and must have covered ten kilometres between my two – very different – runs. I make short work of two croissants; flat flakes scatter the duvet cover beneath me. I will regret those crumbs tonight.

'Ruby,' I say, in a gap between pastry and coffee. 'I assume you'd like to meet her.'

He is silent. It is unexpected, I have only known him as impetuous as his boyhood self – as a human version of Dougal – over the last days.

'You do want to meet her?' I ask. I am surprised at the heavy quiet, incongruous with a summer morning.

'Absolutely, but I'm more cautious now, more aware of what might go wrong.' He looks at me. 'I have been listening.'

'That's OK.' I don't want him to hurt as much as I do. 'We can take it slowly, be cautious. I can't meet her with my face like this anyway.'

'There's something I need to tell you.' He puts his coffee down on the bedside table, on Catherine's little coaster with the seaside joke on it. 'Before we can move on, I mean.'

'Honestly, James.' I risk a hand on his arm. 'I don't think I can take any more.'

'I can't go forward with the rest of this, with Ruby, unless I tell you the part you don't know.' He has his head tipped back. The stubble under his chin is white.

I close my eyes, as if that will close my ears with it. Polly Wright shimmers and shapes in my mind, her red hair, her pale peach skin. The hairs on my forearms rise and I shiver despite the warm air.

'I loved you very much, Judith. Back then, I mean. In the squat.'

It is a tumbling confession for a bright day, out of place, awkward. In a garden down the road, children are playing a game; a bat cracks loud against a ball and they shout out encouragement to someone.

'We – you and I – were . . .' He searches for the word, looks down at his lap. 'We were very close, Judith.' It is the first implied reference to the relationship we had, to the non-stop sex of our newfound freedom: however temporary that freedom may have turned out to be.

I wonder whether to stop him, to explain that I knew there was something between him and Polly. I think about saying that it was a long time ago, that it's in the past. But I can't: it's here and now in front of us.

James looks at me and then at our legs: our feet side by side on the bed as if fifty-six years has disappeared. 'I was going to ask you to marry me. I bought a ring.'

The air sticks in my lungs. My skin crawls with a sticky heat.

'I bought it that day, the ring. The day of the raid. We were going to have supper together, but we quarrelled, you and I.' He swallows. His London voice disappears with his saliva and he talks in his real accent, with his real self. 'We argued about the last raid.'

I remember it. I can still see Polly Wright's face. After fifty-six years, I still recall sleeping in my underwear to put distance between us on the night I didn't tell him.

'I went to the base with Polly.' He reaches across to take my hand and this time I don't stop him. 'And I asked Paddy to look after the ring so it didn't fall out of my pocket.'

All the rings. The pretend rings. Wearing Kay's ring to get contraception; wearing an old ring of my mother's on the drive to Liverpool. The Home gave us rings to wear while we were in labour and all the midwives, in on the deception, called us 'Mrs'. Something so small, with so much hold over so many women.

'I got it at the Barras,' he says and I remember the market, tragic little tables of people's last possessions laid out next to vegetable stalls and butchers' vans. 'It was twelve shillings: second-hand.' He looks at my hand, touches the ring finger.

I pull my hand away. 'I didn't expect that.' I pick up my coffee cup, sip at the cold liquid in an effort to be doing something other than sitting on a bed with Jimmy McConnell, talking about love. 'Let's look forward. We still have Ruby.' I don't want to dwell on these might-have-beens that could, literally, destroy me.

'No.' He leans forward, put his hands on his shins, curls the fingers round his calves. 'Not yet. There's more. And I didn't want to tell you, but I have to.'

I'm not ready for his confession. Some things should be left to die naturally.

'I was in prison for six months.' He stares at the end of the bed. 'And when I came out, I went to look for you.'

I stay very still.

'And I came to your house.'

The room grows cold.

'I didn't want to tell you – not after you told me about my ma. I didn't want you to feel this pain.' He taps his chest with his open palm.

James describes the crescent road my parents lived on, the modern house they'd worked so hard to buy and that I sent Christmas and birthday cards to right up until they died. They always had little messages in the cards, why I couldn't come home for this birthday, that Christmas – but that I would, next time.

James tells me how he walked down our garden path, autumn leaves raked and neat each side of it. He describes the dimpled glass, the wavy shapes of my parents behind it.

James spoke to my parents: he doesn't remember now the details of the conversation, of exactly how it was said, but he stills feels every moment of their bitter news. He tells me how his eyes stung with tears as he walked back to the station and the evening grew cold around him.

'So that was it,' he says. 'They told me that you'd married someone else and I had no reason to think they would lie.'

I am speechless. My kind mother, who in my memory is button tins and church raffles, bring-and-buy sales and Christmas stockings. My father, devoted, who did my homework with me every night. I thought it was their inability to lie that had seen my baby taken from me.

But it wasn't, it was their inability to face the truth.

'I went back to Scotland and I got on with my life. I didn't know what else to do.'

'How could they?' The tears have begun again. In earnest this time. This time I am crying for myself, for my baby, even for Jimmy, for James. The place in my heart where my parents were has filled with a cold, dark liquid, drowned their memory.

I picture James as he would have been after six months in one of Scotland's most notorious prisons, six months that must have all but broken this huge, gentle man.

'It's no different to my mammy, to what she did,' James says, quietly. 'They thought they were protecting us. It was bigger than them: it was what they thought they had to do.' He lifts an arm and puts it round my shoulders.

It should feel wrong, but I need someone. I need him, he is the link to the past and present of this. He is the other person so cheated by this. Him and our daughter.

James pulls me towards him.

I lean my face on to his shirt, screw my eyes tight against the tears. 'I would have said yes,' I say.

Chapter Eighteen

Ruby

I'm beyond excited. For the last two weeks, I have been waking up at three o'clock in the morning wondering, wondering all kinds of things. In the quiet bits, in the dark, I wonder about Mum and what she would make of it all and I wonder if she'd be excited too. She would have been cross at first and I would have gone off on one instantly in retaliation. Bang, yelling that I was only trying to help, that I was doing my best – we've been there a million times, about a million things. I'd give anything to tell her that I'm different now. It makes the skin on my face go hot just thinking about it, about all the things I'd change if I could turn back time.

I know it's true that Mum and me wouldn't still be shouting at each other now I'm twenty-two. But that doesn't actually change anything – that's the absolute shittiest thing about the past: you can't change it.

Dad says he thinks Mum would actually be glad about Judith and James – despite everything she said about it.

'I think the context would be different,' he told me when I phoned to say that Judith and James are going to meet me, that we're all three going to have lunch. 'She was determined not to do it while Granny was alive – which is very understandable. I wonder if she'd have come round to it a bit more in the last few years, you know, with all the TV programmes and so on.'

I snap the dead leaves from the edges of my spider plant: there are a disgraceful amount of them, poor thing. Those adoption reunion programmes are my guilty pleasure. I've watched them since they started, mush though they are, and I've always been hoping to see Mum's baby photo, hear a story that I know is actually her.

Every now and then I'd hear one and think it was her, and by extension of that – of course – me. Then they'd go a bit further into the story and it would reveal that it was the wrong end of Britain or – and this has happened more than once – right at the oh-my-God-that's-my-mum-moment, it turns out the baby was a boy.

My dad absolutely sneers at those programmes – not because of the adoption thing: he feels the same about 'all reality television', quote, because he is a Very Lofty Academic. One day he will find out that those endless cookery programmes to find the best high-end chef in Britain are also reality TV and then his brain will implode.

Anyway, Carmen, a girl I did my first degree with – that still feels so good to say, even if I never do get round to finishing the second – works for one of those television production companies. Carmen says they're all pretending, all those people who burst into tears or go off on one onscreen: not pretending that they're overwhelmed or beside themselves – that's real – but pretending that they don't know they're going to meet their 'long-lost family'. The research goes on for months behind the scenes and only when they know they've got a winner – whole heart-rending story, lots of tearful reunions – only then does it get as far as the actual programme. Carmen says that for every one they show, there are twenty on the cutting-room floor: twenty that ended in fights, or broken hearts, or once – she told me and we shuddered – in an extremely inappropriate relationship. These are the sorts of thing my dad says, which makes me hate that it's true.

But it was Carmen who told me that, if social media doesn't cough up – and it usually does – they get the files from social services. Those reports pretty much tell them everything they need to make the programme out of – and, if they have to, they go to the genealogy sites to put the rest of the family together. So that's what got me off the ground.

Anyway, it's done. Today, I'm going to have my own little moment. I wonder if I'll cry – I'll cry if she looks too much like my mum, that's for sure. Judith looked like my mum in the photo, but she's much, much older now.

James has my mum's eyes – or rather, she has his – so I'm ready for that, prepared. But it's Judith, somehow I feel more connected to the idea of her. Because she's a woman? Maybe because my own women are a bit missing: Mum obviously, and she had no sisters; and my Granny Cooper died a year before Mum; and then Granny Li, who is always either in an exercise class or on a plane. Dad would say that's very unkind, that she also makes a great deal of time to hear how I'm doing and what my latest achievements are. That's true too, but I don't always have the energy to keep up with Granny Li – who is eighty and dashes around like a yo-yo.

I go back to deadheading the spider plant. I will at least have one job completely finished before I go and meet them.

I'm early. I'm early for every appointment I ever have. If I go on holiday with the girls, I'm always first at the airport, sitting in some seedy bar over egg and chips while I wait – bored and numb-bummed – for them to arrive. They have spent the extra two hours they had on getting ready, while I look like the arse-end of a badger.

We've arranged to meet in the cathedral town midway between us where Mum did her architecture degree. It's not far for them and it's only an hour for me on the train. More than that, there's a café splot on top of a fantastic piece of Brutalist architecture that the council tried for years to pull down and my mum fought for years to save. The fact that we're meeting in it says a lot about Mum and her doggedness – the same stubbornness led to us not meeting her natural parents before it was too late, but I will let that go today – and the council didn't get to demolish this crazy old building.

There's a wide square of paving and a set of concrete steps to the terrace. The steps look like they're floating and when I was little, I used to think I'd slide through the gaps and be lost. I did worry a bit that Judith or James might not make it up, but there is a lift in the shop downstairs if they need it.

The steps lead to a plaza that looks like my primary school playground but is a roof-garden, entirely concrete and surrounded by shiny railings with a pattern like waves. There's an Italian restaurant on the top of the shopping centre and it has chairs and tables right out across the roof-garden in the summer. We know the owner – because of Mum – and Dad emailed him to book us a quiet little table right at the far end.

Dad did offer to come with me but, somehow, we both thought I ought to do it by myself.

'It is, after all, your fault,' Dad said. His idea of funny.

I hope Mum is here with me, that the people who think that stuff are right. She described – with an accuracy that made me cringe at the time, and shout at her to stop – how she used to come here on dates with boys from her uni course and they'd drink milky coffee out of weird glass mugs. But then she went to a gig, and met my dad in a sticky mosh pit where the music was too loud to talk. Which explains a lot about how he got away with being him and still got off with anyone.

I order the same weird coffee, only nowadays they pretend it's a 'latte', in the same weird mugs, only now they pretend they're 'retro'. I've been coming here all my life, I know their 'retro' is really 'haven't bought any new ones'.

I can see right across the plaza, almost to the multi-storey car park, from my table in the corner of the terrace. There is a leggy yucca with splits and cracks up its leaves that sort of camouflages me from the street and I peer through it at the crowds.

Judith and James are the fifth couple I think are them. I have followed the rest with my eyes until they pass the steps to the restaurant or turn and go into a shop. As soon as I see these two, they can't ever have been anyone else.

They are tall, both of them. I know without asking that she is going to have big feet like my mum and me. 'Functional over delicate,' Mum used to say as my cousins pranced around in pale-pink ballet slippers at Christmas.

Judith and James look functional – strong – although she walks with a limp.

When they are a minute or so from the bottom of the steps, he stops – slightly ahead of her. People stream each side of them, milling about in every direction. There is the noise of an electric guitar cutting across the rumble of people if you listen hard, and the smell of candied peanuts and tourists rises up to my little corner.

I lean my phone up against the coffee cup, out of sight and behind the plant. I slide the video to 'on'.

James takes both Judith's hands in his, stares right in her eyes. As far as they're concerned, they're the only people in the street. When he's finished whatever it is he's saying to her, he pulls her into his arms and they just stand there, holding on to each other. I wish my mum could see it. And then I think about her and my dad. I wish they'd got a chance to be it.

162

Judith and James separate, and walk the last metres to the bottom of the steps. I wonder if they know I'm watching: if they're looking for me like I'm looking for them.

James gets to the steps, then stands back, makes a gesture for her to go first. She is wearing light-blue linen culottes that flare out around her legs and a short-sleeved button-through top. It is stylish, but it doesn't tell me much. He is wearing shorts, posh ones like suit trousers, and he has a long-sleeved white shirt over them, not tucked in. I wonder if they had other children; they don't look like people with children.

I turn my phone off, slip it into my bag – I'm being polite – and then they're there. They are walking towards me, Judith first, James behind her, his hand on her shoulder.

'Ruby?'

I stand up and my metal chair scrapes across the concrete. 'Hello.' And then, in an instant, it's both ordinary and extraordinary: normal and completely – utterly – bizarre.

'It's lovely to meet you,' she says and we both take an awkward half-step forward. 'I'm Judith.'

'And I'm James.' He crosses the gap, doesn't ask, just hugs me and the awkwardness is broken.

When he lets go, I turn to Judith, hug her too. The hugs are polite though, like the sort you give a stranger. The hugs speak volumes about who we actually are to each other and it's not what I imagined, it's not what I've seen on TV with the tears and the sobs and the longing.

We smile at each other, easier than speaking.

'It's such a beautiful day,' Judith says. 'How was your journey?'

I try not to look at her too hard while I talk. I have always thought my nose was sweet: a version of my mum's but a bit broader. Now I see it on a stranger's face, it looks like a potato. I am trying not to stare.

'Shall I order wine?' James asks and Judith and I both say yes a bit too fast. Everyone laughs, not too loud, just lightly and inoffensively. We're all aware, without discussing it, that our conversation skates over a frozen lake. I'm sure they don't want to fall in any more than I do.

James is sitting to my left, Judith at the point of the triangle we make. I can see her face by glancing up, but I can't really see him unless I pointedly look. And that feels so weird. I don't want him to think I'm staring and I'm nowhere near comfortable enough to say, 'Can you sit really still and look forwards while I stare at you?' So I have to pretend I'm not looking. The sun is just behind him too, so I have to put my hand up to shade my eyes whenever I turn towards him and it makes it pretty obvious.

'You said your mum came to college here,' James asks, and the elephant in the room blunders across the roof terrace: it smashes the plant pots, scatters the glass mugs across the concrete, and trumpets loudly.

'In the eighties,' I say. I tell them about the planned demolition of the spot we're sitting in, and the campaign Mum put together to save it.

The way they look at each other as I say it is both sweet and heartbreaking. They are wearing wedding rings, simple gold bands that catch the sunlight. I want to stand on the rooftops and scream to my mum, 'Come back! It wasn't what you thought, you weren't a secret.' I want to tell her that these two nice old people still have each other, that they must have always missed her. My eyes fill with tears.

'Shall we order?' says James. He is one of those people who can fill an awkward gap, and I'm pleased about that. There isn't the rush of conversation, of questions, that I thought there would be. We've mostly talked about traffic – that they decided to come by train in case of delays on the motorway, about the weather – that it has barely rained since June.

Judith looks at the menu, holding it at arm's length and squinting.

I study her nose while I wait for her to speak.

She chooses an aubergine thing for a starter, goats' cheese for a main.

'Are you veggie?' I ask and she nods at me, smiling. 'How long since you ate meat?'

'About sixty years,' she says.

She didn't eat meat when she was pregnant with my mum, when the egg that would become me was growing inside the tiny foetus that would become my mum. We learnt about this in biology at school – it was part of what made me get so fired up about the whole adoption thing. All the eggs you will ever have grow in your follicles, really early in your development. The egg that made me was inside this old woman once, part of her flesh and blood. My eggs were inside the egg that became me. Like a set of wooden dolls who fit inside each other.

'And the less said about meat and me, the better.' James has sensed another pause in conversation. He smiles and his teeth follow the exact pattern mine did before I got my braces fitted. I still have one snaggle tooth, longer than the others, the front left eye tooth: there it is when James smiles. 'I try though. You?'

'I was brought up veggie,' I say. 'My mum and dad never ate meat.'

That glance across the table again, as if they want to step aside and discuss each sentence, then come back to me and ask more. They must have longed forever to hear about my mum.

'It's hard to know where to start, isn't it?' Judith stretches her hand across the table towards mine.

I stretch my fingers out to mirror it, palm flat against the table. Our fingertips are almost touching. Our hands are strikingly similar, for all the wrinkles on hers: square and wide with whorls like squashed smiles where our knuckles should be.

Judith puts on her glasses to study my hand. She looks up at me. 'That's incredible,' she says and smiles.

I can't speak. The face that looked up at me then, once her eyes were framed by glasses, is my mother's. 'Oh,' is all I can say for a moment.

James goes to speak, to rescue us.

I shake my head. 'It's OK. It's just – with your glasses on – you look exactly like my mum. Exactly.' I dig into my bag, pull out my phone and my glasses case. I swipe across to the camera and hand it to James. 'Would you?' I ask him. I move round the table to squat beside Judith in her chair and put my own glasses on.

I take my phone back from him and turn it round so that Judith and I can see the picture at the same time. My hair is long and dark, hers short – speckled grey and white – but the face inside is the same. Our eyes are different colours, hers are a mossy green and mine are James's ice blue, but the shape is identical. Our eyebrows sit – just above our glasses – in the exact matching arc. Our smiles could be the same mouth set in the same rounded puffed cheeks. It's extraordinary.

I show the phone to James.

'Wow,' he says. 'Just wow.' He wipes the corner of his eye.

'I'm popping to the loo,' I say. Even outdoors and with the slight breeze of being high up, my face is burning. Memories of my mum mixed with new thoughts of what she's missing take turns to stab behind my eyes. I shut myself into the cubicle and sit down on the lid of the loo. A couple of years ago, I was in Ibiza with the girls and I picked up a little shell bracelet for my mum. I got all the way to the checkout before I remembered that she'd died. The gloom that slunk through me at that till, the heat of awkwardness, the bitterness of frustration: that's how I feel now.

I look at the picture of Mum on my screensaver and back at the one of Judith and me. Peas in a pod.

'I'm going to say something peculiar,' says Judith, when I come back. 'Don't be offended.' There is a twinkle in her eye and I feel like I know her. 'You walk exactly like my dad.'

'What?' I've worn a dress, gone a little formal, although I have still got sneakers on.

'My dad had a very particular way of walking, very upright, and he always swung his arms – just so. You have it too, exactly the same.'

I sit down by her, my chair a little nearer to her than before – this gives me a better angle on James, makes it easier to look at his face. 'My friends always take the mick out of my walk.' It's true, they always have. 'But how can a walk be genetic?'

'I suppose it's dictated by physiology,' says James. 'Your hips and your legs are set by your genes, so maybe the way you move is.'

I look at Judith. 'Did anyone in your family worry about their big thighs?' I ask her.

'On the contrary,' she says. 'We have always admired our familial ability to walk great distances. Do you have calf muscles like upside-down skittles?'

I laugh, because I have, and my mum had too.

Lunch arrives and we are quieter while we eat. We swap little facts and we sip cold white wine. There are so many questions I want to ask them but so many of those may be painful.

The food is good, and the sunshine shows this Brutalist terrace and its old-school pot plants off to their very best. The company is comfortable. We're through the second bottle of wine by the time we've finished our main courses. James asks if he should order another and Judith and I both nod a vigorous yes. He turns in his seat, waves at the waiter and gives him a thumbs up that points to the bottle – the universal language, my dad calls it.

James turns back to Judith and me, his big smile wide across his face.

'I've never seen my mum's original birth certificate,' I tell them. 'I don't think she ever did either. Did you name her Penelope?'

Judith looks across at James. He holds his smile just a moment too long, I can see the pain behind it.

Judith reaches her hand out to cover James's. I watch the skin bleach slightly round her knuckles as she tightens her fingers over his. 'I named her Unity,' she says.

There is a long pause. I don't know what to say, let alone what to think. My mum was Penny – having a different name would make her someone else, not my mum.

The waiter comes to clear our plates and we all smile at him, grateful for the distraction.

It's time. The food is done and we have moved on from chit-chat, moved into the meat of Judith and James's story. 'So,' I ask, looking from one of my grandparents to the other. 'How did this all come about?'

We are better starting with how rather than why. Why is the killer.

Chapter Nineteen

Judith

'That was very brave,' James says as soon as we have walked down the steps, said our goodbyes to Ruby and walked away. 'It was very brave to give her a name like that.' He swallows, hard. 'And very generous, when you thought I'd abandoned you.'

It's not an accident that I've kept that word from James – I was keeping it from my mouth, from my ears: trying to avoid the whiplash of that most personal, most identifying, detail.

The lightest flicker of pain passed across James's face as I said it, but he didn't let Ruby see how one simple word chewed him into pieces. Each part of this process is like the rumble of an earthquake: with every word our landscape changes, our feet are less secure on the Earth.

I stare straight ahead, trying to act as if we are shopping, an old couple on a day out. 'I named her for how we made her, what we believed we were.'

'What do we call her now?' he asks me. 'Is she Unity or Penny?'

This is as new to me as it is to him. We slow at a zebra crossing and a large group of students, all wearing the same yellow backpacks, marches past us, oblivious.

'If we call her Unity, we cancel Penny, don't we?' I say, the names jagged and painful in my mouth. 'She began as Unity but she grew up as Penny. We can't deny her parents or the job they did.'

We manage to get back to my house without opening any more wounds, choosing not to slash ourselves with any more what-ifs for now.

Barbara kindly agreed to walk Dougal for me. She didn't ask questions about why I suddenly seemed to be responsible for a large yellow dog, or why he was staying behind in my house while the-skeleton-in-my-closet and I went out for the day. I wonder what she thought when she saw Dougal's bed established in the kitchen.

I'm glad James is here, that we already decided he wouldn't go home tonight. I want to talk about our glorious granddaughter: I want to celebrate what we have, even as I mourn the chance to ever tell Penny the things I've longed for her to know.

James is on the same page, he is sitting right beside me on this rollercoaster – up and down with gut-churning unpredictability – whether I want him there or not. He has a ticket for this ride too.

'Isn't it amazing that she was a vegetarian?' asks James. 'Do you think it's because you were?'

'No, James. I don't.' I put my hand over his to show that I'm not teasing, just gently explaining. 'She was a vegetarian because her parents were, the people who raised her. It's a coincidence that their values chimed with ours. That's all, a sign of the times.'

'But don't you think . . .'

I shake my head at him. 'I don't think political decisions are genetic. Much as I'd like to.' I take the whisky decanter from the sideboard: Catherine's drink, really, but I keep it in out of habit.

He nods a yes and I pour two tumblers.

'Cheers,' I say to him and our knuckles – round the glasses – touch. 'Politics is one of the biggest barriers, usually. One of the things that make reunions fail. Our politics are set in us, hard-wired and fundamental.' I point at him, at me, two deeply political people. Once upon a time, it was what brought us together. 'What would you have done if Ruby was a racist?'

'She wouldn't have been.' He looks affronted. I have accused his granddaughter of something he abhors.

'Lots of people are racist, or horrible, or believe in wars or violence. Lots of people. What if Penny's family hadn't been decent? What if they had brought her up like a little Englander and she'd passed that on to Ruby?'

He puts his glass down. He looks confused, almost cross. 'But they didn't.'

I nod, I totally agree. 'But that's luck. That's what I'm trying to get you to see. We're all products of our environment. Especially in a system as class-based as ours.'

He puts his whisky glass back on the table. I made us cheese and crackers for supper and he picks at a speck of yellow cheddar left on his plate. 'So you can inherit a walk . . . a gait?' He shrugs at me and I nod my head. 'But you can't inherit politics?'

'You can't inherit politics.' I stretch my arms out to illustrate my yawn. I am tired even though the sun has not long gone down.

'But.' He's not going to let this drop. 'Presumably, you could inherit a subversive temperament? Or a tendency to non-conformity?'

'I'll give you that. I think that's a thing.' I've conceded the point because he needs it, not because I necessarily believe it. 'I'm going to go to bed.' I want to see if a bit of space, a little quiet, will make me feel better.

He stands up, catches the crumbs that fell on to his shirt and puts them on the plate. 'Dougal will hoover up any mess,' he says.

He puts his plate on top of mine and carries them both out to the kitchen. The domesticity of it is poignant. It makes me think of the last time we shared a kitchen. It makes me think of Polly Wright.

'I'm going to run Dougal round the block. I'll try not to wake you.' He stands and we are both in the small space between the sofa and armchairs. Beneath our feet is a round sisal mat that Catherine chose in John Lewis.

James reaches his arms out, takes my shoulders and folds me to him. 'Thank you. Thank you for everything, for forgiving me, and for making me part of this.' He kisses the top of my head.

My face is squashed against his chest, his arms are right round me, and – although it is an illusion – for a moment I feel safe. I struggle to remember the difference between forgiving and forgetting, I know that you can live with one and that the other will eventually destroy you. I can't work out what I mean to say so I stay quiet. My hands move to his waist, my fingertips sit, comfortably, against the bottom of his ribs. I let myself be held by him and – I'm sure – we both think the same thoughts.

Chapter Twenty

I had been in the hospital for twenty-three days. I had stayed there through my baby's first smile: lopsided in the beginning, then wide and sparkling – her eyes lit up with joy. We knew everything there was to know about each other. Her tiny fingers fell to the exact same place every time she fed, her cheeks hot against my breast and her little hands soft, warm, either side of her face. Her nails were miniature shells, pink and translucent. The midwife had showed me how to nibble the sharp tops of them away – too tiny to cut – so that she didn't scratch her perfect little face.

I had been there long enough to see many other mothers come and go. Most of them only stayed a week or so, although some were there for two. I had been there long enough to know every midwife and cleaner, to predict what the filling would be in that day's sandwiches or what would arrive for dinner on a green china plate and under a battered tin cover. I had been there so long that it was clear to anyone that Jimmy wasn't coming.

'I'm so sorry, love,' Sister said. 'You're not the first and, heart-breakingly, you won't be the last.' She moved the blanket from the baby's face so that the side of her pale eyebrow showed. 'I thought he'd come. You two had me believing it too.'

The baby smacked her lips, pulled them into a pucker and sucked at nothing. A tiny pink blister sat in the middle of her top lip like a jewel and it wobbled, up and down, as she dreamed.

I looked at Sister, nodded. 'What can I do? I have to find another way out.' My breasts tightened under my nightgown, milk pulsing in at the thought of my baby. 'I can't leave her here. I know I said I would, but I can't.' My voice rose at the end, shy of hysteria but the threat of it cracking at the edges of my voice.

'She won't be put up for adoption until she's six weeks old. That's the law, you can't sign the paperwork before that. Baby will go into a Home for a little while.' The Sister traced her finger down the side of the baby's silver hair. 'You could have her back any time in the next six weeks if you can find somewhere to go.'

My eyes filled with tears, and two spots bloomed like damp flowers on the front of my nightgown. 'They won't take her at the Home. I can go back but they won't let me take her.'

'It's not what I'd normally advise – trying to hang on to Baby,' the Sister said. 'But I am worried for your health, and you're my patient. I only wish you could stay here.'

The Sister knew as surely as I did that I wouldn't survive being separated from my daughter. That it would actually kill me.

'Could you try your parents? Now that she's born. Have you written? Have you told them about her?' The Sister looked up the ward to check we were alone. We both knew that not all her staff would be this sympathetic, that this was not what she ought to be doing.

I had written to my parents, as soon as the baby was born, as soon as I realised she was my moon and stars, that I would never leave her. I debated sending my only photograph of her to them instead of to Jimmy, but I had to weigh up our chances, calculate the risk. I knew that her delicate face, the way she was a softened fresh version of him, would be impossible for Jimmy to ignore.

In the letter I wrote to my parents, I described her tiny self, the things she did, the noises she made. I told them about her fat little tummy, about how she drank and drank until it was as taut as a drum, how she never cried or grimaced with wind like the other babies. I told them of her magic, the spell she had cast on anything she touched, on anyone who saw her. For the last paragraph I begged them, with everything I had, every word, every wish, to let her – and me – come home.

They hadn't replied.

'Do your parents have a telephone in the house?' Sister asked.

I nodded. In the cot beside me, the baby stretched her arms, mewed, and blinked her little eyes awake. Each time she opened them they were a brighter crystal blue, each time she blinked that light – like fire inside ice – shone through more clearly. Jimmy's eyes.

'I have left my office door open. Pick up the telephone, dial nine, then, in a very confident voice, ask for an outside line. I shall be here checking Baby's nappy, so I won't know. And don't tell a soul.'

My hand shook as I lifted the receiver. 'Macclesfield 2997,' I said to the receptionist and listened to a series of clicks as the call was put through.

I counted the rings as my mother walked down the hallway. I imagined her patting the sides of her hair, checking it was neat enough before she picked up the phone.

'Macclesfield 2997,' she said. 'How may I help you?' Her plummy voice, lips pursed against the handset.

'It's me, Mum.'

Silence. Behind her, the grandmother clock in the sitting room struck the hour. The chimes made me scrunch up my toes with homesickness.

After an awkward pause, my mother spoke. 'Are you ready to leave the hospital?'

'Did you get my letter, Mummy?' Her silence let me know she did. 'About the baby. She's so beautiful.'

'Do you have enough money to get to London? Do you have the address?'

I strained my ears to try and hear my father somewhere in the house. Perhaps if they were both there I could convince them. They had been good parents, right up until that moment: they had done everything for me, put their needs second to mine. 'I can't leave her – I'm not going to. But we haven't got anywhere to go. Please can I come home, just for a few weeks until I can find a job, a flat?'

'You have a job and a room waiting for you in London.'

'If you could see her, Mummy, really. Just once, come and see her. You'll understand. You'll see why I can't leave her.' I was trying to keep my voice down, conscious of the patients on the other side of the wall, but speaking as fast as I could to get her to understand before we were cut off. 'You're my only chance, Mummy. Our only chance.' I wiped my face with my hand, tears and snot silver across my knuckles. 'Please.'

'We will not speak of this again, Judy,' my mother said. 'It is over. The baby will go to her new family and be well looked after. You will take up the job in London and start again, get married. Find someone nice.'

My voice rose in pitch, my throat hurt. 'I don't want to start again, I want . . .' but the long burr of dial tone on the end of the line told me that she had gone. That my last chance was over.

I was sobbing by the time I got back to my bed.

Sister was sitting in the chair, the baby curled in her arms. 'It won't be good for Baby to hear you cry, dear.' She shook her head. 'Go and have a bath, compose yourself a bit. I can manage here.'

'Thanks but I'll stay here with her. Thank you. It's what I'd rather.'

'The almoner will come tomorrow, if there's no other way, to collect her. I know how it feels, I really do, but you have to believe it's best for Baby.' She put the warm bundle into my arms. 'Two parents, a stable home. She deserves that.' She stood, brushed down her starched apron front as my heart shattered inside my chest.

'I've helped hundreds of mothers through this moment. Hundreds.' She put her hand on my arm. 'Don't look back, that's the only way. Pack your bag, put on your coat, say your goodbyes to her and don't look back. Make something of yourself, for her – as well as for you.' Sister kissed the top of my head, tucked the blanket round the baby.

'Godspeed, Baby Unity,' she said.

And I didn't look back, the following morning when it was time to leave. I didn't look back as I pushed through the double doors of the ward. I didn't look back when I held my breath through the grey hospital corridors, stared straight ahead as I passed fathers with flowers, grandmothers with toddlers. I didn't look back on the tree-lined walk to the station where star-shaped leaves soaked flat in puddles and tears ran down my face. I didn't look back as I climbed the station steps, crossed to the London-bound platform and sat on the bench – wishing and praying and hoping that the train would never come. I didn't look back as I turned the door of the carriage, put my bag in first and stepped inside.

I used the same survival skills at Catherine's funeral. I kept the screaming inside me, let it boil my insides, burn my throat. I breathed in and out and stayed alive – shallow, calm breaths that were just enough. I chatted about the caterers, the flowers, the melancholy jokes at the service. I remembered the intense pain of that other loss, the months of sobbing, the nightmares that ended with emptiness, hollow breasts of soured milk, with a gap in my arms where her warm weight should have been. I relived the whole thing when Catherine died, every corner of those feelings, every ounce of the loss.

And now, I hardly dare hope, there is Ruby. She is like the sunrise.

Chapter Twenty-One

I don't know exactly how it starts. It is me who taps on James's bedroom door once the dark has truly fallen, when I realise that being alone is not where I need to be, that memories and wishes are not enough. I tap on his door because I can't invite him into our bed, mine and Catherine's, but real life is too wide and cold to sleep alone.

His 'Come in' is instant: I know he is still awake too.

I stand on the edge of the room, the dark shapes of the spare room, the gauzy moonlight at the window, in front of me. I know it is a threshold. I know what will happen if I go in, and I assume James does too.

He shifts over in the bed, lifts the duvet on the side nearest to me. 'I couldn't sleep either,' he says quietly.

I shut the door behind me, let the dark disguise us, forgive us.

I lie flat on my back, my arms at my sides. My fingers spread softly against the linen sheet and it is only a second before James's hand closes over mine. I turn to face him. It seems automatic: in the dark, the old man – his wiry eyebrows, the corrugated wrinkles of his face – becomes the boy again.

We kiss like strangers at first, before the tastes, the smells, remind us of who we once were to one another, of how we once felt.

I can't pretend to remember exactly what it was like to kiss him fifty-six years ago, but my body responds as if it does. My muscle memory takes me back to the squat, to our top-floor room and our gnarled mattress. It feels as easy as breathing to take each other's clothes off, to slip my hand underneath his T-shirt until he peels it away. In the dark, we forget that we are older, that our bodies are larger, less agile, softer.

We are naked, kissing like teenagers, and party to an agreement that it will not stop there.

James leans over, lowers his weight gently on to me.

I can feel the wire of his white chest hair against my skin as he moves his hand down and between my legs.

'OK?' he whispers.

I look up at him, desperate for my body to be able to block out the clamouring of my mind. 'Yes.'

We move together, unfamiliar sensations that transport us both back to another place, an easier time. I let myself believe I'm young again, that there is no heartbreak, that everything we've heard and learnt in the last few weeks can be extinguished.

A muscular pain starts to work through my hip. I move my leg, stretch out the muscle. 'Sorry,' I say.

James stops, leans up on his arms and waits, checking I'm OK. He bends back down and his face is scratchy on my mouth as we kiss, but we push our faces together as if not letting air in will smother the pain.

I push him gently until he is on his back, then I move across his body, my legs either side. I lower myself on to him and rock forwards.

James takes my breasts in his hands and the surge of energy I was waiting for ripples through me.

The last time we had sex, we fitted together perfectly, a well-practised machine. Now, I am conscious that, in order to avoid putting all my weight on to James's lower body, I need to tense my thighs, sit forward on to my calves. When I do that, I feel my belly fill the gap between us, a space where once we were firmly muscled and young. The dimpled skin, slackened by years of pointless diets – up and down, in and out – presses against the oval curve of his stomach: we are not what we were.

'You OK?' he asks, his face just a shape in the dark.

'I don't want to squash you.'

He pulls me down against his chest, purrs in my ear. 'You're not. It's fine.' He raises his hips: I'm immediately conscious of how much I weigh, of the fact that he's seventy-six and more fragile than he was as a boy. 'Don't stop. I just need to . . . Cramp.'

My knee slips forward and the scar from my fall rubs against the sheets. 'Bollocks.' I roll off him. I start to laugh. 'Oh, for fuck's sake.'

He turns to face me, pulls my hips towards him so that we are both lying on our sides. His laugh is a low rumble. 'I'm just grateful anything happened at all. I think the element of surprise helped,' he says. He has one hand over his eyes.

We settle into one another. I am becoming used to the feel of him, his emotional largeness and his capacity to care. It was the same when he was young, that need to touch, mentally or physically, to reach out to other people. He did it to everyone and it was part of what made him such a communicator, so capable when it came to organising us.

When I sleep, I dream of Polly. She is here in the bed, on the other side of James. I see his big shoulder in profile, like a mountain range in the dark: behind it, her hair lights the edge like a sunset. The tendrils of her red ringlets seep and crawl across his skin, reaching out towards me as I sleep, and I can smell the danger on the wind.

In the morning, I think it is best to be honest. Set things straight. I go downstairs while he is still sleeping, let Dougal out and the sunshine in.

I chat quietly with Catherine while I make coffee to take to the sleeping man I had sex with last night. Catherine and I are both glad it wasn't in our bed, and both pragmatic about it being a good idea, a distraction. If it wasn't such awful circumstances, there might be something funny about bookending one's sex life with the person it began with, fifty-six years earlier.

'Darling,' James says as I sit down on the bed.

The word makes this more awkward. I put the coffees on the bedside table. 'About last night . . .' I say, and we both laugh. I swing my legs up on to the bed, sit up against the pillow.

James hitches himself up so that he is sitting too. 'That looks sore,' he says, touching the scar on my leg. The last two stitches are still in there: tiny black staples in the livid skin.

'How do you feel this morning?'

'Quite perky actually.' He looks at me and grins. 'Considering I've been awake all night.' He reaches his hand down and takes hold of mine. This bed isn't as wide as Catherine's and mine – there isn't much space between us. 'It really helped. Thank you. I don't feel so alone.' He lifts my hand, kisses the back of it then puts it down again – as if he knows.

'It helped me too. I needed a bit of a laugh.' I put my head on his shoulder. 'But we should call it quits here.'

James gets up, takes the few steps to the en-suite bathroom. It feels so strange to watch his naked backside, the light dust of white hairs down his back. He turns back slightly, his hands on the door frame. 'I'm still putty in your hands, Jude. I always was. Be gentle with me.'

I don't look when he walks back towards me. I'm not ready for that.

'Shall I make more coffee?' he asks.

I can't quite handle James walking around my kitchen with no clothes on. 'I'll do it.'

'And sit here and drink it?'

'Sure.' It won't hurt to live our pretend life for a morning.

Chapter Twenty-Two

RUBY

Dad and I decided to meet in the cemetery. It's a beautiful day, and it means I can tell him and Mum at the same time. Saves doing it twice.

'So it's their parents that I can't get over. Both sets. My actual great-grandparents. Your grandparents,' I say to Mum. 'How cruel they were.'

Dad doesn't say anything but he makes that face, the solemn one with the twisty mouth, the one that says, *I am about to utter something profound.* I look at Mum for backup.

'Are you going to tell me things were different then, Dad?' I may as well head him off at the pass. I pick at the daisies in the grass, drop the fried-egg heads on Dad's legs.

We brought chrysanthemums for Mum's grave today, a froth of white. I love them when you squash too many stems in a vase and they form a massive flower bomb: they're big and strong and bold despite being made of nothing but petals.

'They were very different. You do social policy: what year did social security start?' He leans back on his hands, his legs stretched out on the grass. 'There was no single-parent benefit in the sixties

– you couldn't move into a flat and get the government to pay for it. And if you didn't have a place to live, or childcare, you couldn't work and you couldn't eat.' He starts putting clover heads between the daisies like coloured buttons down his shins. 'I don't think that kind of support started till Mum and I were toddlers. Maybe even school age. You'll have to look it up. What I'm saying is, there were no safety nets.'

'You sound like Judith and James.'

Dad shrugs. 'I'm sure their parents loved them. They couldn't afford another mouth to feed or—'

'James's mother couldn't afford another mouth to feed, but Judith's could. She said – she said they were really well off.'

'There was one girl in my class at primary school from a single-parent family – and that was in 1972,' Dad says. 'Her dad had died in a car crash. They were different times – there were so few single parents. Lots of very unhappy marriages and domestic violence, but very few single parents.'

I roll on to my front, stretch out my arms and legs in the sun as if I'm swimming on the warm grass.

Dad carries on: he's made up his mind. 'Judith and James's attitude sounds very healthy. It wouldn't help anyone to pin the blame on their parents.'

'They lied though. They actually lied.' He's annoying me now, keeps doing little you'll-understand-when-you're-older sighs without actually saying anything. I set him straight. 'His mother hid her letters, her parents told him she'd got married. It's disgusting.'

He opens his mouth to speak.

I can't let that happen. It's my story, I found it, and it's not important what he thinks about it – if we're honest. 'So, they were part of a splinter group. The Campaign for Nuclear Disarmament . . .'

'CND.'

He is really annoying me now. 'What?'

'CND. No one says *Campaign for Nuclear Disarmament*, CND. I had a badge – when I was about your age – it said "Atomkraft? Nein Danke". It was German.' He stretches out the vowels like he's bilingual and I look at Mum's headstone and roll my eyes, confident that she would do the same at this anecdote.

'Your mum loved it. She was always trying to pinch it.'

'For God's sake.' I make a face at him.

'So, the group Judith and James were part of didn't feel that CND were doing enough, and this Committee of 100 they were into was a bit more political. A bit more dangerous.'

That brings Dad down to Earth. 'Dangerous?'

'Urgh, stop it. Not dangerous exactly: radical.'

He brushes the flowers from his legs. 'Radical is quite a dangerous word.'

'Not that kind of radical. They're dead old, snowy-white hair, sweet – not bloody fundamentalists.'

'One man's freedom fighter is another man's terrorist.' Pompous lecturer Nick has floated to the surface, he can't help it.

'Right, that's it. I'm not talking to you about it any more.'

He goes to say something.

'Nope.' I fish in the pocket of my shorts for my earbuds. 'I'm not talking to you about it.'

'Sorry,' he says. 'I'll stop. Let's talk about something else. Don't dive into your phone.' He has chocolate in the linen bag that had the flowers in. He unwraps the edge, waves it at me like a white flag.

'I guess you don't mean to be a knob, do you, Dad?' I smile and take the bar. It is slightly soft from the sunshine. I snap it in the middle and give him half back. Friends.

He thinks for a second, pushes the middle of his glasses with his forefinger. 'I get mixed up between research and conversation. Don't talk to enough people.' Dad smiles. 'That's not a dig, not a you-should-come-home-more. But most of my conversations are about work.'

The green woodpecker who lives in here flutters – ungainly, like a brightly coloured chicken – on to the trunk of a tree. I point at him in silence.

Dad nods, smiles. He's seen him too.

We wait for the rat-ta-tat-tat of the woodpecker's beak against the bark but the bird changes his mind, spreads his wings and leaps for another tree.

Dad looks back at me and I can smell a lecture coming. 'Judith and James . . .'

'My grandparents.'

He wobbles his head in a maybe-maybe-not kind of way which is weird because 'genes' are irrefutable evidence. 'Yes.' Not a great deal of conviction. 'I'm a bit worried that they'll be a distraction.'

'From?'

'You have a lot on your plate, work-wise. I was talking to Jacqui about it the other day.'

'Pardon?' I say it sharply, two distinct syllables that crackle with anger. 'You did what?'

'We were both at the same conference, a symposium on—'

'You spoke to my MA supervisor? My – my – supervisor, without my permission?'

Dad coughs, shifts uncomfortably on the grass. He puts the chocolate down. 'It wasn't that. I didn't set out to talk about you, it wasn't on purpose. But it would be a bit odd if we didn't.'

I kneel up, my bum on my heels. 'I'm really angry, Dad.' Sometimes, I have learnt, you have to point your emotions out to my dad. 'I'm twenty-two. You have no right to talk about me like I'm a child who didn't do my homework.'

'I worry about you.' He is on the back foot. He knows he was wrong.

'I don't think it's even legal for you to discuss my research with my supervisor. Without. My. Permission.' I pull my phone out of my bag, text the girls to see what they're doing later. I could do with a pint. 'And I've met them once. One time.'

Dad reaches forward to tidy the green glass chips round the bottom of Mum's headstone. 'I don't know how these get everywhere,' he says.

'You can apologise, you are allowed.' I pretend to listen to Mum, cock my head to one side towards her gravestone. 'What's that you say, Mum? He was bang out of order and he needs to say sorry?'

'Who am I to argue with your mother?' Dad says. 'I unreservedly apologise. But you wouldn't be human if you weren't taking up a lot of time thinking about them, getting to know them.'

He's not wrong really: I think about them all the time. I think about how bad it must feel to grow old without their child. I think about how it must be to deal with constantly reminding each other. Imagine never being able to move round it or away from it.

It's hard enough when my dad and I are together. We're always aware of the space where my mum should be. I thought about it so much through lunch that I couldn't ask them if they had other children, just in case they said no. It must be horrendous for Judith and James – all those years of empty.

The glass chips sparkle in the sunlight and Dad pulls out tiny weeds from between them. 'You've come so far: two years of work. Don't throw it all away so close to the end.'

'You have my absolute word that I'll finish my masters, Dad,' I say. 'But alongside that, I am going to get to know my grandparents – with or without you. Your call.'

Chapter Twenty-Three

JUDITH

Today is Tuesday. It is the day for my art class – the group I abandoned a month ago when James tipped my life upside down. I can think of nothing more normal, more levelling, than driving the fifty minutes to anonymity and staring at someone else for two hours.

James has gone home, Dougal too. I will miss that dog's constant presence, the tick of his claws on my hardwood floors and the way he knows instinctively when I need him. James has organised a video-call with his daughters for this evening. Today is the day that he's going to tell them everything. I can't imagine how hard that will be for them to process, what an incredible shock.

Each mile that I travel away from my house lifts a fraction of the weight from my chest. James has been great – he's been my contact with the outside world throughout my recovery, my sounding post since we met Ruby. But it's nice to be alone too.

Today's life model is a man. It's not a surprise: there seem to be so many more men prepared to stand naked in a room full of strangers than there are women. This chap is sitting down though, his legs spread wide to reveal the absolute improbability of anatomy, of evolution.

The model is chubby, and his round belly would obscure his genitals if he were sitting in a different position. I assume he knows that.

I start my sketch at the round hump of the top of his belly, sketch upwards to his doughy breasts. My picture goes the way I want it to: that doesn't happen very often but I'm really glad it has today. I usually struggle drawing soft people but I'm enjoying the shadows of his creases, the texture of the light on his skin. I like how full he is, how stuffed with life.

I've put four pastels in the lid of my box – four shades of green – and I'm making his whole self out of those colours, drawing him dark to light. I think of Catherine, of the way she turned whole landscapes into smudges of colour, colour that shouldn't belong to that scene, and yet did and described it perfectly. 'It's about how I see it,' she'd say. 'About the name I've given it. It doesn't matter that other people thought it was something else. This is my vision, my version.'

At first I think I am enjoying this because I can lose myself in the picture, but – as I make little marks of moss for his toes – I realise that I'm finding myself in this task. I am making marks, my own marks. I am taking the life I knew and I am beginning to re-colour it, to change its meaning. There are feelings in my body again, light and shade. A smile erupts inside me and I try to keep it away from my face, from the seriousness and concentration of the art class.

I work down his body. I have huffed and sworn at the impossibilities of faces, left four green dashes for his eyes, nose, and mouth. I have drawn the strong lines of his legs, the lavish swell of his belly. When I get to the absurdity of his genitals, the smile begins to bubble into laughter. I squeeze my eyes closed for a moment, breathe deeply, but the laughter is inevitable.

I take the brightest green and I colour the model's balls in with a vivid emerald. It is so long since I have laughed out loud, heard the sound of my own happiness, that I barely manage to conceal it as I run from the room, to all intents and purposes in the grips of a terrible coughing fit.

I haven't felt like I could laugh at my life, or even with it, for years. I attribute it to Ruby but, however grudgingly, I have to give James a tiny piece of the glory too.

'I hope he's not going to tell his daughters quite everything,' I say to Barbara when I get to – almost – the end of the story. This lunch, in the bistro next door to the shop, feels overdue. Worlds have collided and collapsed since I last saw her, universes have exploded.

She has ordered a bottle of white wine. It comes with two huge glasses and she puts the barest inch into the bottom of each. 'So there is a "not quite" to tell?' She grins at me over her glass, tipping it right back to get to the wine in the bottom.

'Not that sort of not quite. I mean, yes that sort, but not.' I sigh. That's the closest I can get to my feelings. 'I mean it was just sex.' I wonder what the waiter would say if he heard me. He is young, handsome, he has a faded blue apron tied loosely around his waist. I would put money on him believing sex belongs to the young. I believed it myself fifty years ago.

'Oh, good work,' says Barbara. She pours two more tiny wines. She makes me smile.

I fish for the words. 'It wasn't "just" sex, that's not true. It was pain and sadness and hopelessness and . . .'

'You sought comfort in one another.'

'Ooh.' I manage a smile. 'That's a very elegant way of describing a hasty bunk-up between two sweaty old people. Creaky sweaty old people.'

'We are allowed, you know.' Barbara picks up the menus, hands one to me. 'We are allowed to have sex after sixty.'

'Seventy?' I ask, and I feel a sense of achievement.

'Even eighty.' She peers at the specials board behind me. 'And Charlie Chaplin was eighty-eight when he fathered his last child. Although one can assume – by dint of biology – that his wife was a little younger.' She raises her glass to me. 'Cheers though, whatever your reasons. And I'm truly sorry to hear your story.'

That's the thing about secrets: they make a liar of you, however well-intentioned you are. You can't share your true self with those you love, not if they come in after the fact and the secret is already buried, already sealed away. There are two lives, one before the re-ordering of the facts, and one after. Now, I suppose, I am entering a third life, where the two worlds come together.

'Did it make you miss Catherine more?'

Barbara was married once, a long time ago. It was a union that didn't survive the changes she needed to make to be truly herself but she and her ex-wife have moved on to a fragile friendship.

'I couldn't miss Catherine more.' I sip the wine. 'It made me wonder about myself though. I mean, I'm a gay woman. I lived with the same woman for fifty years. And then I jump into bed with the first single straight guy to stay at my house.'

The waiter puts bread down on our table. I'm fairly sure he heard my last sentence.

'OK, maybe not the first. But still. It's not like I'd forgotten how much I like sex – I think about it a lot.' I raise my eyebrows at Barbara. 'But not sex with him.'

'I think the circumstances are extreme,' Barbara says. 'But even if they weren't.' She drinks each of these tiny portions of wine in a couple of sips. Each time she takes the bottle out of the ice bucket, it leaks drops of chilled water that pucker the brown paper table-cloth. She dabs at them with her napkin. 'How have you left it?'

James has come and gone from my house to his over the last few weeks, sometimes staying over but in his own room, and he has never put any pressure on me to repeat the performance. 'He realises we're not a couple.' I hope that's true. 'And does it really count if you go back to the first of the only two people you've ever had sex with? Especially for a one-off?'

'Exes never count anyway,' Barbara says. 'It's the law. Free pass. In fact, it's a good job you don't have more of them.'

We order our food, chat about the comings and goings in the shop, her brilliant plan to raise money by training apprentices in tandem with the local college. There's a lot to discuss, to catch up on, and a real sense of freedom in someone else taking care of Catherine's legacy.

'And lastly,' Barbara says, wiping her mouth with her soaking-wet napkin. 'Tell me about your granddaughter. What unfettered joy.'

Music plays gently in the restaurant, other diners chatter as background, and the sun leaks across the tables to bathe the room in a glow. 'She is a whole new world. Another chance.'

Barbara nods. Her eyes are glistening. 'I can't imagine what you've been through.'

'I have to control James. His enthusiasm. This is the time when we need to take things really slowly. When the myth becomes reality – that's the bit that's not always easy.'

Barbara unwraps one of the tiny round mints the waiter brought with the bill. She is waiting for me to carry on.

'James's daughters, for instance. What a huge stone in the pond that is for them: acknowledging that their dad loved someone else before their mum.'

'And might still.'

'I'll ignore that.' I throw the paper wrapping of my mint across the table at her. 'That they've had a sister all this time and that they've lost her, that their children have a cousin. The stuff about his mother – their grandmother. And then Ruby, what does she want from us – what are we able to want from her? It's a minefield. Who do you tell? Who do you lie to?'

Barbara waves the bill at me, she's got it. 'Don't say anything about sex for a minute – I'm calling the waiter over. He's already traumatised.'

I shake my head at her, but I smile too. Barbara deftly handles the level of humour I need. She knows instinctively how to value the bits that I'm devastated by and make light – fun, even – of the rest. She and Catherine were very close, they shared this people skill.

'As ever,' she says and puts her hand over mine, 'you sound like you're on top of this. You've got it sorted in your Judith-y way. And I'd like to do something my way too. I'd like to take over running the shop, formally. Without you popping up and interfering.' She grins at me. 'You're far too old anyway.'

'Remind me again, how much younger than me are you?'

'Those three years are vital,' says Barbara, tapping her temple with a forefinger. She lays her palm open before me on the table. 'Keys,' she says, and that's it.

I drop the two silver keys in her hand – it is purely symbolic, she already has a set and I have others – but I am almost overwhelmed by the hope. I'm not sure whether I imagine or hear Catherine's whisper: there – all fixed. Just in time for your next adventure.

'I'm always there for you if you need to talk, any time,' Barbara says. 'And you can always shag James if you need a bit of a morale booster. Ah, thanks.' She turns round to the waiter she knew full well was right there. 'Can I leave a tip in cash or does it have to be on the bill?'

The waiter can't scuttle away fast enough: he rushes through the swinging double doors of the kitchen.

'That made his day,' says Barbara, choking with laughter.

I go back to the office with Barbara, buoyed by the wine and the company.

'I desperately want to march you out with a cardboard box of belongings and a potted plant,' she says.

I collect up a few bits and pieces: some photos and my desk diary. It reminds me that I must phone Gwyn, tell her that I'm mended too – the parts of me that can be – and invite her round for a bit of supper. Perhaps I'll invite James. And Barbara would love to meet James but I'd have to give her a good talking to first. If I really thought she might behave herself, I could play matchmaker with Alan.

'Ah, not Alan,' she says when I suggest it.

'Oh, OK. You move fast.'

Barbara shakes her head, her little pearl earrings remind me of the mermaid. 'I discovered, just in time' – she has raised her voice to schoolteacher level – 'that there is a Mrs Alan. He somehow fails to mention that when he's flirting.'

'Good Lord,' I say, thinking about his little wire glasses, his small, measured movements. 'I didn't think he had it in him.'

'It's always the quiet ones.' Barbara taps the side of her nose in a knowing gesture. 'Back to the internet dating for me. I rather like it – you get a better class of liar.' She grins.

On my desk is the project I am midway through. It is a table lamp with a shade made of tiny glass teardrops. It's the kind of job I've always taken – one that requires patience and commitment, but no specific skill. There is no point in leaving it undone.

Next to the droplets soaking in their bowl, is a bottle of brown vinegar. I pour some of it into a jam jar and start cleaning the pieces, one by one. The sharp sting of vinegar triggers decades of memories: my mother's homemade pickles; fish and chips by the sea with Catherine; the drops of it we put on the dense green peas they served in the unmarried mothers' home.

Once the glass drops have been dipped in the vinegar they start to twinkle under the overhead light. And it doesn't take more than a little buffing with a cloth for them to become tiny prisms – light bouncing off them at all angles, in all colours.

I need to shine. I need to move forward from my grief, make this shop a home for it – a shrine that I can visit and then walk away from. I need to wall the sadder memories into a mausoleum, where they are safe and warm, but where I no longer need to carry them.

I begin the slow and delicate process of tying each would-be crystal back on to its wire, ready to hang them – radiant – round the light.

My phone makes me jump and my heart flutters in my chest when I see the name. I am sure this is something I will never get used to if it happens every day of my life. It's certainly something I will never take for granted.

'Hello, Ruby,' I say.

'Judith. I've been thinking, researching actually. About the rest of your story, I mean.'

She is so like James, that eagerness, that honesty.

She speaks for a minute or two, her voice giddy. 'So, I found your friend Paddy. Tracked him down online.'

'Paddy?'

'The priest. Who you said James gave your ring to. I thought, what if he still had your ring?' Ruby is excited, pleased with her sleuthing.

I don't know what I feel. 'Paddy Gordon. Wow. He wasn't a priest though, not in the end. He'd given that up before we went to Scotland.' My thoughts jumble, I search desperately for the end of the thread. Paddy never did me any harm. Quite the opposite. He was always kind to me, looked out for me. I wonder if he spoke to James about Polly Wright.

Polly Wright. That's the alarm bell I couldn't quite hear over the racket of my thoughts. Polly Wright won't chime with Ruby's vision of James, of her grandfather.

'He is. He's still a priest now. He's not well though, I shouldn't suppose he does priesty things, services and so on.' There is music playing in the background, wherever she is.

'Are you at home?' I ask her. She's told me where home is but I can't picture what her space might look like. 'Or at your dad's?'

She makes a noise that sounds like 'Grufug'.

I take that to be a direct comment on her father. 'Did you tell him about lunch?'

'I did. But he's only really interested in my masters.' She taps something on the phone and it gives a little series of beeps into my ear. 'Anyway, Paddy wants to meet you – I've already told James. Paddy's excited. He was really surprised when I told him you and James are still together.'

'Ruby, I . . .' Where do I find the words? In Ruby's version of life, James and I are married: there is no Catherine, there is no Jeannie, in her version of truth.

My phone rings to tell me I have another call. 'Ruby, James is on the other line, can I call you back? Two minutes.' I am stalling, I need the right words, the most delicate of let-downs.

'I'm not going to see Paddy Gordon,' is the first thing James says. 'There's nothing to be gained from it, from revisiting the past.'

'How the hell did she find Paddy?' I ask, as if James will have the answers. 'Why?'

'She thinks he'll still have the ring I bought you.' He clicks his tongue, irritated. 'I don't think any good will come of this, Judith. Let's let sleeping dogs lie. She says he's got dementia, poor Paddy. Let's leave him be.'

I've walked through the shop, am standing outside on the street for a little privacy. 'It's a chance to spend time with Ruby, a little weekender.'

'It's a bad idea.'

I don't want to push it too far, tonight's conversation with his girls is going to be stressful enough for him. 'Whatever. I'll make arrangements for Ruby and me and if you want to join us, you can. No pressure.'

'I said no, Judith.' His voice is edgy.

I don't argue with him – his loss. But I'm annoyed that he thinks his having had enough of the past means it's time we all stop digging.

'Actually, sod you, James,' I say after I've put the phone down. I will book a deliberately lovely hotel – just for two.

Chapter Twenty-Four

Ruby and I are staying overnight near Paddy's West Country home. He lives in a shared house with other Catholic priests and still, despite creeping dementia, helps with services and Mass – which is how Ruby found him scheduled in on the parish website.

James is staying put in London.

'We ought to be together to tell her we're not an item,' I told him. 'The truth won't hurt her – that's how the truth works, James.' A flash of red hair, blue-white skin. 'She might be disappointed for a minute that the great romance isn't what she thought, but that's all. Weeks of lies will fester into something much bigger.'

'Come to London then, instead. We'll tell her here. This whole trip is a ridiculous idea.'

Even on the phone James sounded stressed. He has been talking to his daughters, trying to field their offers to come over. 'They don't mean it,' he said to me yesterday. 'It's a knee-jerk reaction. They've got kids, jobs. It's too much.'

'It's nice though.' I thought it was very sweet that they'd instinctively and instantly offer to fly halfway round the world. It made me want to meet them.

'I said I'd go there,' James said. 'I haven't seen my grandchildren for months. Maybe I could take Ruby. That would be fab.'

My litany of how James mustn't ask too much, get too involved too fast, is one I almost know off by heart. I have reason to say it most days. It's not his fault: he loves too easily, too enthusiastically.

'Perhaps you'd like to come too. They'd love to meet you.'

I let that one go too, turned the conversation to something else. I am left with the one big issue to clear up on the journey. I've spent the last six hours trying to steer the conversation round to my marital status, but Ruby is focused on the manifesto of the Committee of 100 and the history of unmarried mothers' homes. The satnav tells us we are only seven miles from Paddy's house, so it's now or never.

The countryside is beautiful, wide flat roads with hills like sleeping giants on either side. Cattle graze along the roadside as we get closer, fat black cows who don't seem to be hemmed in by any fields.

Seven miles will take less than ten minutes.

'Ruby, there's something I need to tell you. James and I . . .'

She looks a little panicked.

'Nothing like that. We're not ill or anything.' I look across at her, look back at the road. 'Ruby, we're not married, James and I.'

'Phew,' says Ruby. 'I was worried then. It doesn't matter to me. My mum and dad didn't get married till I was three. I guess it's more unusual in your generation though.' Then she backtracks quickly. 'God, sorry, I didn't mean that you're old or anything.'

I take a deep breath. 'We were married, both of us. At least sort of.' Not exactly. 'To other people.'

'Oh, my God.' Ruby puts both hands up to her mouth in delight. 'And then you found each other again? Oh, that's so lovely. With so much history. Oh, my God.'

She jumps up a little in her seat and I can smell the coconut notes of her sun cream.

'That gives me chills,' she says.

'I'm sorry. We didn't mean to mislead you, and we certainly didn't mean to upset you, but we've never been married to each other. We've not been a "thing" for fifty-six years.'

I made finger speech marks with one hand, the other gripping the wheel. I feel slightly guilty at the obvious omission, but this is a need-to-know-only confession.

I head Ruby off at the pass, in case she asks anything about James and me now. Leaving out detail is healthy – out-and-out lying is not. 'I was with my partner, Catherine, for fifty years. We met at work in 1968.' I let the moment where Ruby digests this percolate in the car. I denied Catherine when James first reappeared: I won't do it again.

'And James met Jeannie in the early seventies. She died a few years ago.'

Ruby starts to laugh. 'Oh my God, I couldn't have got it any more wrong. I'm so sorry.' Her laughter is like warm water, it fills the car with perfect ambience, a feeling I could swim in till I drowned. Tears prick the sides of my eyes and I, too, start to laugh.

I run through the details of James's daughters – as best I can – explain that she has relatives, cousins, that her family just got exponentially larger with people I've not met either.

'So, your wife?'

I indicate left, turn on to a road on the outskirts of town. The countryside peels away in the rear-view mirror.

'Catherine and I were never married.' It's not really relevant but I need to get things right now. 'We had a civil partnership though – in the first week that you could.'

'Where is she now?' Poor Ruby. James and I have both already processed the art of losing people before you even meet them – it is new to her, joining this family too late, after so many of its members have gone.

'She died a year before Jeannie.' It never gets easier to say. 'My partner was the painter, Catherine Rolf.'

Ruby flops back against the seat. She puffs out a big breath from her cheeks and looks like a child. 'No way! We did her for A level. She made all her own paint, didn't she? Out of walnut oil. I could have brought her to school for Show and Tell if I'd known.'

The house Paddy lives in is impressive. It is a gothic building that can only be described as 'looming'. The church next to it is the same grey stone and it makes the ox-blood wooden fascia of the presbytery dramatic. The path leading up to it is bordered with summer bedding plants: violas and foaming clumps of sky-blue lobelia. Amongst them, lupins spill upwards in every pastel shade. It is a real English country garden; Catherine would love it.

We ring on the ivory doorbell and hear it loud through the house. Ruby and I look down at ourselves simultaneously, checking we pass muster for the priests, brushing imaginary specks of dust from our clothes.

I would recognise Paddy anywhere. He looks the same as he did when he sat in my mother's sitting room, in his early twenties and just out of seminary. It makes a pang of longing for my mum rise inside my chest. For a moment, I am breathless.

I would love to tell her this. That I'm in my seventies and here he is, that handsome boy she and her friends used to fuss over, compete over. That he suits a dog collar and that flat-fronted shirt every bit as much now as then.

'Oh, Paddy,' I manage eventually and I throw my arms around his neck. 'It's so very good to see you.'

Paddy hugs me back. 'You too, Jude. It's been a long time.'

'I'm Ruby, we spoke on the phone.' Ruby thrusts her hand towards him, shakes his vigorously. She is beaming.

The room Paddy sits us in is exactly as priests' communal rooms looked in my childhood. The furniture is huge and oak. My grandparents had a sideboard like this, the same folding-leaf coffee table.

There are three sofas forming three sides of a square; they are old and shiny. Paddy gestures towards them.

'Can I offer you tea?' he asks.

It is strange to be so formal with someone I once knew so well. But Paddy, first and foremost, is a priest: not the only thing to bookend my life.

'I didn't think you'd still be a priest.' It's true. I can't imagine the Catholic Church welcoming him back with open arms after his prison sentence.

He wiggles his head slightly, weighing up the years. 'I didn't either, but they needed people to go to Africa. To Algeria actually, and of course no one wanted to go there.'

'Why not?' Ruby asks, her voice quiet in the high-ceilinged room. She is being her most polite self. 'What was wrong with Algeria?'

'We were drawing attention to nuclear testing when we were in Scotland, and before that,' I say. 'Nuclear testing in the Algerian desert – human guinea pigs. Terrible times.'

Paddy is a few years older than me. He must be eighty now. I wonder what that time in the nuclear dust has cost him. The fingers on his right hand are yellow with nicotine and I can smell the cigarette smoke on his clothes. His face is lined like bark around those deep-brown eyes that had my mother's Women's Institute members like putty in his hands. He is still film-star handsome.

'And I proved myself out there – all was forgiven and forgotten, and ten years or so later, I came back to the UK.' He coughs, clears his throat. Looks at me. 'Ruby here told me you and Jimmy McConnell got married.'

'Ah, my bad,' says Ruby. 'They didn't. I made assumptions.' She looks at me.

'That makes this easier then,' Paddy says. 'I thought you were bringing that bastard here.' He stretches out a hand to the packet of cigarettes on the table beside him. His fingers fumble as he pulls one from the packet. 'I'm very pleased to see you, Jude, but I've no desire to see McConnell again. Not in this life – and I doubt I'll be with him in the next.'

Ruby and I look at each other; I don't like the feeling of this. We are uncomfortable and I reach my hand out towards her. Perhaps James was right. 'It was all a long time ago . . .' I start to say.

'I did six years in that hellhole. Six years of close-to-Purgatory. It broke me – Peterhead. Absolutely broke me. I came out of there like a shell.' A single tear ripples down the wrinkles by Paddy's eye, the memory leaves a trail on his skin.

Ruby grips my hand.

'James went to prison too,' I say. 'Barlinnie. That was no picnic.' My voice is raised. The air is charged and frantic. 'It wasn't his fault.'

'I know where he was,' says Paddy. 'But being in a different jail didn't stop men from talking. Didn't keep his filthy secret.'

'I think we should go,' I say.

'Polly Wright.' Paddy spits the two words out as if they are poison.

Everything I ever suspected was true. The list of things I lost because of James swirls around my head until I feel faint.

Polly Wright had porcelain skin, soft peach cheeks like a dream. Her hair came straight from a Titian painting, her eyes were limpid pools. But it was Polly Wright's confidence that shone out of her, her certain knowledge that she was in charge, that she dictated what we did. The ghost of her shakes out her stunning ringlets in the middle of the three of us. I don't want her near Ruby.

Paddy lifts the hand with the cigarette in, points the ember end towards me. 'Polly worked for Box, didn't she? And our Jimmy, he was her informer. He sold us all.'

Chapter Twenty-Five

RUBY

Judith looked like she'd been shot. Seriously. For a moment, I thought she was dead, that she'd just gone – bang – in an instant. People describe colour draining from faces but that's not what happened. Judith looked like she'd been bleached, like a white light had exploded in her mouth. I wasn't sure she was breathing.

And then she got up. Stood up so weirdly she could have been carved out of wood, like she had strings on her arms and legs. She looked at me and said, 'Sorry.' I didn't hear the word, I saw it. It was silent but full of meaning. The 'sorry' was for me.

And she walked out. And now it's just me, stuck in a stinky room with a sweary priest. He sounded so nice on the phone.

'What's Box?' It obviously means something to Judith.

Paddy takes a long time to speak and I start to worry that Judith might drive away without me. But if James and Judith have secrets and this guy is the key, I have to stay and hear him out. I keep one eye on her car outside.

'MI5,' he says, eventually. 'PO Box 500 was where spies used to send secrets back to London during the war.'

This is some kind of alternative universe. I pinch my nails against my fingertips to check I'm awake.

'And this particular wing of Box – of MI5 – worked closely with Special Branch through the sixties. And your grandfather was their informer.' He raises his bony hand at me. 'He was the grass.'

I'm trying to piece this together from Judith and James's story, from what they told me at that sunny lunch, from Judith's explanation in the car on the way here.

'You're wrong.' I don't know why I think I know more about it than Paddy – who was there – but James wouldn't do something like that. 'I don't believe you,' I say to the old man. I say it rudely but I don't care.

'It's true.' He scratches his eyebrow with one hand, doesn't look at me. 'It's all true and it feels good to have that out after all this time.' Paddy breathes heavily, his cheeks draw tightly between the frame of his jaw and eye sockets.

'I was in prison for six years.' Paddy speaks quietly and I have to strain to hear. He tries to stand, leaning heavily on his walking stick, but his legs don't hold him and he sits back down. 'It destroyed me. It broke me. Six years. I'm sorry that it's hurt Jude – she is a good woman.' He looks at me, stares into my face – it feels like he's looking for them in me, working out which one of them I most resemble.

Outside, I can see the roof of Judith's car through the window. 'I'd better go,' I say and stand up to prove it.

He grinds his cigarette out in the ashtray beside him, goes to light another immediately.

'I've never forgiven him. Despite my faith and the words I have preached for a lifetime – I found it impossible to forgive your grandfather. And that's my sin, one I'll carry to my grave.' His voice collapses into coughing again.

I back towards the door. Mostly, I just want to be back at home, amongst the greenery. I want to have never come here at all.

'Why did you invite us, if you knew all that – if you were going to say all these horrible things to Judith?'

Paddy has managed to stand. He hobbles to the big sideboard, pours himself a drink from a decanter on a tray. He turns and lifts the glass towards me but I shake my head.

'You told me Jimmy and Jude were married,' he says. 'I wanted to see what that was like, how they'd got over his betrayal – maybe learn from how she'd forgiven him. You wouldn't understand.'

I hate that phrase. I won't take it from him any more than I'd take it from my dad.

'All I know' – I walk towards the door and I'm literally livid – 'is that I am the person who did nothing wrong. Maybe Judith too. And I feel like dirt because you wanted to shout at us about something another old man did a lifetime ago. You shouldn't have invited us.'

'I didn't invite you.' Paddy holds his whisky glass in his shaky old hand. 'You invited yourself. I tried to stop you, remember?'

I stamp out of the room, slam the door with the bravado of the teenager my mum knew. My hand is on the brass knob of the front door. I pause in the hallway between that wretched room and outside, trying to get my shit together. The tiles are black and white diamonds in a pattern that swims and fades with the ripples of my tears.

It's completely true what Paddy said. When I phoned and told him who I was, who my grandparents are, he didn't want us to come. He told me he didn't remember anything, that he has vascular dementia and we might come on a bad day and that – if we did – he probably wouldn't be able to see us. Paddy didn't want to dig up the ghosts. It was me who wriggled through his protestations. It was me who insisted we come. I didn't take no for an answer and now I really – truly – wish I had.

Chapter Twenty-Six

Judith

I have no choice but to wait for Ruby: I couldn't have driven anyway. I hold both my hands out in front of me, over the steering wheel – they are still shaking uncontrollably.

My mind is a landslide that I try to hold up with my bare hands. Every time I think I've pushed a piece of information back to the top of the slope, it slides down again, suffocating me with pressure.

I lock the car doors. But the information seeps in through the air vents, the gaps around the sills. I close my eyes, but the words hammer at the inside of my head like birds pecking their way through my skull.

I try out words of my own. I say them out loud. 'No.' And then, 'It isn't true.' And 'Why?' because I know Paddy isn't lying, why would he?

The nature of memories means that they are always shadows. Polly Wright cast hers long and dark across decades but everything I believed is upended. A huge chunk of my past is not real, is not true. Someone has torn a strip from inside me – I don't know yet whether it took with it something I need to function.

There is a knock on the car window. I turn my head.

'Do you want me to drive?' Ruby asks through the glass.

'Thank you.' I open the door and step out, walk to the other side of the car.

She moves the seat forward a little, straightens the back of it. When she is settled, she does up her seat belt and turns the key. 'We'll be OK,' is all she says and we drive back to the hotel.

'I've got my mobile,' Ruby says in the hotel lobby. 'Why don't you text me when you're hungry or if you feel like company. I brought a book.' She smiles at me. 'And my walking boots. I will be fine on my own for a bit.'

I'm so grateful to her, this sensitive young woman. I am so in need of peace.

In my room there is the ubiquitous white notepad on the desk. A biro, printed with the logo of the hotel, and a pencil with an eraser on the top are lined up next to it.

My heart is still thumping in my chest as I pull the little stool from under the desk, sit as if I am at school. I pick up the biro and start to write.

At the top of the page I write 'James McConnell'.

I remember his birthday – 8th January. I remember celebrating it with egg and chips the last time we were together. I would have been very newly pregnant, the course of the rest of my life a few clustered cells, dividing and multiplying, becoming the future as I cooked, as we split the sunset-yellow yolks by dipping chips in them.

I write '8th January' under his name.

And then I am lost. Then I run out of certainties about Jimmy McConnell, about James. He is father to two women I have never met. He contains complexities and complications that would take another lifetime to unravel. He is a liar. More than that, a worse crime, he is dishonourable.

Underneath his name I write my own. I add the year of his birth, and then mine. It is the context to the whole long story of us. We were both born in the lea of huge loss and deprivation, against a backdrop of a world war still searingly fresh in our parents' memories.

I leave a long white space on the page and, at the bottom, I write 'Ruby'. I think about freedom and what I want it to mean for her.

Catherine fits in the white space, Jeannie too. I write their names and then I stare at the paper, asking it to fill in the gaps.

I take my swimming costume from the suitcase, put it on under my clothes.

The hotel has a spa in the basement – the original plan was to come here with Ruby. The spa is low-lit and smells peaceful. Candles flicker on the reception tables and throw shapes against a stack of folded white towels.

The pool is lemon yellow at the sides, blue beneath my feet. The lights below the surface cast a glow over my body, make me other-worldly, magical. I sink down, cross my legs and sit on the bottom. I swirl my hands to stay sunken and think of the mermaid snow globe on my table at home. When I open my eyes I see the bubbles spin from my fingers like the glitter in her globe.

I unfurl my body, stretch out my scaled tail and start to swim.

This is not my fault. My arm glides out of the water, slices back in at an angle. James has done James, as Ruby would say. My other arm, sharp-elbowed, scoops the water out behind me.

I have seventy-five years of power in my body: I can separate myself from James, from what he has done. I breathe to one side, exhaling through the edge of the water, my lips leaving foam on the surface.

Tears slip from me and mingle with the pool. They are part of me and part of my surroundings; I float in them and they slip along my body. They cannot hurt me.

My legs are strong and kick out – straight – in rhythm with the action of my arms. My sobs are the least of me, they are merely the stress of the past leaving my body as I get to the end of the pool and attempt a tumble turn.

I dip my head towards the wall and twist my body. This is agility I haven't tried since I was Ruby's age.

I feel for the wall with my feet, push off against it with bent knees.

I explode through the water, born again.

Ruby and I meet for dinner. Her cheeks are pink and healthy, her hair tied back in a glossy ponytail. 'I went for an amazing walk,' she says. 'No phone signal. Just me and a path that went on and on. And loads of those black cows.'

'I'm a bit scared of cows,' I admit.

'I am too.' She smiles and I see that straight white tooth, just proud of the others, that she gets from James. 'I pretended to be someone else while I walked through them. Someone not afraid of cows, only . . .' She takes a sip of her cocktail. 'But that was all fakery because I pretended to be you and you're scared of them too.'

My heart takes a leap. 'You pretended to be me?' I almost laugh at the absurdity of it.

She nods. Her mouth is full of breadstick. A crumb drops on to the pristine tablecloth as she says, 'You're pretty fearless. Apart from the cows, obviously.'

I lay my fingers on top of the silver handles of my knife and fork, and think for a moment. 'I'm not afraid of much any more. When I think about it, the worst of it has happened.' I smile at her, this perfect girl who wants to spend time with me, who doesn't blame me. 'And it didn't kill me.'

The food is wonderful. The hotel kitchen specialises in vegetarian food and tiny dish after tiny dish arrives, smelling of earthy truffle and piquant cheeses. It is a feast we feel we've earned.

Ruby tells me about the rest of her meeting with Paddy. 'It was my fault,' she says. 'One hundred per cent.'

'Oh, let him who is without sin and all that. It was a mistake. People make them.'

We have matching plates in front of us, glazed blue earthenware. Each one has a curl of endive on it, a foam of something divine resting inside it, and pearls of roasted celeriac dotted over that like tiny buttons. A glossy, glassy quail's yolk balances on top of it all like an acrobat. 'And without that mistake, we wouldn't know what really happened.'

'We might be better off not knowing.' Ruby tips the lettuce leaf into her mouth, head back as if she is eating an oyster. 'I liked everything better before.'

'Knowledge is always power,' I tell her, although I am sure she knows. I cut my lettuce in two with my knife and folk. The taste explodes in my mouth.

'I liked the other James,' she says. 'The one who didn't betray you.'

I was getting used to him too. Forgiving him has been a journey – it involved a lot of forgiving myself – but this marks the end of that particular trip. James and I will always exist in this wonderful girl I am dining with, but any personal relationship is ended.

'He's still your grandfather. He made a mistake.'

She doesn't answer me.

'You can't change the past, Ruby, no one can.' I pause long enough that she looks up at me, James's eyes a bright reminder. 'But the purpose of being alive is to curate the future. It's our responsibility.'

Her eyes swim with tears. It's a fresh pain, I didn't mean for this trip to hurt her so much.

'Oh, sweet girl, I'm so sorry.' I can only apologise.

'It's not that. Not this.' She dabs the edges of her eyes with a corner of her napkin.

I can see the mascara stuck to the stitching when she puts it back down.

'I have a thing I regret. Will always regret,' she says. 'And I want to tell you because, well, because of us, but I'm scared you won't like me any more.' She is twenty-two years old. She has a lifetime of regrets and mistakes to swim through – some of them will be so huge they will challenge the very beating of her heart.

'There is nothing,' I tell her, 'that could ever do that.' They are the truest words I have ever spoken: they come from deep within me.

'The day my mum found out she was going to die . . .'

I don't interrupt, don't tell her that we all die – most of us over and over.

'I'd been hanging out with some right idiots. Only I thought they were great. Obviously.' She moves the little blue plate away from her, thinks again and wipes her finger across the droplets of sauce that are left. 'I was a total dick.' She sighs.

'How old were you? Sixteen? Seventeen?'

Ruby nods. 'Sixteen. We'd been hanging out in the park – drinking. I was smashed, worse than I've ever been – before or since – even though I knew Mum and Dad were going to the oncologist, that it was going to be bad.'

I hold my tongue, I will let her finish before I remind her that she was a child, that she's not much more than that now.

A waiter comes and takes our plates, asks if we're ready to move on to the puddings. I nod on behalf of both of us but Ruby doesn't speak until he's gone again.

'Cut a long story short, they got home, I got home, we had the biggest row anyone ever had and I screamed and screamed at my mum. Called her every name under the sun on the day she got her diagnosis, on the day she'd been told how short a time we had.' She dabs her face again. The mascara has run, the contrast makes her eyes look bottomless. 'And the next day, I couldn't remember what had happened, not properly. And so I never apologised. Fragments of it come back all the time, single words, me sliding down the kitchen cabinet and sitting on the floor, my mum crying.' She sips her wine, clears her throat. 'That's it.'

'What does your dad say?'

'We don't mention it. We never have. To be fair, things happened very quickly after that.'

The next waiter excuses herself as she leans across, placing our pudding bowls in front of us. '*Et voila*,' she says and pours liquid nitrogen, smoking, into saucers beneath the puddings. The table turns to magic between us, a lemon grove of swirling smells.

Ruby smiles a little at the theatre of it.

'You were a child,' I say when we're alone again. 'We all make mistakes, but you need to talk about this with your dad, put it behind you.'

'I try sometimes. I really do. But whatever I said was so awful that he stops me every time.'

'This is delicious,' I say, pointing at the yellow ice with the tiny silver spoon. 'There's not much in life that doesn't benefit from talking it over, you know. Most things sort themselves out if you talk about them.'

'Like today?' she asks.

'I can't be right all the time,' I say, and we get on with our evening, with the business of writing our own story.

Chapter Twenty-Seven

Ruby

I'm packing when Dad texts, my swimming costume still wet in a plastic bag, my case on the bed. Judith certainly knows how to pick a hotel.

Dad's timing is hilarious. *Hope everything went OK, love. I am in this with you: I want to be. Do you think Judith and James would come to lunch on Saturday? Xxx*

Ah, fuck, as James would say. I can't even begin to explain.

I'll come to yours on the way home. Xxx

I hope that's non-committal enough. Judith and I have had an amazing morning of saunas and swimming and way too much breakfast, but I'm not sure she's going to be in a room with James any time soon.

I'm in Dad's kitchen in time for supper. He's going all in on cheese and I'm glad I came.

'So I don't know what happens next. With the two of them, I mean. You'll get Judith here, for sure. But I don't think I want to see James again.'

I can't gauge Dad's reaction, work out which one I'm going to get – the sympathy face or the I-told-you-so.

'The problem with these kinds of things is . . .'

I groan inwardly, or maybe outwardly.

Dad gives me 'that' look but carries on speaking. 'This is what Mum was worried about: people are who they are. And sometimes the narrative we tell ourselves, or the picture we paint, doesn't match with reality. It's no one's fault.'

He's chosen to sit on the fence, one leg dangling from each annoying side.

'The reality is that he's a liar,' I say. 'He lied to me about being married, he lied to all of them in the squat. And leopards don't change their spots.'

Dad turns away quickly, but I catch his face before he does. 'What are you bloody smirking at?'

'You,' he says. And I swear if we were different people he'd tweak my nose like Mum used to when I was little. 'I love how black and white you are. So like your mum.'

That makes the tops of my cheeks burn. I'm lost for words so I huff and make a face at him.

Dad sighs. 'He didn't lie about being married. No more than Judith did, and that didn't bother you, did it?'

'He was a grass, Dad.'

A flicker of a smile crosses his face. I might go home.

'I'm just saying give him a chance, hear his side.' Dad pours molten cheese across a baking tray of roasted potatoes and onions. My resolve weakens. 'You can't know the whole story if you weren't there.'

And sometimes you don't know the whole story even if you were there. 'Dad?'

He shuts the oven door and turns to face me. 'Are you all right?' he asks.

My skin smarts and prickles dance across my forehead. 'I want to talk about what happened. About Mum's diagnosis day.'

The only sound is the tiny clock on the cooker. It ticks three times.

'We don't have to,' says Dad. 'We know what happened and we don't need to go over it all again.'

'I need to.' I put one hand against my chest to still my fluttering heart. I take a deep breath. 'Because I don't know what happened.'

Dad puts the tea towel he was holding down on the work surface, spreads his hands across the breakfast bar and looks at me. 'I don't understand.'

'I remember shouting.' Three words and I'm crying. 'I remember falling down.' I take two steps to the side, point at the cabinet next to the fridge. 'Here.'

Dad is silent.

'And I remember screaming and swearing at Mum. Saying horrible things I didn't mean.'

Suddenly Dad is standing beside me, one arm round my shoulders as I cry into my damp hands.

'It's OK,' he says.

'It isn't though. I've thought about it every single day since she died. About how much I wish it had never happened. About never saying sorry.'

My dad pulls me into him. Hugs me like he hasn't in years. His arms are tight round me and he's rocking me, gently, from side to side. I can feel the side of his face on my temple, can feel that he is sobbing too.

'That's not how it was, love. That's not what happened.'

I scan through the images in my mind, flashing tableaus of shouts, of staggers. There is no redemption.

Dad lets go of me, takes my hand. 'You were drunk. You were a child under enormous pressure and you let off steam. Mum and I knew that. You weren't even coherent, just bellowing scribble between sobs.' He sits down on the floor by the fridge, on the lino. He pats the space beside him with his free hand.

I get down on the floor next to him.

'We sank down here with you. Just like this.' His dark eyes swim with tears and they cling between his lashes. 'And we held each other. A team of three.' He gathers me to him, demonstrating. 'You, me, and Mum, and we sat here and cried until we were done.'

Dad is wearing a black shirt. I have left a snail trail of snot on the shoulder.

'And then Mum held your hair back while you threw up in the washing up bowl. And we put you to bed like we did when you were a baby.'

I have curled into him, I am a child again and he is in charge. He is safety.

'And then we came downstairs, Mum and me, and we had a glass of wine and we were glad to talk about something other than Mum, than Mum dying.' The words are foreign in his mouth: I can hear the struggle he has to sound them out.

'I'm so sorry, Dad.'

'It doesn't matter. It never did,' he says.

The smell of blackened onions begins to leak from the oven.

'But every time I try to talk about it you stop me.'

He kisses me on the top of my head.

'I thought you were doing it for me. I didn't realise it bothered you so much.'

He straightens his arms, stretches. 'Onions,' he says. 'I have to rescue the supper or we'll starve. But in future, please tell me if there's anything else you're beating yourself up over. Please. I always want to know.'

We stand up, shake our limbs loose. I am lighter already.

'Feel better for hearing the whole story?'

I nod and he passes me the tea towel to wipe my face – it makes me laugh.

'So call James,' Dad says. 'Hear his.'

Chapter Twenty-Eight

JUDITH

I am so desperate to be alone, I don't even miss Dougal. I loved spending time with Ruby, time as precious as any could be, but the truth has been damaged, the past upended, and I need silence to process the betrayal.

The windows of my house have been closed all day and the quiet has grown warm inside it. It invites me in, gestures – with a finger to its lips – that I should tread softly, make no sound to break the spell.

This is the home I made with Catherine, surrounded – like a moat – with the plants she grew for their tinting properties. This is a space where there haven't been many arguments, where there is no conflict stuck like smoke to the wallpaper, no unkindness hiding in the dust balls behind the log pile. Catherine and I loved each other in this house and we imbued every brick of it with security, painted contentment on to the freshly plastered walls.

That investment was worth it. I can step inside, double-lock the front door and turn off the phone. I close the lid of my laptop, even though it is sleeping. I don't want its screen looking at me, a portal that a wider world might stare through. I need to be here alone.

But even alone, the tears don't come. There is too much to unpack, too much to process. Elements of this have been the best hours of my life: sharing the driving with Ruby, the sense of road-trip – of togetherness. I had to peel back the what-ifs and might-bes of the past, and concentrate on the present to make the most of our time together.

Now I am raw, edges peeled back, staring into the past.

I go into the bathroom and turn on the tap. I pour bubbles into the base of the bath, mix it with my hand. I watch for a few minutes and only then do I think to put the plug in. My brain is full. There is simply nothing more that will fit in there.

I change my mind, turn off the tap.

In my bedroom there is a walk-in closet. It has two white slat-ted doors that open outwards to reveal a rack of clothes, as deep as a jacket is wide, even with my big shoulders. I push through the clothes, most of them smell of me but on the edges of the air there are top notes of Catherine: floral scents, the faintest smell of nut-brown oil. I sink to my knees and crawl to the back wall. I turn and sit on the floor, my back against the wall and our coats and jackets hanging in my eye-line like a childhood dream.

It's there. Wrapped in brown paper that I haven't opened for years. The Sellotape has discoloured, curled in corners. I reach out my hand and tear the paper away from the frame.

It was Catherine's twenty-fifth birthday. Our third together and her second at art school. We lived in a flat in Brixton, not too far from her college. The flat was in a conversion with high ceilings and original features: draughty windows and no central heating. We were still new, still fascinated by the luck that had brought us together. Every morning began as a new chance, the sheer joy of opening our eyes and seeing each other there, head on pillow. Each day began with laughter.

It was a horrible flat. There was a family below us with five children crammed into one room – they had access to the garden and used it to scream obscenities at their kids. We called them Mr and Mrs Shut-up and all the little Shut-ups and made jokes about them to soften the arrows of their screaming.

It was the weekend. Catherine didn't have school and I didn't have work. The little Shut-ups were still sleeping and their parents hadn't embarked on their day-long exercise of slamming the massive front door as often as they could, shaking our first-floor flat.

I made her breakfast in bed. Coffee had just begun: we had a Turkish coffeemaker that fitted on the single gas ring and scalded our hands almost every time we picked it up. I carried the tray in to her. Toast and jam, two slices on her favourite plate.

'I would have picked a bramble from the garden, put it in a jar, but I was scared Mr Shut-up would catch me.' I put the tray on the floor next to the bed, climbed back in under the covers. 'Happy birthday, babe.'

'Where's my present?' Catherine would never lose that buzz of absurd excitement about birthdays, but I wasn't to know that then.

I made it clear that her present was in the bag beside the bed. I also made it clear there was a price to pay before she got it.

'Presents first,' she kept repeating, right up until I covered her mouth with so many kisses she couldn't breathe and she gave in. The coffee grew cold, the toast hardened to a crisp. Downstairs, Mr and Mrs Shut-up started shouting. Everything was perfect.

'Now,' Catherine said, still breathless, her alabaster cheeks pink with excitement. She looked like a Victorian child in the story of a street urchin, tiny fine features and short hair sticking out in messy blonde clumps.

I tutted. 'Patience is a virtue, Rolf.'

'Have I not proved to you that I'm not the sort for virtue?' Her fingers snaked across my hip.

When I got the present bag out, I made a big fuss, smoothed the counterpane out flat. I could see where my hand had been across the pale-pink bristles of the fabric. 'We need a big flat surface. So you can look at each thing separately.'

I earned more than Catherine then. She lived on a student grant and a few pounds a week she got for cleaning for an old lady down the road. We loved the old lady: she'd been an artist in the Newlyn School in Cornwall and she chain-smoked cigarettes as she told us stories of sex and painting, painting and sex. We knew she fancied us, but could never work out which one of us it was.

'It's got to be you,' Catherine always said. 'It's your shoulders, the bit where your arms join them. And the way your mouth always turns up just slightly at the corners, even if you're desperately sad.'

'It's you.' I was certain. 'It's the whole fairy thing. She thinks you're a changeling that someone once swapped for a human baby. You probably are. It's why you have such small ears.'

With hindsight, it was definitely both of us.

The greatest thing about the old lady – beyond how much we adored her stories and her roarin' 20s name-dropping – was that she'd given Catherine a studio. Just like that. One day she invited Catherine to take one of the two attic bedrooms in her huge townhouse – neither of which was ever used – and set up her easel by the enormous skylight. It was an amazing space and Catherine credited the light in it for her success long after we'd moved away.

I could afford much more than Catherine. I was still quite a junior social worker, although nowhere near the bottom of the food chain. Our rent wasn't ridiculous and I paid that. Catherine bought the food, most of which was inedible but the seventies were to blame for that rather than her.

Inside the bag were twists of paper. I handed them to Catherine one by one. No child ever opened a stocking with such wide-mouthed joy.

Her tiny fingers undid one twist at a time. Each piece of paper was a perfect blue and white striped square. I had spent hours in the art shop near the British Museum, relying heavily on the patience of the kind old man who owned it.

Inside each twist was a different pigment. A hundred colours that she took randomly from the bag. With each colour she exclaimed, as if it couldn't be any more perfect. Each tiny portion of powder – not even a quarter of a teaspoonful – received its own eulogy.

'Oh, this orange.' She spoke quietly, terrified of dislodging the smallest grain from the paper. 'It's like that sun we saw on the Heath, do you remember? A massive harvest festival of a sunset.'

I didn't remember, but I didn't tell her. Pictures of days were Catherine's thing, each one slid into place in the catalogue of her mind.

'I've only seen this green once before.' It could have been an enormous diamond and she wouldn't have loved it more. 'My granny had a tea cosy. Its top, like a pompom but not frilly, was this exact green.'

The colours went on, the story she attached to each one was as important and passionate as the one before, as the next. When she had finished, there were a hundred twists of pigment, open on the bed in front of us like a sprawl of flowers.

'Damn,' I said, frustrated. 'This is when you want colour film in your bloody camera.'

'No.' Catherine stared at the powders. 'I'll remember this exactly as it is forever. It's better not to have a photograph.'

'You think?' I asked her, stretching out softly alongside her, trying not to jog the origami garden in front of us.

'Imagine I stare at a photo of this every day, and I would stare at it.' She smiles at me, her eyelashes dark against her pale skin. 'If it was a photo, I'd start to criticise it over time. Wouldn't it be nice if this blue of my brother's swimming trunks were next to the vermillion of a desert cliff? What a shame the stripes of this piece of paper weren't exactly opposite another piece. Stuff like that. If I remember this just as it is, it stays perfect in my mind. It keeps the essence of today, of you, of us. It's filed.' She taps her forehead. 'And so are you.'

Catherine went to Coralline's house most days. Two days a week she was cleaning, the rest of the time she was in her garret, painting under the big Edwardian eaves as artists have done for centuries in one architecture or another.

By the time winter arrived and my birthday came around, I had twigged that Catherine had been painting something for me. My birthday was a work day that year – and a bad one. A day that I'd spent frustrated by the council's inability to house my client suitably – back when emergency meetings were called about one rough sleeper.

I came home tired, grumpy. I was looking forward to 'my surprise'. I was looking forward to cooking and staying in.

Catherine had set up an easel in the sitting room. A white tablecloth was draped over it.

'Is it a book?' I asked. 'Umm, is it a puppy?'

'It could be anything really, couldn't it?' Catherine looked at me. 'I mean, given that it's obviously a painting – it could literally be anything. It could be a holiday in Rome.'

I must have looked bright for a second.

'It's not though,' she added quickly, apologetically.

'Do I unveil it?' My art etiquette was non-existent.

Catherine put her hands either side of my shoulders. 'I'd rather you stand . . . here. And I pull the cover off, so you can see it properly.'

'The tablecloth?'

'The grand antique painting cover.' She moved me to the spot. 'I made every single paint I used in this painting. There's no colour here that doesn't come from your birthday present to me, from the pigments.'

'Is that a double negative?' I was tired, nervous too. I was no artist. I was often left behind when Coralline and Catherine got talking about their work, the history – or the future – of it all.

Art made me nervous back then: sometimes because I couldn't understand it and – worse – sometimes because a sculpture or a painting was so beautiful, so pure and perfect, that it brought back too many awful memories. I shifted awkwardly in my viewing spot.

'Ta-da!' Catherine pulled off the cloth.

I cried instantly. Catherine a few seconds later. I hid in the bathroom while she took the painting down, folded up the easel. She turned the canvas to face the wall and I never looked at it again.

We sort of talked about it, in the days that followed, but mostly I wanted to forget and – mostly – Catherine couldn't understand how much she'd hurt me.

I tear the brown paper away. The painting is facing the wall and the first thing I see is the pale wood stretcher that Catherine made herself. She had a thin little hammer, sharp-ended, as dainty as her own hands. She used to cut the corners of the wood with a mitre to guide her, barely breathing as she concentrated, then I would wait for the tiny taps of that little hammer as the pins went home and I'd know she was happy, that she'd stretched another canvas ready to paint.

The painting smells dry and old. That smell of paint is everything. I wonder if she is in this crowded wardrobe with me, if she is hiding behind the coats, the rolled-up sleeping bag, the black sack of her handbags I'll never use. I close my eyes, breathe in through my nose. I always thought the smell of paint was the smell of history – so it is now: our history, mine and hers.

I turn the painting round to face me. I'm careful, it's not small and I don't want to put my back out. I imagine being found, weeks from now, starved in this cupboard.

And there I am. Just as she painted me.

On the bottom of the homemade wooden frame is a tiny strip of silver. She got someone at college to engrave it. It says 'Judith. Sleeping.'

The picture is utterly beautiful. It is classically stunning. I know enough now, from my day classes, about the rule of thirds and about symbolism and all that art history to see where Catherine has borrowed from, what incredible technical skill is in each brush stroke.

She is me. This nymph, this radiant girl – half-curled on her side facing the artist, with one arm long and languid under her head – is me.

My black hair shines with the silver from the slip of moon I can see in the open window behind the figure. My skin glows like living breathing flesh: like youth if you could bottle it and paint it over the scars of time.

And the scars are the feature of this picture. Along the outside of my thigh run the barest streaks of silver-purple, like quicksilver dropped from the night by faeries. My pubic hair is full, dark, in the tradition of the Renaissance – except there is no censorship of my femininity, my sex. I am not draped in any excuses, not covered by strategic flowers or angels' wings.

My belly is the centre of the picture. Snakes of vivid red writhe from my groin up towards my belly button. They trace, like a bowl, the exact place where the baby grew. Every kick and turn, every swoosh and heartbeat inside me is there. Unapologetic and wondrous.

The skin that hadn't quite tucked back from my pregnancy – what I imagined then as a puckered fold hanging from my body – is the softest mound of womanhood, the tiny rumpled slack proof that she had grown there. My breasts are full and round, the nipples painted in as brown as nuts. The detail of the dimpling on the ends of the nipples, where my baby suckled, is an exquisite pain.

My eyes are closed in the painting, and it is a vision of me I have never seen before. In sleep, I look enchanted, like nothing could hurt me – like nothing ever had.

I am seventy-five years old. Finally, I see myself as Catherine did. Finally I see that those breasts I despaired of for being too big, not round enough – that they were perfect. That they had fed my baby, that they had been part of what magic drew my lover to me and me to her each night. The slack skin I'd been so afraid of is radiant and perfect.

This model, sleeping on a pale-blue sheet with tiny flashes through it where the nylon catches the moonlight, is a beautiful young woman. She is strong, muscled. She has everything to live for.

I hated this picture. I hated the way Catherine had picked up my every flaw and lit it. I was terrified of its nakedness.

We left it in its brown wrapping – for fifty years. I moved it in here from Catherine's studio in case one of the dealers tore open the paper, saw what I remembered as a monster inside.

There is no monster. There is no secret, and no shame. This is a painting about how much one woman loved another: a representation – stunningly lifelike – of how the artist felt about every mark, every place-name, on the map of her subject's body.

I have my hand over my mouth, my fingers are wet from my breath and the silent tears that have slid between them. My legs are numb but I stand, shake them out.

There is a painting above my bed by a friend of ours. I know he won't mind that I unhook it, lean it carefully against the drawers.

I take Catherine's picture and I slide it into position, straighten it in pride of place above my bed. This painting is the truth – I have nothing to hide. I did nothing wrong.

Just Judith. Sleeping.

Chapter Twenty-Nine

RUBY

James is waiting for me in the car outside my flat. I saw him arrive half an hour early and I have been watching him from the kitchen window. His hands are on the steering wheel and he is staring straight ahead. I hate this James. The one who was hiding inside the other one. Maybe when he gets out of the car he won't be as tall, as big; maybe that's how he hid inside the other James. The good one.

I text my dad. *He's here. Xxx*

'Hello,' is all James says when I get in, no drama. He presses the button and starts the car.

On the backseat, and wearing a harness clipped to a seat belt, is a huge golden retriever: the dog in James's profile picture.

'This is Dougal,' James says and, as much as I want to sit in the back with the dog and hug him, I don't answer. 'I thought we could take him for a walk.'

James's is the first electric car I've been in and the lack of sound is eerie. Dougal has his mouth wide open like a smile and the pristine car smells of his warm dog breath. I crack my window down an inch.

James stares ahead, his fluffy white hair silhouetted against the driver's window. 'I'm very grateful to your dad for letting me know what happened.' He clears his throat. 'And grateful for you to give me a chance to explain.'

My dad took advantage of my emotional state last night, got me to agree to this. 'Strike while the iron's hot,' he'd said and rang James from my phone. They spoke for over an hour. 'He'll pick you up tomorrow,' Dad said. 'Hear him out and then decide.'

'Have you heard from Judith?' James asks.

I shake my head. 'Not really. A text during the night.'

'She's not taking my calls,' he says.

'Well, that can't exactly come as a surprise.' Suddenly I'm furious with him. 'You've ruined everything.'

There are teenagers in the playground at the end of my road. They stare at us as we glide past. If I was walking, they would shout out, flip me a bird or two.

Without loosening his grip on the wheel, James extends one finger and taps it against the grey plastic. 'I've never stopped thinking about what I did. But I can't change it.'

I stare out of the window: I don't want him to see the tears in my eyes.

'Firstly, and above all else,' he says. 'It's all true. What Paddy told you is true. I was the grass. I grassed up all my friends, and my comrades-in-arms. They paid a huge price.'

'And Judith?'

'The biggest price of all of us. Along with your mum.'

His honesty disarms me for a second. I'd expected excuses, explanations.

We continue in silence. We drive through the outskirts of the city, past shopping centres and housing estates.

I feel like I don't know anything, like I'm lost in one of those mazes that has a monster in the middle. I reach my hand back between the seats and Dougal nuzzles it.

'There are treats in the glove box if you want to give him some,' James says.

The dog's tail wags loudly as soon as I go to open the little drop-down drawer. We are officially best friends – and I've never been more glad to see a friendly face or tail.

'There's nothing I can say to change this. But I'd be grateful if you'd let me tell you how it happened,' James says, and I shrug a response.

'OK.'

There is a rough sandy car park on the side of the road. The car curves silently into it and we park up. Dougal's tail starts wagging the second we stop.

'He won't need a lead here,' James says when we get out. 'He's too old for rabbits.'

We start down the sandy path. Either side of us are gorse bushes, prickly with green and flaming with yellow, another world from the grey city a silent twenty minutes behind us. I catch my shoulder on a branch and it pulls a thread from my T-shirt. The smell of almonds puffs through the air and it snaps back into place.

The path is only wide enough for one person at a time. James falls into step behind me.

I need to get straight into it or I'll never ask at all. 'Were you a grass when you moved in?' 'Grass' feels unkind, rude, but it was his word – and I feel like being unkind.

He sighs so loudly that I imagine I can feel the exhalation on the back of my neck. 'It's complicated.'

'Everything always is.' I do turn round to say that.

There are so many birds here that their chirping is disquieting if you listen closely: as if they are watching our every move, our every step across their territory. A robin flits on to a gorse branch in front of me and I can read the murderous thoughts in his tiny black eye.

'They were different times.'

'If I had a pound for every time anyone's said that to me in the last month, I wouldn't have a student fucking loan.' I'm only half-joking. 'How different can it have been?'

'Different.' The path widens slightly and James walks next to me. Our feet fall into a rhythm despite his legs being so much longer than mine. 'The most important thing to know is that I loved Jude desperately. Like I'd never loved anyone before.'

'And this Polly?'

'Not at all, nothing even remotely like that.' He stops. There is a crossroads of paths. 'Should we turn round? Or do you fancy a long walk?'

'Actually, I'm starving. Is there somewhere to eat?'

James turns to go back. 'Good idea.'

We briefly talk about food and Dougal, stay off James's treachery for now. As we walk, I silently plan questions and, I can see from his face, he silently sets up answers.

'How come Paddy knew then? And Judith didn't?' I ask him when we sit at our table. It's a greasy spoon by the roadside, red Formica tabletops and grubby wooden chairs. My dad loves places like this. 'And what about the others?'

'None of us ever saw each other again,' he says. 'We were scattered through prisons in Scotland. There was a rumour that a couple of the guys we didn't know well . . .' He lowers his voice. 'The guys with the explosives. I think they were in prison in London somewhere. But they broke us up, moved us around so that we couldn't stay in touch. You couldn't write letters to each other because you couldn't send anything unless it was on prison paper and a guard read it first. There was no opportunity to set anything right. No debrief or decompression. No internet, remember? Just phone directories. Every library had a long shelf of phone books. Every number in the country. But barely anyone I knew had a phone.'

We choose our food and James goes up to order. We both choose chips and quiche without asking each other, and it reminds me again – stupidly – that we're related.

'Were you scared?' I ask him. He's massive and he's old, I can't imagine that he was.

'I lived through a year of hell, before we were arrested. A year of sleepless nights and crying whenever I was alone. Months of trying to wriggle out of it, to get away from Polly. But . . .' He puts his head in his hands. 'It was her life's work. It was unfeasibly hard for a woman to get to that kind of position in the sixties – God knows what rank she made in the end. But she had something to prove and I walked right into it.'

I stay quiet.

'And the worst thing was how cruel she was to Jude. To your grandmother,' he adds in case I think it's another one, another Jude. 'Polly pretended constantly that we were having an affair. I knew she was doing that, but there was nothing I could do about it – bar tell Jude over and over that we weren't.'

He looks at the table while he describes the dirty house, the cold kitchen. He draws a doodle curl in the spilt salt and he tells me that he knew whenever Judith was coming into a room behind him because Polly would move closer, or touch his hand. He would shake Polly off but he couldn't do anything to anger her, to risk immediate arrest.

James's description of the place they lived in is less romantic than Judith's. She didn't mention the money worries, the horrible food that they shared out between them but he remembers it all as if it was yesterday: that's how he talks about it. I think of the photo they sent me at the beginning – the black and white cool, the clothes, the shoes. It didn't look like a freezing stinking hellhole, it looked like a film. But James says it didn't smell like that photo.

He's angry, I can see him shaking as he pushes the pepper pot around with his fingers. It tips over and grey speckles cover the table.

'God, sorry.' He attempts to smile at me. 'They're not easy memories. They weren't easy times.'

We eat in close-to-silence. I feel like James is revving up, like he's getting ready to tell me the rest of it – organising his thoughts. I have a million questions I want to ask him but instead I chew my cardboard food, push the salad round my plate.

He puts his knife and fork together across his empty plate and starts to talk.

'I met her – Polly – a few days after I'd moved in. I knew everyone else, I'd been coming and going for a while, trying to be all things to all people.' He looks up at me, realising I can't know what he means. 'My family were very poor. I mean poor. We never had an indoor bathroom – my mum used the privy in the garden right up until she died. That's not the half of it, but it's the easiest bit to understand. My dad had come back from the Second World War very different to the man he'd been when he left. He found it hard to work – physically. Before the war, he'd been a fisherman, one of the most dangerous jobs on the planet. He couldn't do it any more and – where we lived – there weren't any options. I don't know what killed him – his injuries? The drink? The shame? But he died before my sister started school. I was ten.'

He smiles through the veil of the past. 'Do you know what Judith would say now?'

I shake my head.

'She'd remind us that poverty still exists, even that kind. It never went away.'

I smile, because she would. I remember, with a pain in my throat, that I like her enormously. I like her silly big heart and her over-earnest expression – I like that she reminds me of my mum.

'I left school at fifteen. I'd pretty much stopped going by then anyway, but – to be formal – it had to be fifteen. And I went to work. God, I loved it. I loved coming home with money for my ma and seeing her happier than she'd been in years.'

We both pause. We look just past each other's ears and I think about his mother throwing away Judith's letters. His face says that he's thinking other things about her. Maybe you never get over the conflict of your mum – about mine shouting at me, me screaming at her – not even when you're as old as James.

'I joined the trade union, it was my life. They paid for me to go to night school – I'd be nothing without them. Without that. Education, Ruby, the most precious gift.'

He points at me – at my masters – and it annoys me enough to break the spell.

'Have we got time for coffee?' I ask.

He says that we do and I go and order them. I take my time walking back across the sticky café floor. Maybe James will have got off that particular high horse.

'And I got into CND. I got wise to everything that was going on in the world.' He shrugs his shoulders and I see three small brown birthmarks at the neck of his T-shirt. My mum had almost exactly the same. 'And more and more into it. I started with the Scottish Committee of 100 – I was secretary for a bit – and then I had to choose. I couldn't stay in Aberdeen and do that stuff, I had to leave.'

'So what happened to your mum? And your sister – was she old enough to work?'

He shakes his head. 'I couldn't let her leave school. Things weren't the same for girls and she wouldn't ever have had the chances I did, not then. She had to stay on and do Highers.'

The coffees arrive and James tears the top off a sugar sachet, measures exactly half a teaspoon of sugar out and stirs it into his coffee.

'Is your sister still alive?' I ask.

'Very much so.' His first proper smile in hours. 'A retired GP who plays golf in Ayrshire.'

'That's something good,' I say and I can't help but squeeze his hand across the table. His skin is like soft leather, like the cover of a notebook. He puts his other hand on top of mine for the briefest of moments then we both pull back, wrap our palms round our coffees in the exact same way. It makes us laugh.

'I moved to Glasgow in sixty-four. God, it was a hole. I'd been used to the rolling hills and crashing waves. Glasgow was grey and sooty, stinking pish from the boatyards fogging up the river and your lungs. I thought life would be easy in a city, but it was much harder. Much more poverty. I didn't think that could be true but, Jesus, it was.'

He straightens out his back, sits upright and tips his head back and forwards a few times as if to stretch out an ache.

'Are you OK?'

He stands up, gets his wallet out. 'I am actually, I'm getting there. Let me pay for this and then we'll talk in the car.'

I should never have a pet. I have completely forgotten the dog. 'Oh, poor Dougal.'

'Dougal's knackered.' James smiles. 'He's older than me. And I guarantee he's fast asleep on the back seat.'

We let Dougal out to stretch his legs for a minute.

We settle back into the car, looking forwards rather than at each other for the rest of the story. 'So you'd got to Glasgow?' I remind him where he was.

'Yes, that's my point, that's what I was trying to say. I'd got to Glasgow but I was still responsible for everything at home. I took a job in a factory manufacturing boat engines – and that paid more than my mother could have dreamed of. Most of it went home and that's how my sister climbed out of poverty. That and her bloody hard work.'

You can hear in his voice how much he loves his sister. 'Can I meet her?'

'God, yes, she's desperate to meet you. She was the very next person I told after my daughters knew.' He glances sideways, smiles a little. 'Your aunts.'

That makes me feel better, edges a little light into the conversation. 'I'm looking forward to meeting her too.'

He nods. 'Let's see how you feel at the end of the story.' James looks straight ahead.

'Polly had been on the edges of the group, of the protestors. I learnt later that she was waiting for the right person to get her in, someone with enough to lose. And that was me.' I see his knuckles squeeze a little, whiten across the ovals of bone.

Outside, we have glided through the rest of the countryside in minutes. We merge with a motorway and the rushing lorries to one side of us feel incongruous against the tense past that fills the car.

'I was arrested. It was a pretty major offence, although it sounds silly now. Back then you could go to prison for a week, for ten days, we did it all the time: we were young and we were tough. But this time I was looking at six weeks.'

'James, what did you do?' I am alone in a car with this man, this grandfather I hardly know – and then know less and less each minute.

He pulls a face – I think it's a smile. 'I threw an egg at Harold Wilson.' He looks at me, pulls the closest to a shrug that you can when you're driving a car.

'The prime minister, right?'

'Bastard,' says James. 'Got in on a nuclear-free card and went straight back on it. Put the bombs in Scotland, of course – wouldn't do to have that risk anywhere near London.' He takes one hand off the steering wheel, plants his palm across his big face. 'He deserved it. The fucker.'

He makes me laugh.

'I mean, I wouldn't do it now – non-violent direct action. That was our thing. So I got into trouble on all sides – the Committee were on at me because they saw it as violence, the police because, well, you know, he was the PM.'

'It was just an egg.' I feel indignant on his behalf.

He looks at me very solemnly. 'Actually, I think an egg in the face really smarts.' And then he tries hard to look very serious. But fails.

'Tell you what did smart though, six weeks in prison.' He taps the steering wheel with the flat of one hand. 'More than that.' He waves the hand, animated. 'It meant no income for my ma, or my sister. They wouldn't be able to pay the rent. And I'd lose my job because I'd been off for six weeks and, ah, fuck, Ruby. There's no excuse.'

I don't say anything: I don't know if I know the rules any more.

'In she walks, Polly, and I'm lost for a couple of days. She was out of our league, all of us. Confident. I know now she was at least five years older than me, that she'd been recruited by Special Branch. Hence the confidence.' He swallows like something is stuck in his throat.

I can see this hurts, that it hasn't got better in God knows how many years.

'I was not quite nineteen. I was an idiot. For a couple of days, when she first arrived, it was like Jane Fonda had come to live in our house. And I . . .'

He is silent for a long time.

If he slept with her, if they had sex, I don't want to know. Not because of Judith, but because it would be grim to think about my grandfather – I can't go there. 'I've had a little experience of eighteen-year-old boys,' I say. 'I went out with one.'

'Aye then, so you know,' he says and we leave it at that. 'I'm there in the police station.' He fills his cheeks, exhales, and a little square parking ticket on the dashboard waves in his breath. 'And in she comes. At first, I didn't get it. I thought she'd been arrested too – she'd been at the same demo. And then she sat down, swooshed that hair round her shoulders, and explained. She knew already – their intelligence was frightening – about my mum, and my sister. She described our miserable little house, knew what school my sister was at. I wish they hadn't picked me.

'Ach, Ruby,' he says, his voice cracking. 'By the time Jude arrived, by the time I saw her walking down the hallway with Paddy, soaking wet and looking like a wee drown-ded rat . . . By the time my heart almost broke with the need to pick her up and hold her – I didn't though, not then, not for ages.'

I do not need to know how long my grandparents knew each other before they had . . . Instead of answering him like a grown-up, I turn a beetroot red and my ears feel like they're on fire. I stare straight ahead at the tail lights of the red sports car in front of us, concentrate on the clouds like evening bruises in the distance.

'It was too late. I'd been spared six weeks in prison. Eilidh stayed at school, you know the rest. I belonged to Box. They owned me.'

Chapter Thirty

JUDITH

I have dozed for a few hours, under the painting. Waking feels like coming home.

It is late and the house should be in darkness. Instead, there is a fresh night shadow that darkens the corners, making the edges look bright and lit. I fetch cheese and crackers from the kitchen – I am starving hungry – and a bottle of wine, and I go outside.

I sit at the patio table for a minute or two, eating fast and gratefully. I was too upset when I got back to even think about food; now, Catherine's witness has liberated me. It's not an explanation, or permission, it's a snapshot of the person I was, the person I still am and have grown into.

The night sky is navy blue and studded with stars. I move on to the lawn and lie on my back, staring up at its vastness, grounding myself with its perspective. The sky is stretched wide above me and I reach my arm up towards it, imagining that I can pull it down, scrunch its velvet softness in my hand.

Catherine and I used to lie outside under skies like this, pretending to join the dots between stars. I move my hand across the grass beside me, imagine hers there just inches away.

She used to name constellations and I hear the echo of her voice, warm from wine and summer. 'That one there: those four bright ones with the wobbly one just to the left. Know what that is?'

'No,' I'd have to say – that was my part in the game.

'Labia Minora.' Always her favourite, it would always feature even if it wasn't first in the list. 'And that one? The really long line above the twinkly one?' Her muscled thin arm would point skywards.

'No,' I'd say.

'Occam's Razor.' And she'd sip her wine. 'Oh, and look – you can barely ever see The Laptop.' A sweep of her pointed finger across the sky.

It still makes me laugh now, although one of the things I've found out about living alone is how loud laughter sounds – even when you laugh quietly.

I lie here for a while, feeling the pull of gravity, the mystery of the heavens. It makes me feel smaller on a day when insignificance is welcome, on a day when understanding my place in the universe lessens my responsibilities and my obligations.

My phone is indoors. I do have a responsibility to Ruby. I didn't – just a few short weeks ago – but I do now. It is one of the ripples that she and James have made in the pond of my life, one of the concentric circles we lose control over as soon as we start to open the past.

Ruby has already texted me. *I hope you're OK, Judith. This is all my fault – I should never have been so nosy! xxx*

That makes me think, makes me realise that, no matter how far away the stars or how certain the fragility of life is, our responsibilities are towards one another. I had a pause, after Catherine died, where I could relax mine, where my connections with other humans were less profound than my grief, but that's not where I am now. Ruby is my granddaughter.

It's me who should be sorry, darling. Can I call you tomorrow? xxx I repeat her exact number of kisses: they are clearly what she considers appropriate and I don't want to overstep. If it were left to me, the 'x's would run over the lines, fill the screen, they would be a lifetime – two lifetimes – of kisses. I check the time as I send it. It's almost midnight – still 'today'.

Her reply is a smiley face with two hearts on its cheeks. On the second line, she has written, *Could I come and see you tomorrow? Would that be OK? Xxx*

Nothing would give me greater pleasure I reply – with absolute truth. *Shall I meet you at the station? Xxx*

The stars sparkle with promises. 'Pandora's Box,' I say to Catherine and point at the six stars that mark the corners and the lid. 'And Hope, still fluttering inside.'

'We're crazy alike.' Ruby is standing in my bedroom, staring at the painting. 'If you had long hair, this could be me.' She turns back to look at me. 'Which is a weird thing to say about a nudey painting, no? But you know what I mean?' She gestures, with both hands, at herself – at the length of her, the width of her shoulders.

'And my eyes are shut, so you can't see whether they're green or blue.'

Whenever I look at Ruby, the iridescence of that blue dazzles me.

I met Ruby from her train. Seeing her walk along the platform, brown legs in khaki shorts, a rucksack over one shoulder, was like looking into a crystal ball that only reads the past.

We risked a hug when she reached me, and it felt perfect. 'Going to Paddy's was a bin fire, wasn't it?' she said straightaway.

'It was interesting.' I smiled at her.

She hitched her bag a little higher on to her shoulder. 'And I have a lot to tell you – unless you'd rather hear it from James?'

'Whatever you'd prefer,' I said.

She smiled, fell into step beside me for the short walk back to my house. 'I'll tell you, it's family history after all – and I'm family.' She looked at me, asking for reassurance.

'You are.' I managed to say it without crying. 'We are.'

I've made us lunch and laid it upon the table nearest the double doors of the studio. It's nothing fancy: a salad of croutons and Caesar dressing, a lemon tart that I made this morning – using up the hours of nervous energy that prevented me from sleeping.

'So,' she cuts to the chase. 'How do you feel about James now? Now you know? Can you forgive him? Do you believe him?'

'Gosh,' I say, 'I'm still processing. There's a lot to think about.'

I can't commit to this ideal family of Ruby's: we have to make some rules, some structure. 'I do believe him, although . . .' I say, and I don't know what the 'although' will be. I will have to wait and hear the story from James. A tiny voice inside me keeps whispering, 'Why, James? Why didn't you tell the rest of us what was going on? We could have helped you.' A tiny broken record that won't stop repeating sings, 'What if things had ended differently? What if you could have saved her?'

'Well . . .' Ruby takes the plate I offer her, heaps lime-green lettuce on to the white china.

'Watch out for slugs,' I say. 'The lettuce is from the garden. But I did wash it.'

247

Ruby looks worried but picks at a crouton with her thumb and forefinger. 'So, my dad wants you to come for lunch next weekend. What do you think? He'd love to meet you. Really love to.' She spears some leaves with her fork. 'This is the bit where I'm supposed to say "It won't be anything special, he'll just throw something together." But that's not true. It'll be fabulous – he'll be cooking for two days.'

'That's so kind. And he's in London?'

'Just outside,' she says. 'I checked: it's less than an hour-and-a-half drive from here. Or you can do it in two trains in about the same time.'

'Absolutely,' I say. 'I'd love to.' I think about how hard it must be for Ruby's father to do this: to investigate this whole aspect of his wife's past – a past he can't discuss with her, a past he can't ask her if she wants.

'I'm so relieved,' says Ruby. 'My dad is trying, but it's awkward. He's awkward.'

'There's no rule book for this stuff. Perhaps there should be? It's hard for everyone.' I smile at her to prove that I am part of the team, that we'll get through this together. We have devoured the salad and I slice the tart into four. 'We might have to eat all of this. I think it'll go off, end up in landfill.'

We're quiet for a few moments as we wince and smile at the sharpness of lemon, the cool balm of cream.

'My dad will have to try hard to match this,' Ruby says. 'But he will – try really hard, that is. He's obsessive about cooking, especially for an occasion. James will have to make do with veggie though.'

I don't know why I was stupid enough to think Ruby was only inviting me: of course she wants him there too. I slice my spoon through the tart, concentrate on even breathing, steady chewing, trying to smile.

'Is the painting of you valuable?' Ruby asks. 'I mean it's lovely, but it's not like the stuff of Catherine's that I've seen before.'

'It's extremely valuable.' I spent an hour on the phone to my insurers this morning – them on speakerphone as I wrestled pastry, melted butter. 'And, actually, it makes my house insurance kind of impossible. Not impossible money-wise . . .' It suddenly occurs to me that I need to change my will, that all this will belong to her one day. The freedom that that will bring her stops me in my tracks. I will be able to leave Ruby with choices, options – simply by never having to worry about money. And that will be because of Catherine. The cogs and wheels and might-have-beens of this situation go on forever: I really could do with a guidebook.

'Are you all right, Judith?'

'Sorry, miles away. The insurance for that picture is bonkers. A daft amount to pay every year. Tens of thousands. I already have to have extra locks and special window frames because of the pictures of Catherine's in the hall and the studio, as a condition of my house insurance.' I stand and show her the mortise lock on the double doors. 'This is why people lend pictures to museums – because they can't afford to have them at home.'

Catherine's agent was beside herself today when I told her about the picture. I took the best likeness I could on my phone and emailed it through: she said it took her breath away.

'Do you know that paintings almost always look better in photos? That you should never buy a painting from a photograph of it?' I tell Ruby.

'I can't say I've bought many paintings, Judith,' she says and I realise I'm giving her old lady advice, telling her things she doesn't need and isn't interested in. I am turning into my mother.

When we've finished eating, Ruby gets her rucksack.

'I brought you these to look at,' she says and takes three large photo albums from her bag. The first is the largest, and dark-green leather. The second has a plain black plastic cover, and the third is scarlet, almost a crocodile print. 'The pictures I brought to show you before are the ones from my flat, from way after these. These are old.'

I don't have to ask to know that these contain three eras of a lifetime: they connect the few dots that Ruby showed us before.

'I thought I'd leave them, Judith. And then you could bring them back with you on Saturday. Would that be OK? They're my dad's but he said he didn't mind. Look at this, look at their wedding.' She opens the third album, the red one. '1980s' dazzle,' she says and smiles. She points to a dark-haired man with glasses. 'My dad still looks exactly like this. Confused, and a bit surprised. He finds the world quite complicated.'

I can't look at the other pictures. My heart is in my mouth and if she turns the page it will spill out on to the photographs. I will spill out.

Ruby seems to notice my paralysis. 'Anyway, I'll leave them for you to look at. In your own time.' She shuts the book firmly: she understands.

If someone had asked me, weeks ago, if I wanted to see pictures of my daughter's entire life, I would have torn their arm off with enthusiasm. Now, these books hold the key to her, an edited highlight of what has happened since we separated – I don't know if I can take it.

It's partly that I haven't shared this time with her – I have missed it and it can never be replayed. But it's more than that – it's the secrets and the joys. The memories of the conversations, the holidays, even the dark moments: none of which are mine.

When I open this book, it will confirm how much about Penny I can never know: it will cement us as strangers. Ruby thinks the photographs will build a bridge but, actually, they will make the chasm that separates us real and wide.

Of course I look. I look as soon as I get back from walking Ruby to the station, as soon as I've locked the door and poured a glass of wine and taken some deep calming breaths. And I start with the one that will drive the sharpest shards into my heart. I start with the first.

There she is. The exact face I dream of. She is older though – there are missing days, a few weeks. She will have been somewhere else for the time between when I walked away from her, dragging my heart behind me, and the time her desperate new parents smothered her with kisses, held her tight, salved their longing for a baby. I squeeze my eyes tight shut as if I can make reality change, alter history.

Chapter Thirty-One

RUBY

I'm excited for today. Dad has smashed it with the food: our house – his house – smells like heaven. He didn't need to tidy, although he did it anyway. Everything was already in its place: everything stays where he puts it now it's just him.

Judith arrives after James. He is already sat in the armchair Dad keeps near the cooker, the one Mum used to sit in to talk to him while he cooked. I guess no one's sat in it much since Mum and I went. They've been getting on brilliantly, Dad and James – Dad and my granddad – they have loads to talk about even though I wouldn't have thought they had much in common. There's a lot of 'cool' about James: about his clothes – which could look too young on him, too hipster, but don't; about his career – he's reeling off documentaries he made that my dad enjoyed. He's cool enough to make my dad retreat into his inner spod – I know how much he's always hated small talk – but James makes it easy, keeps the conversation bubbling like the water in the pan below Dad's pot-stickers.

That all changes when Judith comes in. From all angles.

I go and meet her at the door, give her a hug that is getting incrementally bigger each time we meet.

James goes silent, and it's a massive contrast to his tall tales and his loud laugh. It feels like an implosion.

Dad takes a step towards Judith then stops. He lets the tea towel he's holding slacken at his side, holds it there in his hand, and his eyes fill with tears.

Now that I see Judith framed by our hallway, the light from the half-glazed front door softening the edges of her and the colours of the glass casting tiny tiles of green and blue on her shoulders and hair, I see what my dad sees. He sees my mum.

'God, I'm sorry,' he says after a few long moments of silence, where even James didn't know what to say. 'I never expected you to be so alike.' He walks towards her, his hand outstretched. 'I'm Nick.' And then he hugs her.

The hug doesn't take Judith by surprise but it floors me. I am open-mouthed at seeing this Nick in a random display of affection: awkward, blushy Nick who hates meeting people.

'Dad,' I say, involuntarily. 'That's not like you.' And everyone is smiling.

James steps forward and gives Judith a kiss on the cheek. It's very clear, even to my dad I'd imagine, that she doesn't kiss him back.

We shuffle and mutter our way to the dining table. Dad had the kitchen and dining room made into one big oblong space so that he could talk to people while he cooks for them: the only time he really lights up.

Eventually everyone has a full glass. Dad goes to raise his, goes to speak, but the words fail him. His eyes mist over again.

Who do we toast? Does Dad toast Penny: his wife? Or do we toast Unity: their lost baby? Is that even the same person? No one knows, least of all me.

'To absent friends,' James says, reading my mind.

'I brought back the photo albums,' Judith says. 'Thank you so much for lending them to me, Nick.'

'An absolute pleasure,' Dad says and beams at her. 'Your turn next, James.'

It's a good way to break the ice. Judith takes the albums out of her bag, the oldest is on the top, the brown one. It has a ridge of gold embossed around the edge. When Mum died, Dad went through and re-glued all the baby pictures of her, made sure they would never fall out. I remember thinking he was silly to try and stick her past together when we'd lost all our future. But he was right.

I talk James and Judith through the pictures, give them a tour of my mum, of the moments of her life. I've looked at this book often enough with her, with my granny, to know the stories of most of the images. We all pretend that this is a normal thing to do. No one mentions the obvious things – that they never met her, that they were strangers, that all of this happened too late. No one says what we're all thinking and James and Judith say very little to each other.

Dad's food saves the day. He brings pot-stickers full of spiced carrot, turnip pancakes with tiny chunks of chilli rippled through their translucent whiteness. He has made a full New Year's banquet, complete with little shiitake-filled money bags for luck.

'This is your dad's influence, Nick?' asks James, gesturing at the table laden with food. 'Did he teach you to cook?'

'Not really,' Dad says. 'He's more a pie and mash man. I visited my grandparents in Hong Kong every year as a child, the food obsession definitely traces back to then. I've taken a few courses too.'

'It's amazing,' says Judith. 'Thank you so much for going to all this effort.'

It's little things like that, tiny phrases that remind us all – with a jump – that we're in the strangest of circumstances, that we're family and yet total strangers. Every now and again I catch Dad looking at Judith in the same way I tried to peer at her when I first saw her potato nose.

When they've gone, it's just Dad and me, real life again.

'I'll help you clear up,' I say.

'What a good influence they are on you. They can come again.'

I swear Dad still thinks I'm twelve.

'They're not really speaking to each other, are they?' Dad says.

I pretend to be shocked. 'It must be bad if you noticed it.' I flick him with the dishcloth in my hand. 'They left at the same time though, so I guess they have stuff to sort out.'

Dad scoops vegetable offcuts into a saucepan. He uses them to make stock for his over-stuffed freezer of foods we'll never eat. 'How did you and James leave it?'

It's easier like this, both wiping the worktops and putting away dishes, hoovering up dropped rice and flaked pastry. I tell the whole story like James told me, like I told Judith. No more secrets.

'Jesus,' Dad says when I finish. 'Those poor people.'

The kitchen is almost finished. He pours us both wine, sits down at the table. 'It's some story. I can't imagine having to live with it.'

'Weirdly,' I pick my words, 'I didn't think you'd be like that about it. I thought you'd be . . .'

'Judgey?' he asks. My favourite word as a teenager.

I shrug, nod, smile. He's hit the nail on the head.

'I'm a historian, Ruby. I study the outcome of human nature, of what's been before. We can't judge people by our standards, by what we'd do out of context. Learning from history is all about context.'

'You don't think James was wrong?'

'Not as you tell it. I think he was trapped.'

'And Judith was trapped.'

He makes a rueful smile, it doesn't reach his eyes. 'And Mum was the one who had no say in any of it, despite playing the biggest part.'

'Do you think she'd like them?' I ask, although I know the answer.

'She'd like them very much indeed,' Dad says and he raises his glass to mine. The little 'ting' they make when they knock together tolls like the tiniest of bells.

Chapter Thirty-Two

JUDITH

I can see James's car parked ahead of mine despite being three streets away from Nick's house. There are only a few cars between us, I don't know why I didn't see it when I arrived.

'Judith, we have to talk,' he says as I take my keys out of my pocket. 'Properly.'

'I can't talk about it.' I can barely look at him. Meeting Nick with him has been tense and pressured. I'm sure Nick was as relieved as I was when we left.

James puts one hand on my shoulder and I shake it off. 'Please don't touch me.' I'd like to say more but my voice fails, swallowing so many words over lunch has caused a blockage – to un-stopper it here would be dangerous.

'I have to talk to you.'

'I get it. It all makes sense. But the end result will always be that you saved your mum and sister and you didn't save me – or her.' I open the car door. 'It's better for me to walk away. There are no winners.'

'I don't want to do this here . . .'

He has that way of making me turn around to face him – he always has had – of knowing the minimum number of words to catch me. I get into the car and reach out to shut the door.

James puts his physical bulk between the door and the car.

'Fuck off, James.' I will not be bullied.

'Don't make me do this here.' He has an envelope in his hand. The envelope is small and square, the back flap of it is open.

I've had too much James McConnell lately. I've had too much drama, too much shock. 'Leave me alone.'

I don't react quickly enough when he opens the back door, throws himself inside my car. 'No. You have to talk to me. I brought this to give to you but I couldn't do it at Nick's: it wasn't the right time. It arrived yesterday.'

He passes the envelope over my shoulder.

I can see straightaway that it's a photograph. On the back, in the pale copperplate people slightly older than me still write in, it says 'with love from Rose'.

I can see the front of the photograph without turning it over. I know it exactly. At least, I think I do – but my exact memory of scenes is not as accurate as Catherine's. The baby is just as I remember her. In the corner of my mind, where moments are stored, I hear Rose's husband's voice: 'My missus asked me to take a photograph of your baby.' As he speaks, I look down into my arms, and there she is.

The baby looks straight into the camera. Even in black and white, her eyes are already the oyster shell blue of James's. They reflect every beam of light in the room, refract it down and down through the depths of her. Her tiny mouth smiles that lopsided baby smile, one side not yet completely under control. Soft downy hair floats around her like a halo, each single hair perfectly focused in the camera's lens. This is exactly as I remember the picture.

What I have forgotten is the background. That the baby sits, propped up and her head protected, in my arms. I can see the floral pattern of my nightgown behind her, my hand running protectively along her blanket in the bottom of the shot and, at the edge of the picture, the profile of my face as I bend down to kiss her.

I haven't heard James open the door, move into the passenger seat, but he is there. He stretches his arms across and pulls me to him. And we sit there, crying like babies, the single picture of our daughter – while she was still our daughter – between us.

I couldn't have driven. It was come back with James or be marooned outside Nick's: go back inside and tell them that I'd need to stay, that the new grandma was moving in.

'We can be back at mine in forty-five minutes,' James had said. 'We'll come back for your car later.'

He had moved me, like an invalid, to his car and then checked the parking meter, made sure – ever practical – that my car could stay there.

His house is beautiful. It is an Edwardian red brick that sits a stone's throw from Paddington Old Cemetery. It has black iron railings and a tiny front garden, elegantly planted with sage greens, tall spikes of slate grey, lavender that has dried to the colour of Ruby's eyes.

'No one wanted to live here when we moved in,' he says. 'Just Jeannie and me in a street full of other immigrants.'

Inside is neat, fashionable. Everything looks very expensive and as if it was made for the space. The back wall of the house has been replaced by a wide conservatory that runs across the width of the house and opens on to a garden.

259

'It's silly just for me, isn't it? And the occasional Australian mob.' He is talking softly, gently, and he guides me to the sofa.

In the corner, above a bookcase, is a print of Catherine's painting: 'Artemis. Waking.' Jeannie's favourite, James had said that first day in my house.

I have never considered the title before. It is part of a series – all goddesses, all abstract. It is only now – in the incongruity of James and Jeannie's house, looking at the blooms of pinks and purples, the movement between textures that appears so effortless – it is only now that I see where it fits. Judith. Sleeping.

It's a message from Catherine delivered by Jeannie. My heart aches for both of them.

It takes Dougal a full minute to hear that anyone is in the house. When he does, he trots in and welcomes me, doesn't stop to wonder for one minute what I am doing here, in his master's house, on his mistress's furniture. I hug the dog tight, burying my face in his fur.

'My sister sent the picture down yesterday. She was careful, couriered it – and she's had an exact replica made. She found it in our mother's things.' James sits down beside me, strokes the dog's head. 'Eilidh has had it since my mother died. My ma didn't have many pictures, literally a handful. So Eilidh thought it must be one of the two of us, but she could never work out who. She knew not to throw it away though.'

'She kept it.'

He nods.

'I mean your mother.'

He nods that he meant that too.

'She kept the picture of her granddaughter, but she threw away my letters.'

'They wanted the best for us, our mammies,' James says. He slips his hand into mine, rests the two – interlinked – on his leg. 'They loved us and they wanted to protect us.'

I think about speaking, even open my mouth. James shakes his head lightly.

'When I turned up at your mother's door, I'd done six months in a violent jail. Six horrific months. I'd a shaved head with bald patches of ringworm on it.' His accent deepens with the past. 'I'd not eaten properly in months or had access to dental care. I must have looked like a huge filthy spider. 'N' th' ah opened mah geggy. Spoke like that, like a man who's been in a Glasgow jail for half a year. A criminal.'

My mother would have been scared of him. I know that. Her life revolved around the church committee and the Women's Institute. The focus of it was my dad's hard work and my bright future. We were her life.

'She probably thought I'd been through the worst,' I whisper. 'That the baby had been born and it was all over, as much as it ever could be.'

I am staring straight ahead, trying to put myself in my mother's pale-blue housecoat, her black leather driving shoes.

'We wouldn't have been able to get her back, you know,' I say. 'Together. That's not legally possible. It wasn't then, it isn't now. Adoption is the only law that binds in perpetuity.'

'So it was already over by the time I was released?'

Tears run down my cheeks. 'And you'd betrayed me anyway. You'd already betrayed me.'

He gets up, strides across the room. He leans his body against the fireplace wall, his hands either side of his head. He lifts one palm and smacks it down again in the same spot. I can hear his breath catching, stuttering through his throat.

James turns to face me. His blue eyes are burning, wild with anger, loss. His accent has gone again, he speaks in his most clipped voice, slowly, one word by one word.

'I did it for you.'

'When you walked into that filthy, low-lit kitchen, I wanted to grab you, squeeze the water out of you and protect you. I knew right then that you were The One. I never had to doubt it,' he says. 'You had red welts on your palms. Remember?' He unrolls his clenched fists, shows me the inside of his hand. 'Huge red marks across your hands where you'd carried that case. They were nearly bleeding but you never even thought of letting go, of letting Paddy carry it.'

James has moved to the sofa, not quite next to me. He taps his fingers against his cupped hand until I glare at him to stop. The noise is childlike, annoying.

'I could see the fire inside you, through that rain. I saw it smoulder through your slicked wet hair, your angry mouth curled up like a stone. You spoke to me, to the core of me. I knew there was a version of you right inside me, at my very heart we were the same.'

My lungs are tight. I can feel my heart thudding in my chest. Without making it obvious to James, I slip my fingers over my wrist, feel the blood racing over my bones, beneath my skin.

'And she saw it too. Polly. She saw it the second I did, the second that light switched on in me and I realised what I'd been missing. She saw what she'd been missing too – the tool to exercise absolute control.'

He leans forward, that familiar gesture of separating his fingers through his hair. White tufts sprout from between his fingers, the picture of benevolence: the fluff of every Father Christmas, every fairy-tale old man. 'Polly realised at the same time as I did, that I would do anything for you.'

'You betrayed us.' I move slightly along the sofa. I haven't got the strength left in my soul to get up, to walk out.

'I was already in. Special Branch already had me. But I had been doing my best to get away from it. I'd been misleading them, withholding facts. And it was working.

'I realised there was nothing I could do to make them let me go, so I tried to be less useful. To stand back and know less, so I had less to tell them.'

He sighs. Sits up straight, his hands flat on his legs. He is still. 'And then you came.'

He takes me back in time, reminds me of how we met, how we began to notice one another. He remembers – in searing detail – our first months, of accidentally touching my hand as I passed him cutlery, of waiting outside the library where I worked so he could pretend to be walking past, to come home with me in the grey sleet. He tells me that he never needed to wear a coat when he walked me back, that he couldn't feel the rain, that he only saw the blurred light on the silvered pavements.

When he talks about our moving on, our becoming a couple, he remembers every detail of the room, of our clothes. James says he cried afterwards, when I went to the bathroom. Not from the beauty of us, but from the guilt, from the weight of the thirty pieces of silver dragging down his heart.

'We were in so much more danger than we knew, Jude.' He turns slightly, takes hold of my hands in his.

I haven't the will left to shake mine free.

'Polly said they would let you go. You and Kay. She knew they had got everything from me that I was going to give, that I'd risk prison if I had to. That I couldn't go on as a grass.'

I remember Polly's face when she looked at me, how she'd let her fingers trace across the back of his hand and he'd jump, stung, when he saw me looking. Polly shoved me away, belittled me, whenever she could – and Jimmy never stopped her. I think how he used to come to bed and lie, staring at the ceiling, for hours without moving. That I knew he was awake because I could see the moon's round shape reflected in his dead eyes, that sometimes I imagined he was crying.

'You and Kay were each looking at three years. Six for Paddy and the others. They didn't believe that women could be as responsible for revolution as men.'

He squeezes my hands, his thumbs rubbing the bones of my palms.

'One morning, not long after you and I became a couple, Polly told me I had to come with her.' His thumbs stop moving, press against my palms. 'There was a black car waiting round the corner. They bundled me in and drove me to the Craigie Street Police Station.' James still says 'Po-lis', even now.

We all knew stories of Craigie Street, of how perfectly fit people came out of there limping and bruised at best, of how sometimes – if the police were feeling benevolent – they'd leave the station in an ambulance.

'They were putting together the first anti-terrorism squad. Polly was part of it, of the very beginning. And we were their prototype terrorists. They held me in an interview room, there were loads of suits, as well as uniforms. And they spread photos of you across the desk.

'Pictures of you leaving work, one with me. Crossing the road with your silly wee umbrella up above you like a sail.' He makes the shape of my arms and the umbrella.

'I thought it made me look grown up,' I whisper.

264

'And they'd watched us out at Faslane. They'd watched us handing out leaflets. Always you. All the pictures were of you.'

James gets up, stretches to his full height. He starts walking up and down the smooth wooden floor in front of me. 'And they promised me you'd do three years. They promised me that you'd do three hard years in prison, that you'd likely not even survive it.'

He drops to his knees in front of me, holds my knees with his huge hands.

'Those places were a horror. And if you'd made it, then what? How would you ever find me again, how would we put it behind us? They'd tell you how you'd got there and you'd hate me forever.'

He leans his head down towards me. 'I didn't know that you'd end up hating me anyway, that you sat in that hospital believing I'd let you go. So I did it, I signed a document that had your freedom on it, yours and Kay's, and I committed to doing whatever Polly asked of me. To leading a revolution that led you all right to them.'

He doesn't look up. James looks like he is praying, perhaps he is. The back of his neck is wispy with hair, two lines of muscle stand out either side of his spine.

'"*You don't know anything about him.*"' I am speaking very quietly. 'That's what Polly said to me in the dark, in the back of that van. "*You have no idea who he is.*" I didn't, did I?'

I put my hands either side of his head, raise his face towards me. 'I didn't know that you'd saved me.'

I think of all the years that I spent believing that he'd been unfaithful, that he had abandoned me in favour of Polly and her pre-Raphaelite beauty, the sparkling flint of her eyes, and her lips so blood red she must have bitten a cursed apple.

James screws his eyes closed. Refuses to look at me. 'A coward dies a thousand deaths, Jude. And a hero only one.' He presses his face against my knees. 'And even then, I didn't save you. I didn't save either of you.'

I stroke the hair back from his face, as if he is a child. 'I had three beautiful weeks with her, James. Twenty-three days of staring at her face. The most magical time of my life.'

He traps a cry in his throat and I hear the edges of the word 'No'. He is afraid to hear this.

'If she had been born in prison, I would have never even got to hold her.'

'You can't know that.' He is openly crying now, wretched sobs that boom from deep inside him, bass notes of distress too funda-mental to suppress.

I hold my hand still on the side of his head. His ear is below my thumb, his skull cradled in my hand. 'I was a social worker from 1968 onwards, James. I know that if she had been born in a prison hospital I would barely have got to hold her before she was taken away. I might have never seen her face.'

I turn his face towards me, make him look at me. 'You did it. You saved us.'

It is inevitable that I will wake wrapped in James. That it is a part of closing this episode, of saying goodbye to the past. Finishing as we began.

He sleeps quietly for such a large man, and the memory makes me smile – my tiny elfin painter snored like a train.

He has one arm underneath me, and the other covers me like a blanket. My back is spooned against his front and I pause, take in all the sensations of how different this is – of his large feet against mine, the hair on his chest that tickles my back.

'Are you awake?' I whisper. The morning is greeting us through a gap in the curtains. This is James's room, not their spare room. It is masculine and bare, the only clothes are folded neatly over the back of chairs, the wardrobe door shut without anything shoved in and poking from the edge of a door. There are paintings on almost every surface of the walls, but no ornaments or knick-knacks on top of the drawers, on the top shelf of the bookcase. I think if he did share this room – this bed – with Jeannie, he has hidden away the more painful memories.

He groans that he is half-awake, that he is conscious.

The night has taken its toll on both of us. Our emotions are fragile and frayed. And yet the dust of sadness, of lost opportunity, that has lived with me for five decades has settled. It is – somehow – calm. I had never realised that what I experienced could have been worse – that there was worse. There is no hierarchy of grief, of experience, but I am glad that my own bereavement came at the end of a short blissful time. I am glad there was sunshine.

'Are we taking Dougal?' I ask James once he admits to being fully awake.

'I think not. He'll be fine.'

I nod. 'Flowers though.'

'Definitely flowers.'

'This is a strange conversation to be having naked,' I say.

'At least we're not hiding anything,' James says and, despite all the sadness, all the heavy grief, we can smile.

Ruby told me how to find the grave. She asked if we'd like her to come with us: to facilitate an introduction, she said.

I thanked her for the offer, declined it, but I didn't remind her that her mother and I need no introduction – that we have known each other always.

We stand, James and I – hand in hand – reading the inscription on our daughter's grave. He squeezes my hand tight, and I return the gesture. Neither of us speaks.

I don't think we're praying. We are just being, listening to the birds behind us – a scatter of starlings angrily discussing the future of food, of when they should leave; the clipped chatter of a magpie. The grass around our feet is tidy and well-kept, and I bend down to take the white chrysanthemums – that have started to brown around the edges – out of the pot on the bottom of the headstone.

James and I brought autumn colours. We chose the flowers – together – from a florist near James's house, both hoping that the florist wouldn't ask us who they were for, that we wouldn't have to say those words. He didn't ask: he helped us to choose blue-grey thistles, papery orange physalis. He interspersed them with long blond grasses that bend gracefully in the light breeze, with gerberas in hot colours on green-wired stems.

'The flowers are perfect,' I say at last in the calm of the cemetery. 'They say *not quite an end*.' I swallow, lean on James's arm to get back up.

'I don't want this to be an end,' James says. 'Jude, I want this to be another beginning.'

It is two days since I left James at the cemetery. I have thought, long and hard, about what he said. I have considered it from every angle. The only thing I haven't done – can't do – is discuss it with him.

I've kept in contact with Ruby, swapped light text messages, talked about her dad's cooking, about – genuinely – what a nice man he is. But I've ignored James's calls.

We have wound the clock back as far as it needed to go. There is nothing to be gained now from starting again, from remodelling my entire self, my whole lifestyle, for the sake of a few years of . . . what?

These thoughts have gone round and round in my mind for forty-eight hours. I am in my sitting room, looking at the local dog rescue site. I've enjoyed my time with Dougal – he has been a welcome asset. I can't commit to a new dog, at my age, but there seem to be several old dogs who might be able to commit to me. I am in my running kit – I have neglected my fitness these last few days, Catherine would be cross with me. 'The day you stop is the day you can't do it any more,' she used to say – dragging me back out on to the streets after a cold or giving me a second pair of socks to wear if it was icy. As soon as my breakfast has gone down, I will pound the streets.

The doorbell goes and I wonder if I am expecting any parcels. I fight down an idea that it is James: I don't want to be rude to him, but I'm not ready to see him.

It isn't James, or the postman. It's Ruby. My heart leaps and my face smiles involuntarily. 'What a very welcome visitor,' I say. 'You must have left home so early.'

'It's fine,' she says and leans in for a hug. This hug is long and unaffected, totally natural. I hope she feels that too. 'I thought I'd have a day off. I've got some stuff to talk to you about and I wanted to find out how you got on with Mum.'

'Let me get changed. I can run tomorrow.'

'What size are your feet?' she asks, looking down at her own.

'Whopping great eights.'

She laughs. 'Oh, then I can blame you. Although I suspect James's are even bigger. My feet are the same size as my dad's. Can I borrow some trainers? Maybe a T-shirt?'

The idea makes me laugh out loud. 'I can't think of anything more perfect. Do you run?'

'No way,' she says. 'I haven't run since primary school – but how hard can it be?'

Chapter Thirty-Three

RUBY

It's fun at first, funny even. Pounding the streets with a seventy-five-year-old beside me, looking for all the world like someone out running with their grandmother – which is, of course, what I am – even if we don't call it that.

Judith runs so slowly I could keep up with her if I walked fast. When we set off down her road, an avenue of sweet cottages, each with their wide front gardens, painted gates, our pace is comically slow.

'Takes a few minutes,' Judith says. 'To untangle the muscles, put the creaks to bed.'

She drops her hands to waist height, shakes them out. She runs with her chin up, slightly in front of her chest and the rest of her body. She blows air out of her puffed-up cheeks. 'It's important to smile,' she says. 'Makes you relax.'

I am smiling like a mad thing. I never imagined this moment. We run past the end of her road, round the corner and on to a long, straight lane. I can see the sparkle of sun on sea at the end of it.

There is a slight pain building in my lungs and I cough to try and shift it.

'Are you all right?' asks Judith, not breaking her stride, not even breathless.

My armpits are uncomfortably damp and I can feel mascara sliding down below my eyes. 'I'm fine, just a bit . . . I didn't realise "5k" was quite this far.'

She looks at me – grins – her teeth white in a face that hasn't coloured up, isn't even sweating. 'That postbox is the one-kilometre mark.'

We are nowhere near the postbox.

'But we've been running for ages.'

'Eight minutes,' she says. 'I always get to the postbox bang on nine and a half minutes in.' She looks at me. 'I have an app,' she says like she invented it.

We pass the postbox. Judith asks me twice if I want to stop and I pant that no, I'm absolutely fine and loving this shared experience on a bright warm day. We get on to the promenade and I spot my first bench. 'I do need to stop, Judith. I do. Just five minutes and I can start again.' My heart is hammering and my breakfast is very close to reappearing. I hang my head down between my knees and try to stop feeling so sick.

'There's a tap a bit further along, if you need a drink of water.' Judith points down the length of the long concrete prom.

'This is very similar to somewhere I used to go with my granny when I was small,' I say. 'With my mum's mum.' It takes a millisecond to realise what I've said. Luckily I can't go any redder. 'Shit, I'm sorry.'

'Don't be. Your granny was your mum's mum. I gave birth to your mum. All these things can be true. You and I are, whatever we are, whatever we want to become in time. It doesn't change anything that went before.'

We stare out at the sea. It's the kind of blue that you think is tropical, if you've never seen anything tropical. I think of the adventures my family went on when I was small, before I demanded Wi-Fi, and other human children, before I would only go places where I could shake off my parents. I'd so travel with my mum now, we'd have a laugh. I resolve to take a trip with my dad; after a moment or two, the romance wears off and I think that perhaps we'll start with a day in Brighton or a trip to Chinatown for lunch.

'It'll probably be full of lead, the beach tap,' she says, 'but short-term use shouldn't harm you much.'

My throat is so tight from the running, so parched by gasping for breath, that I nod.

Judith and I walk down to the tap and I splash my face with water, suck some in. It tastes of fish.

'Can we just walk for a bit?' Being outpaced by a septuagenarian is even worse than the ritual humiliation of school PE. 'And chat.'

'Nothing would give me greater pleasure,' says Judith and for a few minutes we stroll in silence, while the blood returns to my feet and the pain in my lungs fades.

'Have you heard from James?' I put on my most nonchalant voice, but she still flinches. James called me yesterday, said he couldn't get hold of Judith, that she was still ignoring him.

'You know you've got your phone set to alert the sender when you read a text?' I say when she doesn't answer me either. 'So he does know you're ignoring him.'

'Did he tell you . . .'

'He squared the circle,' I say. 'I know what happened. I'm so sorry for all of you.'

We reach another bench and I sit down, pat the wooden slats for Judith to sit beside me. 'I've decided on my dissertation subject, cleared it with my supervisor.'

'That's wonderful.' She's genuinely pleased.

'And after that, when it's all in and marked and finished, I'm going to get a job in a florist. I'm going to train up, learn everything I need – about house plants too – and then one day, I'm going to open my own shop. It's what I want to do with my life.'

The smile that breaks across Judith's face is real and I will bathe in its warmth. It will be slightly harder to have the same conversation with my dad. Maybe I'll make sure Judith is there when I do.

'What a wonderful idea.' She puts her hands beside her on the bench. I look at our matching knees, the giant kneecaps almost square and definitely identical. Hers have more scars than mine, more rough pink patches, but our bones are the same.

'James wants to try again, doesn't he?' I smile. I'd be a bit more graphic with my friends. 'He told me that he's in love with you, that it hadn't ever really died and now it's . . . He called it a "wildfire".'

'He's a silly old sod,' says Judith, but she smiles. 'He has the best of intentions.'

A fat gull worries at a chip on the ground in front of us, his yellow beak bright against the grey of his head and body, of the tarmac path.

Judith turns towards me. Her face is suddenly serious, the wrinkles deepen and darken, and it makes her look old. 'I can't go through it again. I can't change my whole self to be with him.'

'I don't see why—'

'Ruby, I'm a gay woman. A lesbian.'

I don't get it, she's made no secret of her sexuality, why would she.

'I'm a gay woman who lived with her partner – with the love of her life – for over fifty years. I can't suddenly jump ship and be straight or bisexual. Nor do I want to.'

A jet ski blares across the water in front of us, far too close to swimmers. People on the beach shout at him, the plume of water behind the ski says that he didn't hear them.

'Ruby, I can't have a relationship – not like that – with James.'

'Why?'

'I'm gay. My friends are gay, my clothes are gay.' She points down at her Lycra shorts, her trainers. 'Christ alive, even the paintings in my house are gay.'

That makes me laugh. 'And you're invested in that?'

'It's who I am, it's how I've spent the last fifty-something years.'

She leans back on the bench, stretches out her legs – points her gay trainers towards the sea.

'I have those trainers,' I say. 'And I'm not gay.' It's a lie – about the trainers – I wouldn't be seen dead in them, and nor would any of my gay friends. 'Are you trying to tell me that because you and Catherine were married, as it were' – I add the last bit so she doesn't jump down my throat about there not being such a thing as equal marriage when they were young – 'that you can't have a relationship with a man?'

She looks at the floor, flexes her feet. 'Yes.'

'Even though you and James clearly were a thing before or I wouldn't be here?'

'Mm-hmm.'

I wrestle my phone out of my bra: there are no pockets in Judith's shorts that I'm wearing, and I wasn't leaving it behind. I've been looking at this video over the last couple of days.

'Watch this,' I say to her.

She looks puzzled at first. It's a video of a city centre, the height of summer, hundreds of people milling about in no particular direction.

I can see in her face when she realises who she is looking at. She and James cut through the people: she is limping and he is holding her hand.

'I didn't want to use a walking stick,' she says, mostly to herself.

'I filmed you,' I say. 'Because I wanted to remember the first time I saw you both.'

Judith and James walk towards the camera. I can see exactly why I thought they were a couple: they look well together. They look easy.

At the bottom of the steps, James turns to her, takes both her hands in his, stares into her eyes. She touches the screen with her finger.

'I remember the flutter of adrenalin when I saw you look at each other,' I say. 'Like there was no one else in the street.'

Her voice is quiet. 'He said he'd fight for me, that he was on my side no matter what happened next.'

In the video, James lets go of one of Judith's hands, leads her on to the steps, up to meet me – and I stopped filming in case they saw me.

'Did you see the look on his face?' I ask her.

'I did,' she says and shrugs like a petulant teen.

'And did you see the look on yours?' That shuts her up: she's thinking of the evidence she's just seen, of her gazing up at James like she doesn't ever want to look away.

I stuff my phone back down my bra. 'Shall we try and run some more?' I don't want to: my lungs don't want to and my feet don't want to – Judith's old-lady trainers are giving me blisters – but she looks so sad.

'I'm ready.' She smiles again, waits for me as I get myself upright, apologise to my poor body that hasn't suffered this kind of horror since school.

Again, that slow, slow running. Like I filmed us then turned the speed down. But this time it's a bit easier, especially as we're headed home instead of into the wild blue yonder.

'Hi!' The hottest guy I've ever seen in shorts jogs past us. He looks back over his shoulder and flashes Judith an enormous grin.

'Do you know him?' I ask, my eyes following his firm, tanned legs down the promenade.

'No, he's just a runner.'

'He's a crazy hot runner.'

'Was he? I didn't notice.' But even I can tell she's joking.

He jogs into the distance ahead of us. A glorious speck on the horizon. 'Why did he say hello to you? If you don't know him . . .'

'Because he's a runner.' She smiles. 'And so am I. We're a team.' She shakes her arms out a little. 'And now so are you.'

'So . . .' I catch my breath, try to find enough puff to speak. 'I'm going to find the man of my dreams by becoming a runner.'

'Stick with me, kid. They all smile at me: I'm cute.' Judith pats her short hair, pretends to shake it loose over her shoulders. 'I'm old, and I'm jogging. Every good-looking young man that passes me thinks I'm adorable. Maybe one day they'll stop and ask who my friend is.'

'So, we've sorted my lack of boyfriend. But that still leaves you – and James.' I know she doesn't like it, but I promised him I'd try.

'And I told you how that goes.'

I swear she speeds up. I put on a spurt of energy, much to the distress of my lungs. 'You know that that's not who we are nowadays? Who people are?' I watch our feet hit the ground in rhythm: heel first, Judith told me, come off on the toe. Use your natural springboard.

'Sorry?'

I've confused her. I stop running for a moment – to the eternal gratitude of my heart – and look at her. We are standing opposite each other on the pavement: same height, same build, same size feet. The consequence of three generations.

'We don't tie our colours to the mast any more. People, I mean.'

She doesn't answer, maybe she doesn't agree.

'Judith, at the risk of straightsplaining, sexuality isn't a hill we die on – in my generation.' I'm embarrassed talking about her sex life but I stare right at her, pretend I don't feel awkward. I pretend I am my mum, giving me one of her talks on how not to care what the other girls say. 'We've moved on. For us it's about who they are, not the body they wear.'

'I'm too old. I'm not going through all of this again.' She looks up at the clear blue sky as if someone will send her an answer, but I'm not giving up.

'You can love who you want, Judith. Even if they're not the same gender as the last person you loved. We're allowed.'

She mumbles: they're not even real words – just muttered sounds, excuses for why she can't try. .

I put my hand out, nip a dark-green leaf from the privet hedge next to me on this suburban road. I break it in half with my fingernail. 'Do you know what my mum used to tell me when I was being a bolshy teenager?'

She looks up because I mentioned my mum.

'She said we have a debt to history. That other women's experience paved the way for our choices and it's our duty to take all the opportunities we're given. To respect their battles.'

She opens her mouth to speak but I cut her off. It's time for her to listen to me, to what I know. 'You are that history, Judith – you and all the other women who had no choice. My freedom has been paid for by all the things that happened to you and the women who went before you.' I need her to believe me, to give herself a second chance. 'My mum would say that you paid for yourself, Judith. And now you can do anything you want.'

There's a single tear running down her soft, creased skin. I want to reach up with my finger and rub it away, but I don't.

Judith could be my mum standing there with her hands on her hips, her jaw set strong.

'Well?' I ask her. 'What do you think?'

'I think your granny raised her well,' she says.

Chapter Thirty-Four

JUDITH

The knock at my door is the sort that an urgent parcel-delivery man does. The one where they have to make you hear them because they have thirty seconds till the next drop-off or they won't get paid.

I wonder all the way to the door what I've ordered, what someone might have sent me.

'There is a bell,' I say to James, on the doorstep. 'That civilised people use.'

'Why are you ignoring me?' He steps inside as he speaks, knowing full well that his bulk will make him difficult to get rid of. 'I've rung and rung. I must have sent twenty texts.'

I don't want to admit I'm ignoring him: it sounds childish. I turned the notifications off on my phone after Ruby told me about them, so now he doesn't know whether a text is delivered or not. But it wouldn't take a rocket scientist to work it out.

'Dougal sends his apologies. He's feeling old and creaky and he thought the journey might be a bit too much for him today.'

'That makes it sound as if I invited you.' I walk away from him and down the hall. I know that's a lot easier than trying to throw him out. 'Also, Dougal has an open invite. He' – I stress the word – 'can turn up any time.'

I go through to the kitchen and I know that he's behind me. 'I'm having some soup. Do you want some?' I wasn't going to eat for a while yet but I don't want to stand opposite James in a show-down, hands on our hips like gunslingers. I want to pretend that I'm in the middle of something, that I'm far too busy to look at him.

'Thanks. That would be great. Can I help?'

That's the last thing I want. 'No. Not really. You can go and wait in the garden or' – I gesture behind me – 'you can sit on that stool in the corner.'

He chooses the stool.

I snap open the Tupperware, drop the soup into a pan. I made it from tomatoes I grew in my own garden. As it warms, the colour comes to life, and the fading summer revives.

I slice bread as if it were the most intricate of tasks, as though I can't look up for fear of disaster, of losing a finger. When I've cut four slices, I take an age to pick up each crumb, clean the board.

'How have you been?' he asks.

'Fine.' I haven't been fine. I've been trying to roll up the past and stuff it back into a box it no longer fits in. That takes up all my energy, sucks all refreshment from my sleep. 'There's a lot to think about.'

James stretches his legs out, balancing on his heels. He's wearing plain black trainers with three white stripes. His long legs are bare and brown and his linen shorts are neat, ironed.

'There's a lot to talk about,' he says. 'Thinking about it is all I've been doing. You too, I'm sure.'

I turn round. I am holding a wooden spoon, its end pale red with soup. 'I'm exhausted James. I'm totally done.' Soup drips on to the floor and I tut. 'Let's just talk about soup.'

We both reach for the roll of kitchen towel at the same time. I acquiesce, let James clear up the blood-red drops on the white floor.

'I'm not done, I'm just starting,' he says. He pushes the pedal of the bin and throws away the paper towel. 'I've woken up from the longest sleep and I find myself here, with you, and looking at another chance. Another life.'

'We don't have another chance, James. I don't know what you and Ruby have decided between you, but it's not for me. I can't do it.'

He doesn't speak. Opens the cutlery drawer, takes out two spoons, two knives, like he lives here.

The soup burps a bubbling geyser on the stove. We both jump.

'You can't come round here pretending we're a thing. We've slept together twice.' I take two bowls from the cupboard, put them on to the work surface with a bang.

'With respect,' James says, 'we have slept together considerably more times than that.'

I glare at him.

'Sometimes several times a night.'

'That was an extremely long time ago.' He has made me laugh, but I keep that to myself. I take the soup across to the kitchen table, keep my back to him.

'Judith?' When I turn round, James is sitting at the kitchen table looking at something tiny he holds between his finger and thumb.

I put the bowls down in a rush, a tide mark of red sloops up the sides of them. 'No, James. Don't do that.'

'We have a grandchild together, Judith. I want to grandparent with you. I never stopped loving you – not in the conventional sense. And I don't believe you ever got over me. Not really.'

I look at the ring he's holding. It isn't ostentatious or shiny. The band is dull gunmetal grey; I presume it's silver under its history.

282

The stone is the blue of James's eyes, that deep pool water, diluted by light from the sun.

'I wondered whether it should be a ruby,' he says. 'But this is, almost exactly, what I got from the Barras. The ring I gave Paddy to look after.'

'I'll never marry you.' I feel sick with panic. 'Whatever happens between us, I'll never marry you.'

'This isn't that sort of ring.' James puts it into my open palm. 'It's not fancy – it's certainly not expensive. It's just a ring, as close to the one I bought you – once upon a time – as I could find. It doesn't have to mean anything. It's just a gift.'

I sit down. The chair moves on the tiled floor and it covers the noise of my sigh.

He holds the palm of my hand in his, both turned upwards, and his large thumb across the centre of mine. His thumbnail is as big as the ring.

'It might fit here.' He takes the ring, wriggles it on to the ring finger of my wrong hand. 'What about that? It's different to the one I originally wanted you to wear and on a different finger. And that marks the fact we're different people now.'

'I wanted to marry Catherine, desperately. But I couldn't. And so, whatever happens, I couldn't ever marry you.' He's not leaving me room to be angry, to throw things at him – insults, rings, soup.

'And I don't think Jeannie would be particularly happy to be called my "first wife",' he says and smiles. 'But plenty of people are happy without being married.'

He starts to eat as if nothing has happened, as if everything is normal. He looks up at me as his lips suck soup from the spoon, dares me – with twinkling eyes – to speak.

I give in: ignore him. As I butter my bread, the ring sparkles in the light of a fading summer.

'What if you die?' It comes out so loud but I can't control my voice. 'What if you die and I am alone? Or I die and you have to go through it all again? We're too old.'

James springs from his chair and covers the two steps between us in one stride. He puts his hand flat against my sternum. The bottom of his palm over my heart. 'Judith. Stop being so afraid of your heart breaking that you can't feel it working. Living hurts. Taking risks hurts. But I promise it's worth it.'

I have cried more since I found James – since he found me – than for five decades. Back then the tears dried up, staunched themselves inside me quite quickly. I realised only weeks after I'd left her that it was impossible to live with that level of grief, that I had to make it part of me or carry its bulk around awkwardly – first in one hand, then the other, forever shifting to manage its weight.

James puts his arms around me, smothers that grief against his expensive shirt. I feel the dampness that my eyes and nose leave on it, pressed against my face.

'We're so far away from finished,' he says. 'We need to start a family – to fit Ruby in with us, with everyone else in our lives. And we're going to make it work.'

'I've got plans, James.' I wriggle my hand up between my chest and his, wipe my nose. 'I've decided what I'm doing next, and it doesn't have you in it. I have a project.'

'Everything is easier with someone beside you.'

I picture myself as a social worker, coming home some days and slamming my briefcase against the wall in the hallway: Catherine waiting, arms outstretched. I would curl around her and paint would clot on to the suit I'd worn to court, bloom fresh despite my losses, my failures.

I fit against James in the same proportions that Catherine fitted against me. I release myself, take his hand and walk through to my bedroom.

He stands with his hands at his sides, his eyes wide and staring straight ahead. 'It's perfect,' he whispers. 'It's perfectly you.'

I can only nod as he takes the painting in, steps closer to it to trace the curves of my hips, the defined edge of my jaw.

'This is the you I fell in love with.' He turns to me. 'This is the you I see in front of me, the you our granddaughter loves so much.'

I sit on the edge of the bed, gesture for him to sit beside me. I lie back, my legs bent at a right angle and my feet almost on the floor. I used to lie on my bed like this as a teenager, feeling myself stretch out and wondering what I would become. Whatever that might have been, I am it now. I am seventy-five years old: I am the finished article.

'I'm going to sell it.' I have made my mind up.

'Really?' James looks surprised. He is trying not to say more, trying to stop himself from saying that I shouldn't, from telling me what to do. He manages it well.

'I have something I want to do. A project. And this will finance it – for a long time, I should imagine.'

James flops back beside me. We stare at the ceiling and he moves his hand across to mine. 'Good for you.'

I smile at him, satisfied by his confidence.

'You know there are people you can get to copy paintings?' he says. 'Incredibly talented artists who can reproduce every brush stroke while you sell the real thing.'

'Nah.' I sound like Ruby. 'The magic of this painting isn't in what we can see. The magic is deeper than that. It's done its thing.'

James touches the ring on my finger, turns it round and round, and we lie there for a while, side by side.

The studio lights are bright. This kind of television isn't the same experience as having nice young people with cameras bundling into

Catherine's shop, but the intention is exactly the same. We're going to drum up some worldwide interest for Catherine's final gift to me. Her final piece of repurposing.

This is the kind of studio I used to visit back when Catherine did arts shows, interviews: the sort with a breeze-block-walled green room, and fruit bowls and wine on wet tables.

When Catherine did her first chat show, in the early eighties, I was madly excited about the other guests, about who I might meet in the green room. But I learnt really quickly that the stars are in a rush, and the more famous someone is the less time they spend on these uncomfortable vinyl sofas with the lingering smell of cigarette smoke in the corridors.

James set all this up, along with a number of newspaper interviews later on. He has confidence in it.

'We're not live,' the female presenter says, 'which takes the pressure off.'

Her glossy-haired co-host speaks from the other side of her – they sit together on one sofa, and I'm on the other, opposite. 'But we try and steam through as if we are. It keeps the studio manager happy.'

'Too right,' the woman with the clipboard shouts from behind the lights.

James is out there with her somewhere, but everyone is a silhouette in the half-dark, only the outlines of bodies and absurdly large headphones. 'Cans,' James had said as he put his on.

Between the two sofas, between the hosts and me, is Catherine's painting. It's been carefully lit, as it would be in a gallery, and radiance shines from it. It's hard to believe that this vividness hid in a cupboard for decades. This bright young woman feels as if she will stretch and rise and walk towards her life at any moment. And so she will.

'Judith Franklin,' the female host says. 'You have an extraordinary claim to fame, don't you?'

I smile and nod. I know that this is my cue: I was given a loose script in the green room and James went through it with me a couple of times.

'You'll be fine, darling,' he said, squeezing my leg. 'You'll be better than fine, you'll be great.' He kissed my cheek despite the thickness of the studio make-up, wiped the powder off his lips afterwards.

'Judith,' the male presenter says. He's quite thickset and his face rumples up when he smiles. 'You were the model for a lost Catherine Rolf painting. It's from what year, Judith?'

'From 1969,' I say and try to keep my voice steady. I think about how Catherine taught me to run – that if you smile your face will automatically relax, your breathing will slow. I make the most of it, in, out. 'We lived together in a flat in south London.'

'Many of us have prints of Catherine Rolf paintings.' The woman has mastered the art of smiling and talking at the same time. 'I actually have one in my bedroom. But the originals are in art galleries around the world.'

She talks about where I kept the painting.

He asks me questions about the change of style, the paint she used, and then he asks me why this is the only figurative painting Catherine ever did.

'Maybe because I hated it so much?' I say.

'And this painting is for sale now, isn't it? It's going up for auction at Sotheby's next week and is expected to fetch over a million pounds.'

'It is,' I say, and swallow as quietly as I can.

'And with the money, you're setting up a foundation? A club for girls?'

That wasn't what she was supposed to say, the presenter has moved from the script. James warned me that she might, but I've let myself relax – they've stuck to the letter until now.

I shake my head. 'It's not for girls,' I say. 'It's for women. Women of all ages, all identities, to come together. But it's also open to anyone else willing to talk and listen.'

'And learn to run? I believe the running is very important?' It's the male co-host. I can see the sweat rolling into the neck of his shirt.

He touches his tie.

'Running was important to Catherine. To her mental health. No one denies the effect of exercise on mood, but this is more than that – this is a safe space to talk about what bothers you and listen to someone else's experience of it. Someone older than you, or decades younger. The running club aspect is what will draw us all together, but you're every bit as welcome if you want to sit and drink coffee with us.'

'And it's called?' They know what it's called, but I'm supposed to announce it.

The lights are hot, I can feel them on my scalp. It makes my skin prickle. 'The project is called Walk Run Talk. It's the last word that's the most important.'

'Thank you, Judith.' The female presenter looks away from me, smiles into a camera on the other side of the dais.

'So many women live with secrets.' I say it loudly into the darkness of the studio.

The two presenters look back towards me. They are clearly shocked. The woman goes to speak, to stop me.

'We live with secrets and we live with the results of them, and those things roll down through generations. If women know that they are not alone, that other people have carried the same burden and survived, it will make everything different. If they know that

288

their problems are not new, that they happened to their mothers and their grandmothers too.'

'Judith,' says the female presenter, stretching out one hand towards me. 'The internet is full of places to talk. There are forums and support groups for everything you could imagine. We have women's groups, knitting clubs. How is what you're doing new?'

I look over at her and then remember, look back to face the camera directly. 'This is new because it brings generations of women together. Walk Run Talk asks older women to share their years of lived experience, and to use it to support younger women. And we encourage young women to share their feelings with the older generation. It is never too late to heal if you have the right tools, the right support.'

And I realise that I'm going to say it: that I'm going to announce her birth to millions of people, live on TV. My baby never had the typed newspaper entry that she should have had. I didn't receive telegrams of congratulations on the occasion of her birth, or cards that I keep in a yellowing box.

'When I was nineteen years old, I had a baby. I wasn't married. I was allowed to keep her for twenty-three days, and then she was taken from me and adopted. I had nowhere to turn. No one to help me. I thought I was the only person in the world to go through that experience.'

There is silence in the hazy dark in front of me.

'There were no demonstrations, no marches, no letters to MPs. Just hundreds of thousands of women thinking they were the only one.

'So many women – young and old – still go through things today that make them think they're the only one experiencing that particular pain, that exact suffering – whatever it may be. We are going to show them that they're not alone. We are going to reclaim those streets, run through them, and raise our voices for each other.'

I stop before I cry. Take a deep breath in. In the darkness, clapping starts – I know it's James. Other people join slowly at first, tentative, and then louder. The whole studio is whistles and cheers and clapping.

The male presenter is wiping tears from his eyes. The woman is standing up in her tight red suit, her hands above her head – clapping and clapping and clapping.

'That's a wrap,' says someone from the studio floor and I can breathe out again.

Chapter Thirty-Five

RUBY

I've never been to Scotland before. Which is crazy, given that I've been to mainland China.

It feels strange to be in James's car – without him. Like trespassing or reading someone's texts. Judith says she drives it because it's greener than the one she used to have – but as we change each track on the playlist, or adjust the heating and air con by the individual degree, we both know it's also a far nicer ride.

'What you see when you cross the border is up to Scotland,' says Judith. 'You'll either be welcomed with a vista that lasts to the ends of the sky, with huge curled hills in the back of it. Or rain so fine it doesn't have drops and visibility of about ten feet.'

It welcomes us all right. Nothing changes on the motorway when we first see the big metal sign that marks the border but soon the road changes, and the countryside changes, and everything widens into blue and green and vivid purple.

'He'd love this,' I say, leaning forward to be part of the rugged moors, the colours. Boulders of grey stick up here and there like frozen elephants, like lumps of history dropped in a field.

Judith nods. 'I'm over that everyday grief, the sort that catches you every time you come into a room, wake up in the morning. But then there are things like this and it starts all over again.' She smiles. 'I never thought I'd get that used to him, to having him around. He'd only been living with me for a year but it feels like he'd always been there.'

It makes me teary. My eyes fill up – but in the best way, in the way that says it was unconditional love: that feeling that tells you it was the real deal on both sides. It took me a while to get to that point with my mum – guilt clouded everything, the same way that the pink and purple heather clouds in these lowlands before me. Literally the landscapes of my forefathers.

'Losing him has helped me accept the other stuff, put it in perspective.' I am comfortable talking like this to Judith. We don't have secrets: we vowed to base our friendship on that. 'It's bitter-sweet, isn't it.'

We drive along in silence, thinking of his soft paws, the way he would nudge you with his nose if he wanted your half of the sofa. 'I never loved a dog before,' Judith says. 'I didn't realise how good it is for your soul.'

I nod. 'Me too. And I don't think I've ever cried so much in my whole life.'

'A prince amongst hounds, Rubes,' James had said when he called me to say Dougal had gone: to tell me they'd been to the vet's for the last time and that he'd left 'the old boy' there. 'Not all of Dougal, though,' he'd said, and I could hear the crack in his voice. 'Just his body.'

And that made me feel differently about Mum. About how what I've lost is her body, I haven't lost her. I carry her in my heart like Judith did for all those years.

James can't come to Scotland with us: he says it's because he's looking after the new dog but Judith says it's more than that, that this part of their story is too painful for him to return to. 'Maybe it's shame,' she said. 'Maybe it's sadness. But we need to leave him to it, whichever it is.'

The new dog is a rescue so she has to stay in their house until she knows she belongs there – that Judith and James are her family now and they will never leave her. She doesn't know how lucky she is, how much love there is to spare.

'I've never had a dog that wasn't yellow,' James told me when Judith brought the new dog home. 'And I've never had a dog that wasn't called Dougal.' He held the new dog up to me on FaceTime: one of those dogs that's so ugly, they tip over the other side into beautiful. Her fur is muddy brown in places, off-white in others, and it all sticks up and out like a loo brush. Her tail is a pink corkscrew covered in tufty white hair that makes her look like a pig. 'This is Dougal the fifth,' James said, kissing her ears. 'And the first girl.'

It's still light when Judith and I get to Glasgow, so we go to the squat before we check into our hotel. The road is wide and clean, and the houses along it are red brick at first, long, low blocks of flats. The stairwells are beautifully tiled and the windows edged in stone detail.

'I love those buildings.' I point out of the car window.

'They're very different today.' Judith is leaning forward slightly over the steering wheel, trying to work out where we are. 'Those are the tenement blocks – life in them was very difficult. I'll take you to the museum tomorrow and show you. Whole floors shared one lavatory, all the flats. The water froze in the winter. It was a hard life.'

'They're beautiful now.'

'And they cost a fortune,' Judith says. 'But they were the last resort when we were here.' She sighs and the car fills with wishes.

I turn away from the neat red-brick flats. 'Are you sure you want to do this?'

Judith nods. She turns the indicator on and pulls in to the left of the road. 'We're here. It looks very different, but it's definitely here.'

There is a small green surrounded by a painted iron fence. Inside it are a couple of benches, a children's play area with a slide and two swings. Next to that is a row of modern houses, small and neat.

'Where is it?' I ask.

Judith purses her lips, gets out of the car. Despite the glorious weather on the way here, the air is colder than I'd expected and I reach back into the car for my jumper. We walk uphill to the end of the road, then Judith turns and looks back.

'Imagine this lined with huge Edwardian houses – like big, tall versions of your dad's. Big enough to have cellars and servants' quarters in the top.'

'Where the new houses are?'

'All the way up the hill,' she says. 'And along there' – she points to the bottom of the road where another wider one intersects it – 'there were abandoned tram tracks: wires hanging down and tiny smashed-in traffic lights. I used to be afraid the wires would still be live when I walked past in the rain.'

Her face is soft: she is years away. But she doesn't look sad.

'Do you wish it was still here?' I ask her.

'No. No, I don't.' She smiles at me and her silver earrings catch the sun: they are tiny little feathers. 'It's all over now. All behind us. I wanted to stand here, on this road, and watch some old ghosts go by – but that's it.' She raises one arm. 'I wanted to wave them on their way.'

I join in. There's no one around, although I don't think I'd care if there were. Judith tells me stories of where she worked, of the songs they sang in the squat at night, of the slogans on the leaflets she handed to people who would take them.

And my grandmother and I stand in the street waving goodbye to the past.

This morning, the Glasgow Walk Run Talk group are taking over the city park – this is the event that brought Judith and me here, although we would have come sooner or later, settled the story.

Judith and I meet in the breakfast room.

'Look at you all raring to go,' she says as I kiss her soft cheek.

I have my own running kit now – trainers much nicer than the ones Judith first lent me. I started running properly after the horror realisation that not only could this grandmother outrun me, but Granny Li's non-stop fitness classes probably meant that she could too.

Dragging myself out through the first months of winter was the worst bit, and then I joined a Walk Run Talk group that starting meeting not far from Mum's cemetery. I ran my first 10k early this year and I know that, in this bizarre new me that I'd never antici-pated, my next stop will be a half-marathon. The biggest change is in my friends: twice a week I meet up with people I would never have got to know before. Women of all ages, all backgrounds. I don't believe there's a question I could ask that someone in that bunch wouldn't have the answer to – or know where to find it at least. It makes me feel protected. Protected and proud.

Judith isn't even the oldest here. There are so many people I can't count them and everyone is chattering, smiling. It's a beautiful September day with no need for coats or jackets.

We're in the park we drove by last night, a vast glittering hot-house at its centre – the biggest I've ever seen. I can't wait to see the huge green leaves that press against the windows up close.

'It's called the People's Palace,' Judith tells me. 'That name always meant so much to me.'

To one side of the towering glass is a banner strung across the path. 'Glasgow Walk Run Talk' it says in huge red letters and I take photo after photo of Judith standing underneath it.

The organisers want Judith in the front row. 'I'd far rather be in the middle somewhere,' she says. 'This isn't about me.'

I squeeze her hand. 'It kind of is.'

A woman beside us holds a microphone. 'Three, two, one . . .' she says and the crowd erupts in whoops and shouts and whistles.

We start to run. I have to slow down now to stay with Judith – I don't know why I'm so smug about that, I am twenty-three and she is seventy-six – but we make sure we're side by side.

I turn round. Behind us, hundreds of women surge: singing, shouting, talking. They are bright colours and loud noises, they are flushed cheeks in every skin tone, their feet march forward, unstoppable.

Happy tears sting in my nose as I run and I squeeze Judith's hand tightly.

Together we are powerful.

Chapter Thirty-Six

JUDITH

There are many places I could go to show Ruby where I belong within the story. I could have started at my parents' house, knocked on the door and asked the current owners if I could crawl into their under-stairs cupboard, sit there in the dark imagining the custard-cream biscuits and the lidded buckets. I'm sure they'd be shocked to know that the space where they keep old tennis racquets, piles of shoes, was a nuclear bunker for a little family who were happy in that house, once upon a time.

There is nothing to be gained by standing on the edge of that leafy park in Liverpool, looking for my memories around the boating pond. I will feel no better from staring through the bars of the big gates outside the home and picturing myself inside, sad and small.

Glasgow is different. We had such hope when we lived in that house – we were young people who thought we could change the world. And we did, in our own tiny way.

Ruby has done her best to put the group back together. She is using us, and everything that happened to us, for her dissertation:

writing our story, telling our truth, trying to explain what we meant to do, what we thought would happen.

Kay was the easiest to find. Kay became a politician, a member of parliament. She really did it, followed the dream to reality and spent her whole career standing up for the underdog, putting things right. Ruby and I will meet her for lunch tomorrow.

Kay and I will be two old ladies talking on the shores of Loch Lomond, throwing pebbles into the still glass of the water and watching the ripples widen, concentric circles that will run on and on.

Dougie and Angus eluded Ruby's sleuthing skills: they may well both have died, although she has dived into archives and brought both men into the present day with us. Ruby has copied piece after piece of faded newspaper: cuttings and trimmings of everything we did – the times we were arrested, the times the boys went to prison: a week here, six days there. It was a very different time.

As for Polly Wright, that wasn't her real name. Ruby could probably find out who she was if she tried hard enough, but there's no need. Polly was a victim of this in her own way: doing everything she could to be the best in a profession that was stacked so heavily against women – whatever it took. Maybe Polly thinks about it every day too, in this brave new world.

Ruby has talked a great deal with Paddy, on the days when he is bright and lucid. His knowledge of the peace movement is encyclopaedic, even now. She has hopes that he and James can find their own peace, whatever that might turn out to be. Time will tell.

The run has been a special joy – and to be here with Ruby is extraordinary – but the place I really wanted to go, the place I needed to see to end the story, was Faslane itself. What was a slippery field when we knew it is a state-of-the-art nuclear submarine base now – but there has been a peace camp here since we left. Year after year, people have kept up our fight, demonstrated for what they believed was in everyone's best interests. They risked the cold, the mud, the fierce Scottish winters, to stay here – dwarfed by the sides of the glen, awed by its silent beauty, holding up against the forces of the world.

Ruby and I park the car beside the river – at least a mile away from the fence of the naval base – and we walk together towards the camp. The hills are still and sweeping. It is only if you stare that you see hares dashing for the cover of the brush, hawks hovering above, their wings vibrating on an empty sky.

There is a fire burning somewhere up ahead, and songs of peace float upwards in its wisps of smoke until they are too pale to be seen or heard in the green hills.

I am reminded of what I have always known: that it isn't hope that moves mountains – mends hearts – it is unity.

AUTHOR'S NOTE

I was born in one of the 252 unmarried mothers' homes that existed in England and Wales during the fifties and sixties. A staggering half a million British women lost their babies to adoption over those two decades.

When I started the journey to find out about my birth family, I discovered that most of my history had been lost: the records of my birth were destroyed in a fire at the hospital I'd been born in, and the records of my adoption were missing, all except a single A4 form with my mother's 1960s address on it. From this, I eventually traced my natural parents.

I met my father, Ian Sutherland, in 2002. He had been one of the secretaries of the Scottish Committee of 100, and that's when I first heard the history that would inspire this novel.

I didn't get to meet my mother, Christine Harris, a lifelong peace campaigner: she took her own life in 1970. Christine's death meant I would always have unanswered questions, not least – where I was for the first nine weeks of my life, before my parents collected me.

In 2020, I did a book event in Liverpool with the author, Catherine Isaac. During the event we talked – with the audience

– about my history with the city and its unmarried mothers' homes. Catherine suggested I put something in the local paper to see if anyone was still alive who remembered Christine from the Home.

A few days after the piece came out, I received an email from a man named Terry McLoughlin. Terry's mother, Rose, had given birth to her first baby at the time I was born, and she and Christine were in hospital together. The first thing Rose told me was that Christine had a Scottish accent – I hadn't known that, nor would I ever if Rose hadn't met her. These are the kinds of things that can't be recompensed or restored to adopted people whose parents have died or who remain estranged. We will literally never hear our mothers' voices, never see their handwriting – just some aspects that can be hard for non-adoptees to comprehend.

Rose told me something else that has been life-changing. She is a Catholic and, knowing that Christine had to leave the hospital without me and that I was to be adopted by persons unknown, Rose has prayed for me every week since I left Christine. To discover that someone was thinking of me, my entire life, sending love and good wishes every week for fifty-six years gives me a continuity that I never thought I'd find. I'm not religious, but that sentiment, that care, means the absolute world to me.

I am lucky to have written this novel in an era where real voices are becoming valued, where we are calling for representation to be accurate. Adopted people see their story every day depicted in books and films – but the story portrayed is nothing like our lived experience. We see reunions, mistaken identities, unlikely coincidences, but we seldom see the loss, the assumptions, the secrets and lies. We rarely see *us*.

I wrote Judith and Penny's story to give me – and the half a million like me – a voice, and to remind those of you who have not been through this that it is an inhumanity we must never return to.

This book is dedicated to my mother and my mum, two strong women who did the best they could for their baby, and to all the other millions of mothers and babies who had no choice.

ACKNOWLEDGEMENTS

My heartfelt thanks to . . .

Firstly, like last time, the time before, and as much a part of my writing process as a keyboard, to Phil McIntyre for his amazing gift of being able to make a gently low-key suggestion that becomes the entire book.

To Sarah Hornsley for her constant encouragement, sage advice, and UTTER SKILL. My students will forever treasure the editing style hereafter known as 'page 77 & page 88'. If you are reading the acknowledgements of books in your genre to find good agents, you just spotted the absolute best.

To Victoria Oundjian and everyone at Lake Union for wanting to share Judith's story with the world, and to her and David Downing for their outstanding edits.

To Sarah Blair for 'straightsplaining' and to Clare Baker for trudging up and down windswept beaches, Covid permitting, listening to the same plot day after day (and still smiling). To Chris Wallis for casting an older eye over it, and to Ann Morris for talking to me about what it was like to be a woman at that time.

To Fionnuala Kearney, Jess Ryn, and Jacqueline Ward, the best writing buddies anyone could wish for, and to the Mhor Maniacs, for the brain- and soul-food you've been over the lockdowns. To

Janet, Hattie, and Bex because. To Susan, Tony, and Judith for the reasons contained within this book. To Jane, always.

To Parul and Matt of the London Writing Salon and the hundreds of other writers in that Zoom room. If you are a writer struggling with discipline or concentration, wherever you are in the world, go to Londonwriterssalon.com and find a brilliant writing tribe.

To Colin, with all my love, and to our children and grandchildren.

And, finally, to Scotland. Thanks for having me back.

ABOUT THE AUTHOR

Photo © 2019 Andrew Hayes-Watkins

Anstey Harris was born in an unmarried mothers' home in Liverpool in 1965. Now a mother and stepmother herself, she lives in Scotland where she runs a writing retreat. She has been inspired by her family history, and hopes to give a voice to the women and children – 16,000 a year during the 1960s in the UK – separated from each other by forced adoptions.

Anstey won the H. G. Wells Short Story Award in 2015 and her debut novel, *The Truths and Triumphs of Grace Atherton*, a Richard and Judy Book Club choice, won the Sapere Books RNA Popular Romantic Fiction Award in 2020. Her second novel, *Where We Belong*, was shortlisted for the RNA Book of the Year Award 2021 and she numbers Libby Page, Katie Fforde and Beth O'Leary among her many fans.